One Night of Love

It was Lammas Night, when anything was possible and all things were permitted. Marissa knew quite well that only on this night would she find herself alone in the moonlight with Lord Tristan Lynton. Only on this night would he be looking at her in so ardent a fashion.

It was Lammas Night, and he had found her in the woods, a fair maiden, just as in the old tales. Smiling, he trailed his fingers across the creamy skin of her cheek, then brushed them down through the silk of her hair. When he came to the back of her head, he cradled it in his hand, and lowered his head to kiss the mouth turned up to meet his.

As Marissa's mouth softened, Tristan's kiss deepened, and pulling her closer, his hand traced her spine to her waist and then beyond, toward a moment of madness that he would most certainly regret with the dawn—and that Marissa would never forget. . . .

D1453364

Exeter's Daughter

by

Emma Lange

A SIGNET BOOK

SIGNET
Published by the Penguin Group
Penguin Books USA Inc., 375 Hudson Street,
New York, New York 10014, U.S.A.
Penguin Books Ltd, 27 Wrights Lane,
London W8 5TZ, England
Penguin Books Australia Ltd, Ringwood,
Victoria, Australia
Penguin Books Canada Ltd, 10 Alcorn Avenue,
Toronto, Ontario, Canada M4V 3B2
Penguin Books (N.Z.) Ltd, 182-190 Wairau Road,
Auckland 10, New Zealand

Penguin Books Ltd, Registered Offices:
Harmondsworth, Middlesex, England

First published by Signet, an imprint of Dutton Signet,
a division of Penguin Books USA Inc.

First Printing, September, 1995
10 9 8 7 6 5 4 3 2 1

Chapter 1

Lady Marissa Portemaine opened the door of her room only to shut it again with a sharp thwack. Oh, she did resent him and never more than when she looked at his portrait, directly into those amber eyes whose steady regard seemed, as thoroughly as they did in life, to fault her.

But of course, the viscount did not have a proper home with a proper portrait gallery. No, he lived at Tremourne Lodge, traditionally a dowager's house, and there was only one portrait, his, hanging on the wall almost directly opposite her room.

"Why, whatever is it, lamb? What have you forgotten?"

"I have not forgotten anything, Wren. I am confident I shall quite dazzle all of Lady Lynton's guests as I am."

Marissa spoke offhandedly, as if she either did not believe she would dazzle the people assembling even then on the small, but well-tended lawn beneath her window, or as if she didn't care. Wren, Marissa's former nurse become present abigail, only cast her mistress, whom she still considered her charge, a single, searching glance before she returned to putting the small vanity table to rights. Lady Rissa, she knew well enough, would speak when she wished and not before.

Marissa allowed the gossamer thin wisp of silk that was her shawl to drop from her arms. He could return today. In his letter to his mother he had said he intended to visit an estate in the south of France on his way home from Italy. He was, he had said, interested in what was grown there, for the climate was similar to that of the Roseland peninsula of Cornwall, Tremourne's location. Marissa doubted the excuse. No one was so interested in crops, for the love of God. She thought he lingered in France with a woman, but whatever the real reason he did not race home, he knew the date of his mother's garden party. Lady Lynton's darling roses were at their peak at the first of July, and he would try to arrive for her one annual affair. Marissa had not needed to observe the great affection with which Lady Lynton referred to her son to know that Tristan cherished his mother. The honey man—her secret epithet for him derived from both his coloring and his temperament—would be the best of sons, cherishing as readily as he cherished. He was so very good, disciplined, reasonable, and righteous!

"I've no need of this shawl, Wren. It is bothersome, in fact. However, if Lord Lynton should return, I want you to bring it to me at once, before he makes his appearance in the garden."

"Ah," Wren said, casting her mistress a shrewd glance as she took the shawl, "I do believe his lordship has put you in a pelter since the first time he came to Pentworth with Master Kit and caught you in the stables in the arms of that groom, Billy or Willy, wasn't is?"

"I was not in Billy's arms!" Marissa flared as fiercely as if the incident had happened the day before, when in fact, it had been five years since she had been fifteen and Tristan had stumbled upon her. And judged her for all time! "Nor was I kissing him, either," Marissa added, but more on a mutter and more to herself than to Wren. Abruptly, she paced to the window to look out upon the guests, consciously searching for a head of light hair. Golden brown hair to be exact, and golden brown eyes to match. The honey man. "Billy was only pretending to kiss me, holding me lightly by the shoulders while he told me a remarkably unacceptable version of the three pigs." For a moment Marissa's mouth lifted. It was an expressive mouth, shaped like a Cupid's bow with generous corners that remained all but invisible until she smiled—or scowled—and then the corners could lift—or turn down—in such a way that her face came alive. Thinking of Billy's story, she smiled, until she recalled Tristan and what Wren had said, too. Immediately she whirled back to Wren. "Furthermore," she said, the controlled tenor of her voice pitched so that the abigail's graying head came up. "I wish you to understand that Tristan St. Aubyns, Lord Lynton, has never put me in anything so vigorous as a pelter, my dear Wren. I simply do not wish to cause Lady Lynton embarrassment before her guests, and I can assure you the welcome her son will give me would almost certainly cause her that regrettable emotion."

"Aye then, m'lady," Wren agreed, for while she did not think his lordship would embarrass his mother, she knew how important Marissa's dignity was to her. Indeed, at times in her young life, that dignity had been all she had. "I'll see you're warned before his lordship takes you by surprise."

"I'll box your ears, if you fail."

It was an old game between them, the haughty duke's daughter threatening the lowly servant. The so-called lowly servant smiled. "You'd not touch a hair of my head. 'Tis beneath you now you've grown so tall." She chuckled at her own joke and waved a hand at the door. "Get on with you, lamb! They'll be waitin' on tenterhooks to see Exeter's daughter for themselves, for even as far away as we are in Cornwall, they talk of your beauty."

Oh, yes, Marissa thought, sweeping from the room, they were waiting. But to judge her beauty? She doubted it. Beauty could be found anywhere. But not notoriety.

In the hallway, she paused and narrowed her eyes, catlike, at Tristan. She was under his thumb, or would be when he returned. The thought was insupportable. Her mother and father, agreeing for once—if through their secretaries—had sent her to the home of the one man in all England who had never expressed anything toward her but disapproval. Of course, the duke and duchess had had in mind Lady Lynton, not her son, but Marissa knew Tristan.

He had come too often to Penhurst and Exeter House with Kit for her not to know him. The viscount would be the master of his household, his mother a treasured dependent. Well, by heaven, it did not signify, Marissa vowed, swirling away from the bothersome portrait. She would not be dominated by anyone, man or woman. She would behave precisely as she pleased during this exile in Cornwall, the viscount be damned.

On the lawn of Tremourne Lodge sat two women known to everyone at the garden party, for the Tregaron sisters had lived all their lives at Rose Cottage only a few miles distant from Tremourne and just outside the village of Penryn. Native Cornish, they were small-boned and dark-haired, though fair-skinned, and living on a pension left them by their father, spent their days gardening, writing drafts of Minerva Press novels that were regularly rejected, and informing themselves through observation and direct questioning, if needed, of the affairs of all the people around them.

The younger of the two, Miss Millie, had finished the small glass of sherry she allowed herself whenever she visited Tremourne, for if the fortunes of the St. Aubynses were at a low ebb, they'd still have the best sherry of any household in the parish. Her cheeks flushed a little as a result, she peered a trifle myopically in the direction of her hostess. A young girl was just approaching Lady Lynton from the direction of the house, and Miss Millie chirped excitedly, "Is that she, Hester?"

Miss Hester preferred lemonade to sherry. She liked to keep a clear head, and she bestowed a disparaging glance upon her sister. "Lud, Millie! You are in need of spectacles, if you believe that lumpy chit is a duke's daughter. And her coloring is all wrong. I have told you that Lady Marissa is the height of elegance. And beautiful with hair as black as midnight and eyes the blue of the sky mixed with . . . silver. Wide, and almond-shaped, they are further enhanced by her heavy, thick, dark lashes."

Miss Millie's head bobbed up and down and she let out a

contented sigh, for if Miss Hester spent a part of every afternoon writing Cornish versions of the popular penny-dreadfuls everyone read, it was Miss Millie who loved to listen to her read these efforts aloud. "Lady Marissa sounds like a Cornish princess of old!"

"In looks, perhaps," Miss Hester conceded. "But by birth and by temperament, she is Exeter's daughter. No Cornish princess of old dared do as she pleased."

Miss Millie's eyes met her sister's and after a silent exchange, they turned as one to consider the array of guests on the lawn.

"There are quite a few people here this year," Miss Millie murmured.

Hester nodded authoritatively. "More than last year or the one before. Lady Marissa may be whispered of the length and breadth of England, but everyone wishes to meet her."

The sisters' dark eyes met again. "No one knows what she did to get herself sent to Cornwall in the midst of the Season," Miss Millie remarked tentatively.

Miss Hester snorted. "Thanks to Hermione Compton's prosy letters to Agatha Kendall, we know all else, however."

"I did think the dampened undergarments a bit fast," Miss Millie admitted with a hesitant look at her sister. When Miss Hester offered no rebuke, she went on. "But I cannot see that visiting Tattersall's in male disguise was so dreadful. How else could she have decided upon the horse she wanted for herself? Really, it seems rather silly that women may not go there. And as to dressing in masquerade in order to visit a gaming house," Miss Millie tittered, "why, it sounds remarkably exciting to me. Do you suppose she won?"

"Naturally," Miss Hester replied, adding, "She is a Portemaine. It is said Exeter never loses," though she had never so much as set eyes on a Portemaine before Divine Providence had dropped Lady Marissa down a trifling three miles distant from her.

"Of course, Hermione Compton never reported that," Miss Millie observed, a somewhat sly note creeping into her pleasant voice.

Miss Hester heard it and responded in kind. "No, she did not. Alas, poor woman. I imagine she is beside herself now she realizes she had taken Celia off to acquire a little town bronze the very Season that Exeter's daughter is sent to live in Lynton's own home."

"But he is not here," Miss Millie observed, not without a hint of frustration. "And even if he were, I wonder if the boy is not too steady and sensible to have his head turned by a girl of Lady Marissa's uncertain reputation and temperament, no matter how fetching she may be. Very likely, Hester, he will ask for Celia Compton after she has had her Season, just as Mrs. Compton has long expected he would."

Miss Hester pondered the clearly unsatisfying thought for a while, her eyes narrowed. "Perhaps he will, but there were rumors, you will recall, that the Comptons were displeased when Lynton did not follow them to London but chose instead to travel to Italy to console poor Matthew Haydon."

"And you know how vehemently Hermione Compton disapproves of Mr. Haydon. Why, she went on most uncharitably in our presence, and it was after church, even." Millie, considering further, brightened another degree. "And there is the matter of our new curate, as well. While Mr. Compton strongly disapproves Mr. Seaton's Wesleyan notions, it is said that Lynton defended the man and even went so far as to urge Redding, the vicar in Falmouth, to allow him to purchase the living here in Penryn."

"Yes, yes, I recall Tilda saying as much." Tilda, their housemaid, was valuable for more than her efficiency, for she was not only a voluble girl but was related to servants at many of the houses around Penryn village, including Sedwick Place, the Comptons' home. "Yes," Miss Hester mused with growing confidence. "Yes, it is quite possible our Lynton has already seen for himself how unworthy the Comptons are of him."

"But Celia is a pleasing girl." Miss Millie fretted. "She is pretty and has very nice manners, though I have, I must say, always thought she lacks a certain something necessary for a proper viscountess."

"Breeding," opined her elder sister succinctly. "That is what she lacks."

"Her mother is an Arbuthnott of the Sussex Arbuthnotts," Miss Millie prided herself upon being scrupulously fair.

"But Celia's grandfather was a tin miner," replied Miss Hester, who prided herself on plain speaking. "To be sure, old Compton became rich as Croesus, but even he never pretended he had breeding. And as to the Arbuthnotts, they are not so influential a family as they once were. I never see them mentioned in the *Lady's Magazine* anymore," declared Miss Hester, and as she pored over the monthly journal with meticulous care, she had every right to speak with her customary authority. "Undoubtedly the waning of their standing accounts for Hermione Compton's insufferably pretentious manner."

"You truly think so, Hester?" Miss Millie looked unexpectedly pleased. "Lady Lynton has never failed to invite us to Tremourne, but you will recall that we have never received an invitation to the Comptons' Christmas affair."

"And our father was a vicar!" Hester declared indignantly.

The sisters fell silent, both contemplating the unfairness rampant in the world, and after a little, how those who perpetrate that injustice occasionally do receive their just deserts.

Which brought both ladies' thoughts back to Lady Marissa. Miss Hester thought how striking a dark-haired girl would look beside Lynton, and how pea green Mrs. Hermione Compton would become, watching the pair. Miss Millie's thoughts took a different tack. She considered the girl, herself. Lady Marissa was undoubtedly beautiful, for Hester had had the great luck of seeing the girl and had said so. And she was well-born. That was indisputable. Her father was the Duke of Exeter, while her mother was the Duke of Marleigh's daughter. No tin miners there. Suddenly Miss Millie's forehead knitted anxiously. "Hester, are you quite persuaded that Lady Marissa will condescend to speak to us this afternoon? I know we are guests, but . . . well, but she is Exeter's daughter."

"Of course she will speak to us!" Hester declared roundly. "Have I not told you she spoke to me while she was out riding on that splendid black mare of hers? She'll come and take tea with us one day at Rose Cottage, I promise you. She's the manner of a queen, and mark my words, if she didn't like him, she'd snub a royal duke before she'd snub a common man. She has breeding."

"Oh, la! I cannot wait to see her. I wish she would come. "

At a short remove from the Tregaron ladies, another pair, a man and a woman, also discussed Lady Lynton's guest of honor. Standing a little distance apart, and almost never exchanging a direct look with one another, they appeared, by mutual design, to be two people only marginally acquainted with one another.

The man was young, in his midtwenties, and attractive, with dark hair and sparkling dark eyes. The woman was older, but also attractive, with a pleasingly full figure, thick russet-colored hair and the milky skin and dark blue eyes that often go with such hair.

"I believe you may be in difficulties, Babs," the young man, Jack Fitzhugh, remarked softly and not without amusement to the woman.

She understood him, for her brow lifted sharply. "She is too high in the instep for Lynton. I have been in company with her three times as opposed to your two, and I vow that if it had rained, she would have drowned, her nose was fixed so high in the air."

"It is a slender and exceedingly refined nose, however," Mr. Fitzhugh countered equably. "And a thoroughbred such as she cannot be expected to hold her nose level with the rest of us."

"She is scandalous as well, and due to his father likely, Lynton has little liking for those among the nobility who believe their birth entitles them to behave as recklessly and scandalously as they please."

Mr. Fitzhugh slanted the woman, Mrs. Lowell, a sparkling glance, but he refrained from remarking aloud that were everything known about Mrs. Barbara Lowell that could be known, she herself would scarcely be considered a model of rectitude and sobriety. "What did she do, Babs, that was so outrageous she had to be exiled to Cornwall, in the middle of the Season, yet? Have you learned?"

"No," Mrs. Lowell admitted, clearly piqued. "My few sources in London say no one knows, though surely the truth will come out eventually. It could have been anything, though. I think the only outrage she has neglected to commit is to be caught in a man's bed. She's gamed at the most infamous house in town, though she is only just twenty; encouraged one young man to kill himself over her; and it is said, worn her undergarments dampened."

Mr. Fitzhugh's dark eyebrows lifted. "She possesses a figure more elegant than lush, but still I imagine it would have been a pleasure to see that figure on display. Ah, look, Lynton's greatest admirers, the Tregaron pair, are craning their necks to be the first to catch a glimpse of her. I told you, did I not, that I met Lady Marissa, leading her mare and speaking, seemingly uncoerced and quite amused, with the elder of the crones?"

Mrs. Lowell's mouth pursed faintly, and her tone, when she spoke, was rather more biting than playful. "You are singing Lady Marissa's praises most assiduously today, Jack. Are you losing your interest in little Tory, then?"

Mr. Fitzhugh did not reply at once. His shifting gaze found Victoria St. Aubyns, Lynton's sister of seventeen. Tory, as she was known, was not so elegant or striking as the tall, slender beauty staying at her home, but she was comfortably pretty and the curves of her young body promised to become very nice, indeed, when she reached her full maturity. Slowly, Mr. Fitzhugh shook his head. "No, Babs, Exeter's daughter is not for me." He gave a wry laugh. "She is too sharp for one. Lud, when we met and I trilled all the usual compliments she gave me a look that not only cut through them as if they were air, but went on, I am certain, to fathom the admittedly shallow depths of my thoroughly self-centered soul."

"While little Tory adores you?"

"Do you know, Babs, when you repeatedly refer to her as little in that way, I am reminded how old you are, and for my part," Mr. Fitzhugh went on smoothly, "though she is pleasingly young, I find Miss Victoria St. Aubyns to be far from negligible."

"You find her to be the perfect girl to give you the political career you desire," Mrs. Lowell snapped, not well pleased with the young man's reference to her age.

She did not disconcert Mr. Fitzhugh, however. He agreeably inclined his head. "What she does not bring to a man in wealth, Miss St. Aubyns will, indeed, bring to him in influence as her brother is exceedingly well respected in political circles. I am certain Lynton could have had any position in government he wanted had his father not lost the family fortune and so forced him to concentrate his attentions here in Cornwall. I wish him well in his efforts to recover, but having no interest myself in managing the estate my dear uncle John left me, I shall be delighted to be the one in the family to go to London to look after our interests there, while Lord Lynton attends to our land here."

"Our interests, Jack? Our land?" A throaty chuckle escaped Mrs. Lowell. "For a certainty, you don't lack for audacity. I only hope you can persuade *little* Tory to abet your schemes."

"Oh, I shall," he said, and without any smile at all, dark as he was, Mr. Fitzhugh reminded Mrs. Lowell fleetingly of a wolf. "I've no talent for farming, nor interest in that direction, and yet I've no intention of losing the inheritance that has, all unexpectedly, made me a member of the landed classes. No, Babs, whether by virtue of my charming personality or the ruthless streak I undoubtedly possess, I intend to rise further still, so far, indeed, that I cannot even look back upon my lowly upbringing in that dreary, hopeless corner of Dublin."

Chapter 2

M arissa could hear the muted sounds of Lady Lynton's guests, but just for a moment, catching the smell of beeswax, she lingered in the shadows at the top of the stairs inhaling the scent that reminded her of a childhood that only seemed distant. She could not be seen pausing there, even from the front door, for there was no grand entryway at the Lodge. The house really was small. There were only two reception rooms, while her father's seat, Penhurst Place, boasted by comparison two dozen reception rooms, but it was true, too, that the Lodge was not the seat of the Viscounts of Lynton. Tremourne Abbey had burned some six years before. Lynton's father had been the only one home that night and had died in the blaze. Perhaps Tristan had not rebuilt the Abbey because he thought the place haunted? Despite her dislike of him, Marissa smiled a little. He'd not be daunted by anything so fanciful as a ghost. Judging by the look of him, she'd have said his ancestry was more Viking than Cornish, and like the former, he would live where he, not superstition, willed.

Standing there, her gloved hand lightly touching the redolent stair rail, Marissa half smiled. She looked for melodramatic answers, when the truth was likely simple. Tristan had probably come to like the Lodge. It was not such a farfetched notion. Upon arrival, she had sneered, but she had been bitter then. Almost as soon as her second day, she'd admitted that she liked the Lodge. It was comfortable, well cared for, well loved. She also liked the people in it, currently. Lady Lynton was one of the few adults she held in high regard, and Lynton's sister, Victoria St. Aubyns, she'd found to be unexpectedly endearing.

As to Cornwall, she had thought she was being buried in a dull, unbearable backwater for her sins, but had found, instead, a lovely place of winding lanes enclosed by gracefully arching trees; slate-roofed houses with whitewashed walls; and on the high, bare cliffs facing the seas of the Channel, there were the mysterious stones of the ancient Cornish.

If only *he* were not to come, she would laugh, knowing the punishment her mother, at least, had intended for her, was pleasure, instead. But *he* was coming. Her eyes closed briefly. And she saw the viscount as clearly as if he stood before her. Not as he looked in the portrait. He was almost smiling there. No, she saw him as he had regarded her one night in London.

Lady Renwick's invitation had specified fancy dress. Marissa's costume had merely been fancy undress, but Marissa did not smile as she remembered the clinging Grecian gown covering one shoulder only. Like the ladies of the previous decade, when the style had been fashionable, if scandalously so, she had also dampened her undergarments, and would never have gotten out of Exeter House had Wren not been ill. Her mother, as ever, had been distracted by the guests with whom she surrounded herself to make up for Exeter's glaring absence, and unaware that Wren was indisposed, had not thought to look beneath the unexceptional cloak Marissa had wrapped around herself.

Beneath the cloak and gown, the wet underclothes had felt clammy. Marissa rocked a knuckle against the hard stair rail, recalling too vividly how the dress had stuck to her breasts, her belly, and her thighs as she moved. She had felt as good as naked, but she made herself recall Leicester, as well. The earl, urged on by her mother, had been insistent with his attentions, refusing to take no for an answer. Marissa's mouth lifted as she remembered the look on the earl's heavy face, after he took in her costume—and after his pale, narrow eyes had all but crawled over her. Well, he had not pressed himself upon her again, but then her mother had seen the gown and seen Leicester's shocked face as well. Her hopes of the earl having been high, the duchess had been livid. Marissa had allowed the consequent harangue to wash over her; and knowing it was fruitless, had not even put herself out to inquire, scathingly, why the duchess was so determined to marry her off when her own marriage was so infamously awful. Having gained what she wanted, Marissa had not allowed her mother's anger to affect her, until they had reached Exeter House. There, by the worst luck, Kit had been standing in the entry hall with Lynton. Marissa could not remember what they had been doing there, or even if Tristan had been staying with them, as he often did when Kit was home from the army. She could only remember how her mother had appealed to both men to witness how lost to all reason her daughter was, how reckless, how insupportable.

Kit, bless him, had refused to cut Marissa to pieces, saying she could be kept, though he had said, ruefully, that the dress must go.

But it was Tristan's perusal she remembered. His golden brown eyes had registered disdain alone, after he swept over her with a single, cool glance. Speaking over her head to her mother as if she were a child of five or six, at best, he had said, "I suspect that without any attention Lady Marissa will reject the costume on her own, Your Grace. She looks cold." Suiting his actions to his words, he'd turned away without another glance, making it clear that the sight of her body and long legs outlined by the clinging gown interested him no more than if she really had been a child.

"Thank you, Hobbes. I am glad to be home. Yes, please do tell my mother I am here, and that I'll be out, after I've changed out of these travel-weary clothes."

Marissa's eyes flicked wide open and her hand tensed on the stair rail as tightly as if she held it in a death grip.

She could not see him. She could only assume from the direction of his voice that he was standing at the front door.

Perhaps he had only that moment arrived. Wretched man. He'd given no warning at all. And now what was she to do? Retreat? Let him learn from his mother of her presence in his household? But if she moved, he might investigate and find her slinking into the shadows as if she were afraid of him.

Which she assuredly was not. She merely did not like him and desired to delay until infinity seeing him again. He always found fault with her. Even in small things. Lud, when she had once stupidly asked his opinion of a bonnet that was prettily decorated with cherries, he had told her derisively that the bonnet was very well, if she wished to impersonate a fruit vendor.

No, she did not want to see him. He was inevitably either derisive, disgusted, or simply disapproving. But she could not hide from him either, for it was not in her nature to retreat, and so, torn, Marissa stood still as a statue near the top of the stairs, waiting for she knew not what, her heart pounding.

She could hear the sounds of laughter from the lawn. Soon she would have to go down, or Lady Lynton would come to look for her. What was he doing? Why did he not go to his study to look at his mail or some such? There. She heard his footsteps. He was approaching the stairs. His head came into view, and his shoulders. They were broad as ever, but his light brown hair was shot through with new lighter streaks of blond, thanks doubtless to the Italian sun. In the next moment he would lift his head and catch her with his eyes. They would be the same amber, the same shade as the darkest gold in his hair. Honey man. Lud, she only wished she did not like honey.

She did not like Lynton, however, whatever her opinion of honey. Before he could catch her standing frozen at the thought of facing him, she deliberately extended her foot.

Almost directly before the stairs then, Tristan lifted his head and began to smile. He was expecting Tory, of course, and the change in his expression, when he took in who she

was, might have been funny had Marissa been in the mood
to be amused.

She was not. His eyes had locked with hers, and she
could not think of much of anything but that she had never
before seen a smile actually die.

Tristan stared at her, not as if he could not believe his
sight, but as if he did not want to believe it. "You will undoubtedly understand my distinct surprise to see you here,
Marissa. I was not warned of your presence. To what, I
wonder, do we owe the pleasure?"

He might have been asking why he had the pleasure
of an asp's companionship. Knowing Tristan's height,
Marissa remained where she was. It was a novel and grati-
fying experience to look down on him.

"I doubt your pleasure was much considered, Lynton,"
Marissa replied with studied lightness. "It is to your mother
I have been sent, in the hopes that Lady Lynton can mend
my ways."

"Mother?" he repeated, his strong, handsome features
hardening. "It would require a regiment of crack troops to
mend you."

"Oh?" Marissa's thin, delicately curved eyebrows lifted
faintly. "Well, I am flattered, Tristan, to know you think
I've such a strong character."

"What did you do?" Tristan demanded flatly, ignoring
her little sally as if it were too absurd to remark.

She held his gaze without blinking. "I attended a masked
ball."

"Girls do that every day of the week."

"Perhaps they may go to Ranelagh every day, but I do
not believe they go so often to Mrs. Daviess'."

He stared, but even as Marissa experienced a perverse
spurt of satisfaction at the thought that she had robbed him
of the ability to speak. Tristan repeated slowly, "You attended a masked ball at a house of ill repute? I see you
have moved beyond your usual, petty scandals, Marissa.
Were you trying to shock your mother into an early grave,

or were you seeking a position with Mrs. Daviess? The duke's daughter as whore?"

Despite every effort Marissa made to control her response, she felt heat flood her face. At least at that distance, she could hide it and did, looking down, to smooth an imaginary wrinkle from her glove. "Actually, I don't think I've the temperament to be a whore," she said with every evidence of sophisticated ease, her eyes on the soft, supple kidskin she smoothed. "I'd not care to be at the beck and call of any man with tuppence to rub together."

"Oh, I am sure you could command more than tuppence, Marissa."

She lifted her head at that, in control of herself again. "How complimentary you are in the late afternoon, Tristan. I shall have to remember it. But as to your question, I went to Mrs. Daviess' to taste the lobster patties. They are reputed to be the best in London." He gave no hint whether he believed her. He only studied her so that Marissa began to fear he might be able to see into her mind. "And they were superb," she added flippantly, as, throwing caution to the winds, she began to descend the stairs.

"Who took you?"

Finally, he said something for which she'd prepared an answer. "That," she informed him airily, "is none of your business, my lord."

"No, I suppose it isn't," Tristan agreed, but not pleasantly, his golden brown eyes seeming to kindle the closer she came to him. "But neither is riding guard over you my business. I cannot imagine how it came to pass that we were selected to be your jailers, but I cannot allow you to remain here."

"Finally something upon which we agree." Marissa gave him a sickeningly sweet smile she guessed, or hoped at least, he would like to strike from her face.

And his eyes, a darker gold now than they had been, did narrow. "My mother is unaccustomed to tigresses. You would put her weak heart to the test."

"No, she is not at all up to me. And there is Tory, too,"

Marissa went on in the same light, reasonable tone. "I daresay I'll have her permanently ruined in another week. You'd best work quickly."

The anger that flashed in his eyes prompted Marissa to recall suddenly how Kit had once said that Tristan was one of the few younger boys at school the older ones had not tried more than once to dominate. He did not allow her to bait him further, however, only said levelly, "I will speak with Mother tomorrow."

"Excellent," Marissa replied in a tone of one who has had a matter settled to her immense satisfaction. "I wish you success, of course, my lord, and should you take it into your head to have me sent on my way sooner than the morrow, you've only to send word to Wren. She's an efficient worker and will have my trunks packed in a trice."

Tripping lightly down the remaining steps, Marissa brushed by Tristan, doing her utmost to conceal how aware she was that, though she was tall for a woman, he was imposingly taller than she. And imposingly broad-shouldered.

"Now then, don't allow our reunion to keep you from your mother and her guests. I know Lady Lynton, and Tory, too, have been looking forward most excessively to seeing you."

"Excessively, Marissa? They are my mother and sister."

She had set the bait, and he had taken it, albeit dryly. Looking back over her shoulder, Marissa gave Tristan a limpid smile as reward. "Ah, but I was judging by my own degree of eagerness for your return, my lord." And with that return for his reception of her, she waltzed away down the hall, taking care to flaunt that she could walk with regal ease, though she felt the weight of his hard gaze every step of the way.

Chapter 3

"Oh, Tristan, let me look at you!" Lady Lynton relaxed her hold upon her tall, very much grown son only enough that she could lean back to look at him.

Tristan laughed. "I'd have thought you looked your fill yesterday. Did you think I might get lost betwixt England and Italy?"

"No, of course not," she said, smiling mistily as she squeezed his strong arms. "But one never knows what may happen, and I confess I am rather attached to you. Oh, it is good to feast my eyes on you, Tristan. I know I am prejudiced, but the Italian sun agreed with you. You look like some bronzed god now."

Her son's smile deepened. "I have not had my vanity fed so nicely since I left, but now that we've established that I am hale and hearty, I wish to know how you are. Hobbes says you are napping every afternoon."

"What I am is possessed of a prosy butler." Lady Lynton smiled, and giving Tristan a last squeeze, released him. "It is the gardening season, Tris. I have been resting because I have been working hard with my roses and my herbs, not because my heart has given me difficulties. I promise you that. Now, tell me all about your trip. And about Matthew. How is he taking Carlotta's death?"

"He is bearing up, but to have her die so tragically in a carriage mishap . . . well, it is not easy, and there is his son, Will, for him to think of. As I said yesterday, he has decided to return to Penryn. He should arrive in a fortnight or so, but our discussion of Matt and the reception he may expect here will wait. The issue of Lady Marissa Portemaine will not."

The smile had faded from Tristan's face, and looking up from the comfortable chair in which she had seated herself, his mother sighed. "Oh dear, you've your I-am-not-pleased-but-do-not-wish-to-upset-you look on, my dear. Perhaps I should have written to you, but the duke and duchess needed an answer immediately."

"The duke *and* duchess wrote to you?" Tristan asked, momentarily diverted.

"They each wrote separately, I should have said. No, I cannot report that Exeter and Catherine are reconciled after all these years, but as the letters were similar in substance, both communicating an urgent desire to remove Marissa from London, I can say there has to have been some sort of communication between them."

Tristan shrugged his shoulders dismissively, for in truth the infamous estrangement between the Duke of Exeter and his duchess did not interest him half so much as the daughter they had produced and now foisted off onto his mother. And him.

"What were you thinking of, Mama, when you agreed to take her?" he asked, standing before her, imposing without intending to be. "She is not some wounded animal you can nurse back to health. Simply put, she is trouble, and you are not strong enough to manage her."

"Actually I had not thought to manage her, but to befriend her," Lady Lynton said, a smile in her voice. "As to why I agreed to invite her to visit—I was moved by more than my schoolgirl acquaintance with Catherine, for frankly, we were never terribly close and have not even seen each other since your father died. But if I am to explain myself, I do not wish to have to crane my head, Tristan. Have a seat. The wing chair has always accommodated you comfortably."

Tristan heeded his mother's wishes to the extent that he sat, but he chose the window seat. Sitting on the edge of it, his long legs stretched before him, he crossed his arms over his chest and prepared himself to listen to his mother's reasoning.

She smiled faintly. "You look as if you may give me a hearing, but not necessarily a sympathetic one, my dear."

"You are perceptive as always, Mama. I've little sympathy for her, and I know her better than you."

"You know her better now, but I knew her a child, though not well, of course. Even in those days, I did not always accompany your father to town, but we did visit Catherine at Penhurst several times. I remember one visit in particular. Catherine had a good many guests, as she is wont to have, and wanting to escape the crowds for a bit, I went into the music room to play a little for myself. Marissa was there, reading a book. I thought at the time it was an odd place to read. The chairs are all very stiff and upright, but she had dragged two of them together and managed to curl up, and so I asked her if I would bother her. She could not have been more than eight, Tristan, and yet she studied me in the oddest way, almost as if she were judging the sincerity of my concern. I must have passed whatever test she applied, however, for she said, sounding even as child both lofty and self-amused at once, that she would be pleased to have music, if I would be pleased to have an audience. I played for some time, and when I was done, she clapped and thanked me, saying with a smile that she had never had a private performance before. I remind you how young she was. Of course, I laughed, taken with her, and then went on my way. Or almost did. I had reached one of the many doors in that quite grand music room, when the door closest to Marissa flew open. It was Catherine. She never saw me. All her attention was upon Marissa, with whom she was furious. It seemed Marissa was supposed to have been presented to some of Catherine's guests but could not be found at the appointed hour. For the crime of making her mother's guests wait Catherine struck her hard, ringing blows to each cheek, screaming as she did that Marissa was a wretched child whose only desire was to embarrass her mother. I thought to come forward and take the blame somehow, I was so shocked, but, I did not think quickly enough. Marissa spoke before I could. Standing very straight before her mother, her cheeks flaming red, she said in a tone that would have been unnaturally cool for an adult that the time had gotten away from her, for she had been reading. And then she added, on a deliberately defiant note, I admit, that her father wanted her to read.

"You can imagine Catherine's reaction. By then it had been at least five years since she had allowed Exeter's name to be spoken in her presence. I thought she would strike Marissa again, but what she did was, perhaps, more deadly. Lud, I can hear her even now. 'Is he here?' she shrilled. 'Has he been here for years?' Of course, Marissa had no recourse but to shake her head no. 'That is how much he loves you. He has abandoned you as easily as he did me and for no more than his own decadent pleasures. I'll not let you be like him. I'll root out every trace of him in you. See if I do not!' With that she grabbed the book, threw it to the floor, and half flung Marissa out of the room."

Lady Lynton looked almost upset as she had been that warm late summer's day over a decade before in Suffolk, and Tristan's voice was sympathetic. "It is not a pretty story, I grant you that, Mama. I knew the duchess was a cold woman, but I did not know she had treated Marissa so harshly. However, we are not living in the past but the present, and that young girl has become a heedless vixen who is bound to exhaust you."

"If she causes an upset that is too great for me to bear, then I will simply return her to her mother, Tristan. In the meantime, however, I shall enjoy her company. Yes," Lady Lynton insisted when her son eyed her skeptically. "I shall. Do, actually. We take chocolate together most mornings and among other things, I admire her spirit."

"Oh, come, Mama!" Tristan's eyes flashed with an impatience that his mother had rarely seen. "That spirit of hers has run roughshod over half the world. Dear God, there is no end to all the reckless, self-indulgent things she's done, not least of them causing a young man to try and take his life for want of her!"

"That was young Westerly, was it not?" Lady Lynton asked calmly. "Yes, I heard of his attempt to put a period to his existence when she refused him . . ."

"After she told him she was indifferent to whether he killed himself or not over her refusal to marry him. And I am not telling tales out of school. She admitted to Kit that she said it."

"Did you see the marks Westerly made on his wrist?"

Tristan gave his mother a look as dry as the desert. "Actually, I spared myself that pleasure, Mama."

"Edith Carrington's son, Geoffrey, was not so squeamish, and he reported to his mother that the marks were rather faint in all, and high, too, on the arm more than the wrist, as if he had not so much tried to take his life as tried to make it appear as if he had tried to, perhaps in the hope that Marissa would relent."

"Well, he did not succeed there."

"No," Lady Lynton agreed, smiling faintly. "Geoffrey reported to Emily that Marissa told the boy she had little liking either for Cheltenham tragedies or bumblers."

"Which remark is reported to have very nearly caused him to try again," Tristan responded rather curtly. "And though you may say that he did not do it, still, the point is that Marissa would not have cared. Think of Tory, Mama, if you will not think of yourself."

"I am," Lady Lynton said clearly, and wanted to sigh, when Tristan's handsome face tightened. It was not his way to argue and protest, but sometimes she thought she'd have preferred ranting to that taut-jawed look. "Tristan, I know you do not care for her. You've never hidden that, but just think what her life has been—given that she was born resembling a father who all but deserted her and lived with a mother determined to eradicate every trace of him to be found in her. Perhaps she is not redeemable, but I should like to cosset for a time the little girl who was struck viciously yet never even cried out. Not once."

Tristan knew his mother to be a woman of quick sympathy for any mistreated or injured creature. The Tregaron sisters had once said they thought there was a secret path to Tremourne known by all stray dogs and most wounded birds. But Lady Marissa Portemaine, despite her sad history, was no easily cuddled and mended mutt.

"Do you know, Mama, what she has done that even Exeter would agree she must be sent from town?"

"Yes, of course. Catherine told me in her letter that Marissa attended a masked ball in a, ah, house of ill repute."

"You can scarcely bring yourself to say the words!" Tristan exclaimed. "And she went to such a place in order, she said herself, to taste the lobster patties."

Lady Lynton said quietly, "In strict confidence I inquired of Edith Carrington what she knew of the house, and she reported it is rumored to be the one Exeter visits the most frequently."

"Great God!" Tristan rose abruptly, his hand going to the back of his neck, as if he were suddenly weary and aching.

Lady Lynton watched him for a moment. "I cannot say precisely why she went to such a place, Tristan. I have not asked her. But in my heart, I know it was not for lobster patties."

"She could very easily have been dragged into a room in that house and raped, Mama." Tristan turned wearily from the window, to find, as he had expected, his mother's hand at her throat. "You shrink from my plain speaking, but my point is that, whatever her motive, Lady Marissa Portemaine demonstrated that she lacks sense as much as she lacks sensibility, which brings us back to Tory. I cannot think you want to put her in such close contact with a girl who may well lead her into harm."

"Marissa has never involved another girl in one of her scandals, Tristan, and I do not believe she will lead Tory to harm. In fact, I think she has done Tory some good. Cast your eyes up to the heavens all you like, but Tory is at an age where she wants to know all the latest fashions, wants her hair done attractively, wants her clothes to be stylish, and so on. And I am sadly lacking in that area. I would much rather while away my time in a garden than pore over *La Belle Assembleé*, but Marissa has impeccable taste, and I believe, if you will look, you will see that Tory is measurably more confident these days."

"Because she admires the elegantly turned-out duke's daughter already! Is that what you want? For Tory to admire a young woman who has attended a ball wearing dampened underclothes?"

"Tory is sensible enough to know she would be cold in dampened underclothes, Tristan." Despite her wry response, it was obvious that Lady Lynton's mind was elsewhere, and when she continued after a moment, her tone was decidedly more militant. "In truth, I hope at least a spark of Marissa's spirit will rub off on her. If I had had an ounce of it, I'd not have allowed your father to ruin us."

"Mama!" Tristan's strong features softened instantly. "You cannot hold yourself responsible for Father's weakness for high-stakes gaming. He's the one . . ."

"I was too timid even to ask why the roof at the Abbey was not repaired in a timely fashion or to protest when he said he must sell one after another of my jewels! Do you think Marissa would have stood by and allowed her husband to drain her son's patrimony so there would be nothing left with which to rebuild the house that same husband madly burned down about himself?"

Tristan sank down on the footstool before his mother and took her hands in his. "I cannot say what Marissa would have done with Father. Likely she'd driven him to an even earlier grave, but that is neither here nor there. What is here, is that I will not have you blame yourself for Father's faults. Besides, we are recovering. My balance with Greeley in London is less with every year."

"But you haven't a proper home, Tristan!"

"I lack a proper home?" Tristan squeezed her hands

tightly. "I've bedrooms aplenty, reception rooms, a dining room, a kitchen, efficient servants, and thanks to my mother, a particularly lovely rose garden."

Lady Lynton bowed her head, unable to speak for several moments, and even when she did look up at her son, her smile was tremulous. "You are so very good to me, Tristan. So good, I regret asking more of you. But I do wish Marissa to stay, at least for a time. Please, Tristan, I like her, strange as it may seem to you."

"It does seem strange," Tristan allowed with a wry look that conveyed concession, too, somehow. "But if you wish her to stay, then she shall . . . until she does something to discomfort you."

Lady Lynton laughed, pleased, but amused, too. "I've a notion you might want to wager that will be sooner rather than later."

"I would never make such a wager with you," Tristan replied, the ghost of a smile curving his mouth. "I care for you too much to milk your purse so readily."

Chapter 4

"It was a great scandal eight years or so ago, and though it may have been forgotten in town, no one in Penryn has forgotten." Tory sat on a stool in the library, swinging her legs, while she watched Marissa lift a fencing foil down from the wall and whip in back and forth, testing its flexibility. "The principals all resided here, you see, for Lord Bessborough owned Sedwick Place, where the Comptons live now."

"Lord Bessborough?" Marissa asked, making a feint with the foil.

"Lord Bessborough was Carlotta's husband," Tory explained. "He was nearly thirty years her elder. Can you imagine? But he had not gotten an heir by his first wife, and when she conveniently died, he sought a replacement who would be up to the task." Tory giggled at the raised-eyebrow look Marissa gave her. "That is the way the Tregaron sisters put it," she confessed. "They are also the ones who said Lord Bessborough beat his wife black-and-blue. Tristan said only that he was a beastly man. At any rate, Mr. Haydon found her one evening in the woods. One of her arms was broken. Yes!" Tory nodded in answer to Marissa's exclamation. "Bessborough had beaten her so brutally he broke her arm. I believe Mr. Haydon was in love with her already. Tris won't say so, but Miss Millie and Miss Hester say Carlotta was very beautiful and she was often in company with Mr. Haydon, as they were neighbors. At any rate, after he found her so beaten, Mr.

Haydon helped Carlotta to flee Bessborough for Italy, where they married, after Bessborough died."

"That is quite a scandal. And your brother is still friendly with Haydon?"

Tory watched Marissa execute an intricate series of passes ending with a flick of her wrist that would have left a scar on the cheek of her imaginary opponent.

"Tris believes, and Mother agrees, that had Mr. Haydon not taken Carlotta abroad, Bessborough would have gotten her into his clutches again and likely ended by killing her. That is why Tris does not fault Mr. Haydon for the course he chose and believes he has the right to return and raise his son in his home."

"Does he believe Mr. Haydon will be will be forgiven his past deeds by the others because he's a grieving widower?"

"He hopes so," Tory said, watching Marissa whip the foil through the air again. "Particularly as everyone around Penryn knows how poorly Mr. Haydon's agents managed his estate without anyone to oversee them."

"Could not your brother have done that?"

Tory said something about her brother's own affairs absorbing him, but Tristan, standing in the doorway of the small library at the Lodge, attending to the girl executing another graceful lunge, did not listen. Her black, silky hair flowed loose and free down her back, looking so much like it had the first time he had ever seen her that he felt almost as if he were there in the stables at Penhurst, looking into the shadows.

She had been in a man's arms. Her groom's, as it had turned out.

He had not been in the best frame of mind to encounter a reckless, willful girl. He did admit that. He would never have gone to Penhurst with Kit in the first place, had he known the duchess had a large party visiting. But he had not known, and he had not wanted to go straight home from town. Understandably. The Abbey had been a still smoldering ruin, and he had just learned from his father's solicitor that its charred stones and the land around it were all his father's reckless, willful obsession with gaming had left them. And the debts, of course. That he could not honor his gaming vowels had been the reason his father had put a period to his existence.

No, he had not been in any frame of mind even to exchange smiles and pleasant banter with the duchess's guests and at the first opportunity had escaped to the stables, ostensibly to see a new hunter Kit had purchased.

He could not have been at Penhurst more than two hours by then, but nonetheless he had heard idle talk about Kit's younger sister. Though she was only fifteen, she had defied her mother by joining the guests at dancing the night before and now had the Earl of Chandos' son panting after her. Tristan had not attended closely to the talk. Kit had spoken of his sister since they had been at school together, almost invariably with rue, and Tristan had long since dismissed her as a spoiled, willful brat.

In the stables, he had paused at the door for his eyes to adjust, and so before he saw the couple, he heard a man whisper low as if to a lover and the soft shuffle of feet moving in straw. Staring into the shadows, Tristan had distinguished the young woman first. Her hair hung loose, and it had diverted him momentarily, for the thick, glorious cloud tumbled nearly to her waist.

Distracted, it had taken him a moment to realize a man held her. But she was not lost in the embrace. Perhaps Tristan made a sound, or perhaps she had known he was there all along, but whichever, the girl, and Tristan did not mistake who led during that particular dance in the stables, half pushed, half nudged the man around so that she could peep over his shoulder. When she saw Tristan, she stared a half second, completely undistracted by the man apparently nibbling at her neck. Then, abruptly, she jerked away from her partner as if he had suddenly become a bramble.

"Who the devil are you?" she demanded, seeming utterly unconcerned that he had caught her in a man's embrace. "And what the devil are you doing here?"

She was quite incredibly beautiful. Tristan had expected her to resemble Kit, who had his mother's blond hair and gray eyes, but she was all black hair, remarkable dewy skin that gleamed even in the dim light of the stable, and a perfectly shaped, oval face with every feature a pleasure to regard, from her wide, perfect Cupid's bow mouth, to the slim, straight nose, the delicate jaw, and even the high, thin, arching eyebrows. In the light from the door he could see, as well, her eyes: wide, slightly almond-shaped, impossibly light blue, and set off by thick, feathery, coal black lashes. Her youth, the shock of her feminine appeal in spite of her youth, all startled him for a moment, and as he was registering who she was—she looked too like her father for him not to realize—a young man's voice intruded. "Rissa! Rissa! I know you are here. I saw you coming toward the stables, and I followed as soon . . ."

The young man's voice trailed away the moment he stepped into the stables. Tristan recognized him as Chandos' son, a full-lipped, weak-chinned boy who had at that moment a hot light in his eyes. The light began to fade, though, when he saw Tristan and was doused completely when he registered how closely Marissa stood to the ruggedly built groom just behind her.

"Yes, Charlie?" the girl who was Lady Marissa said. "Was that you calling me by my pet name just now, though I have never given you leave?"

"Well, ah, that is, I did not think . . ."

"No, you did not think," Lady Marissa, all of fifteen years old, cut in, her mouth curling contemptuously. "Had you, you would recall that I have never given you leave to address me as my friends do."

The boy began to sputter. He must have flushed as well. Tristan could not see the telltale pink, but he could see the unmanned look the young fellow cast his way. Instantly, Tristan's temper had ignited. The girl was using him. She had meant this Charlie to find her with the groom, but that plan having failed, she had regrouped alertly and seized the opportunity to humiliate him in another way: belittling him before a peer.

Tristan had extended his hand to the boy. "I am Lynton."

"Durston, here!" the boy said too quickly. "I'm honored, sir! Indeed, I am. I've heard how you raced Portemaine's blacks."

Just then, with his father's death and his debts weighing him down, racing Kit's matched black seemed the frivolous feat of another person altogether, but Tristan had not followed his inclination to snap as much; had, instead, mindful of the she-cat who wanted to strip the boy of his pride, even invited the boy to ride with him later. "Just now, however, I've been sent by Her Grace to fetch her daughter." He had turned to address Marissa directly then, his eyes narrowing on her. "You will come with me, Lady Marissa. Your mother wants you."

Tristan did not think he would ever forget the look she had given him then—shrewd, amused, and caustic all at once. "That is a patent lie, sir," she had drawled languidly. "My mother, her sainted grace, would never send a stranger after me. She is much too much the stickler, but I will go. Though you are a dissembler, you are preferable to present company."

With that she had glanced disdainfully to Lord Durston to be certain he had taken the hit, and then she had departed the stables like a queen, neither waiting for Durston's response, nor for Tristan to join her.

Even now, five years later, Tristan could recall the urge he had had to throttle her. He had never felt anything like it in his life.

Tristan moved from the doorway, catching his sister's attention. "Tristan!" she cried, jumping off the stool to run to him. She was smiling broadly and tipping her head from side to side to show off the little gold earrings he had brought her from Italy. When she embraced him, he flicked the other occupant of the room a glance. When their eyes met, hers gazed steadily back at him, intensely blue and absolutely unrevealing.

"I adore my earrings, Tris!" Tory leaned back, bringing her brother's gaze back to her. And at her he smiled. "They are so pretty! Rissa says they would be the envy of everyone in town, because they are so delicately wrought."

He had bought them in Florence from a fine goldsmith, but despite their delicate filigree, the earrings were very small, and Tristan doubted they would even be noticed in town, but he did not look again to Marissa. Lightly flicking the earrings, he smiled at his sister. "I am glad they please you, Tory, and as they are as pretty as the wearer, I would be content to admire them all day, but alas, I have been sent to fetch you, my dear. Mama wishes you to help her with some embroidery thread."

"Ugh! I thought Baines would finish untangling it, though I suppose I'd no right to leave her to the task, as it was I, after all, who took a kitten into Mama's room."

"Ah. That will be the tiger I saw stalking a shadow in the hallway?"

"The very one." A rather shy grin crept over Tory's pretty rounded face. "Mr. Fitzhugh gave her to me. He is Admiral Stone's nephew, and he said he met you once. Do you remember?"

Tristan frowned, trying to remember, though it was not easy to think of anything but the girl waiting in such stillness to hear if and when she was to be sent away. "Yes, I do have some recollection of meeting Stone's nephew. It was several years ago. The admiral was very proud of him, as I recall, proclaiming the boy the best of his sister's offspring or something to that effect, and he was undertaking the expense of sending him to school here in England."

"Yes, that's right. Mr. Fitzhugh went to Cambridge where he became very interested in political matters, but you will be able to learn that for yourself, as Admiral Stone left him Ardmore House in his will and he is living in Penryn now."

"Ah, the admiral made him his heir, then. I did not know

that, but it is a bit of luck for Fitzhugh, I would think. Ardmore is not a large estate, but the land is rich. And his cats
fertile, it would seem."

The color in Tory's cheeks deepened even as she
grinned. "He'd three cats produce kittens at once! It was
quite a sight. Mother and Rissa and I went with Elise and
Mrs. Kendall simply to marvel at the number spilling out of
the stall where they were housed. There is only one left
now, however, and Mr. Fitzhugh has persuaded Mother that
our little tiger is lonely for a companion. You can see why
he ought to do well in politics. He's very persuasive. But
you may judge him for yourself later, for he is to come this
very afternoon with the little mite. Lud!" Tory laughed at
herself. "If I don't stop this rattling on, Mama will have
tossed out the present kitten with her thread. Will you come
with me, Rissa?"

"I would like to speak to Marissa a moment, Tory," Tristan intervened to say. "She can follow you in a moment."

Marissa smiled when Tory looked to her, as if she had a
choice in the matter, and affirmed that she would be along
in a little.

Marissa had not moved from where she stood when Tristan first entered the library. Some twelve feet separated
them, and as Tory departed, Tristan looked at her fully for
the first time, taking in the fashionable striped morning
dress she wore. With its high waist and full skirts, it con-
cealed much of her figure. But he had seen her in the Grecian gown and dampened underclothes, and so he knew her
breasts were high and firm beneath the muslin, the shift and
the stays; knew her belly was slightly, sensuously rounded;
and her thighs were long and supple.

Perhaps Marissa guessed his thoughts, though Tristan's
perusal had taken no more than a blink of an eye. When he
glanced up, he found her cheeks had colored. Faintly, but
perceptibly. If she was abashed, however, she was not entirely so. He saw she held the foil still, waist high, and
pointed at him.

Tristan made no move to take it from her. Indeed, he

stood with his hands at his side, his chest quite undefended. It was his golden brown eyes that joined battle with her, clashing with her light blue ones. "Mother wishes you to stay."

Her beautiful face seemingly carved of alabaster, Marissa made no response. She might have been disappointed. She might have been glad. Tristan could not tell. Then abruptly, she lowered the foil and swung about, turning away from him to replace the foil upon the wall.

Marissa had to stretch to reach the hooks, but her body was lithe, and she managed easily. When she was no longer distracted with it, Tristan continued. "Because this is Mother's home as well as mine, you may stay as long as she continues to wish it and so long as you don't upset her."

When Marissa swept around to face him, the look in her eyes was cool, the tilt of her chin regal. "I take it those terms are not negotiable."

He could see no reason to respond. She had not put it as a question, really.

One corner of her mouth lifted. Had he forgotten how expressive her mouth was, Tristan would have been reminded then, for there was no mistaking the sarcasm in the slant of her lips. "I see," she said. "Well, though you'll not believe it, I have no wish to upset your mother, and so I suppose you should prepare yourself for a long visit. Good luck."

With that, she gave him a cryptic smile and left the room by the French doors, presumably so that she'd not have to walk near him. Tristan thought she'd made a wise choice, for though she was all of twenty now, he felt very like throttling her again.

Chapter 5

"**D**o ye ken the course then, m'lady?"

Ben Hawkes, at nineteen the eldest and best rider of Lynton's two grooms, strode to Marissa's side, leading a powerful gelding by the reins. They stood upon a rounded hilltop, in a gravel lane marked off from the fields around it by one of the thick briar hedges that served as fences in that part of Cornwall.

"I know we shall begin here," Marissa said with a laugh.

"Aye, and we'll leave the lane at the woods, o'er there." Ben pointed down the long slope of the hill to a thick woods. "Ye can see the path through them, lookin' like a tunnel. 'Tis a half mile or more to the great rowan tree in the midst o' the woods, then once out o' them, we'll cross the drive. You can see it?" Marissa nodded. Bordered on one side by the woods, and on the other side by orchards, the drive curved in a long crescent to the Lodge. "On t'other side of the drive, 'tis easy sailin' to the finish, only that bit o' park land slopin' down to the river."

Ben referred to the Penryn River, down which the fishermen of Penryn village rowed each morning in their brightly painted wooden boats. To reach the river, Marissa and Ben would have to race over a quarter mile of Tremourne's park. It was not a broad park. Tristan, in a move Marissa thought characteristically as well as excessively purposeful, had planted fruit trees in most of what had once been an extensive park, but he had left a swath of open, purely ornamental space so that the river could be enjoyed from the Lodge.

"All of the park down to the river is visible from the Lodge," Marissa observed neutrally.

Ben glanced down at her sharply. "Now then, I thought ye said his lordship was away."

"He has ridden out with his bailiff to look over the estate."

"Aye, he does that regular," Ben mused. "His lordship's not like some o' the Quality that wouldn't know their own land—and after he and Thompkins are done, he'll stop off like as not at his huntin' box in the woods, though he doesn't hunt much as far as I can see."

Marissa could easily imagine one other use for an isolated hunting box, but saw no reason to mention to Ben that it was surely the perfect place for an assignation.

"Ye've not told anyone about our race, have ye, m'lady?"

Ben had gone straight to the point of Marissa's earlier remark, and now she sighed. "No, Ben, I have told no one, but Dorcas told Miss Tory."

"Thet hinny!" Ben smacked his cap against his thigh. He and Dorcas were courting, but that did not mean, Marissa noted wryly, that he was blind to his beloved's faults. "She wants to watch the race. 'Tis why she spoke. Do ye think Miss Tory will tell his lordship?"

"Not if he doesn't ask," Marissa said succinctly.

Ben nodded. "Well then, there's naught amiss. His lordship won't be askin', if he's away with his tenants."

"What about Tibbs?"

Ben shook his head, dismissing Tremourne's head groom as a concern. "Tibbs may say a few choice words to me afterward, but seein' it's you I'm racin', he'll not say overmuch. Eats out of your hand, Tibbs does, m'lady. Can't say often enough what a rider you are."

Marissa's mouth lifted with pleasure. She liked Tibbs. The stocky Cornishman had a magical way with horses. "Right then," she said, her eyes lighting. "Are you on, Ben?

My fifty pounds against your agreement to ride out with me as my escort as Lord Lynton wishes but then to go your own way, if I wish it once we are away from the Lodge?"

A wide grin splitting his cheerful freckled face, Ben held out his hand. "Aye, m'lady, with fifty pounds, I'll be that close to askin' for Dorcas."

While, if she won, Marissa would be assured at least a modicum of freedom. After she shook the young man's hand, they mounted up. If she did not win . . . but she did not want to think of how it would be with someone always set to watch her. That was Tristan's goal. She knew it, and that he had set himself to be her principal watcher.

Not that he had spent the previous day staring broodingly at her after his mother had overruled his wishes as to Marissa remaining at Tremourne. He had done nothing so Gothic. Tristan wouldn't. The honey man would do only what was golden and right. Still, by his lights, that meant keeping a steady eye on her.

Jack Fitzhugh had come with the second tiger kitten and another young man, a close neighbor, Gerald Kendall. In his early twenties and chafingly overawed by her, Gerald did not inspire a great deal of patience in Marissa, but as he and his family were friends of Lady Lynton's, she had tolerated him politely enough since she had come to Cornwall. The day before, however, she had been more than polite. She had been positively cordial, and all because she had felt Tristan's golden gaze stray to her repeatedly. Perhaps he was on the alert lest Mr. Kendall should threaten to kill himself over her as Lord Westerly had absurdly threatened to do. Absurd honey man, Westerly obviously had somewhere in his family tree an actor, or even two, and both of them proficient at grand tragedy. Prosaic Mr. Gerald Kendall as obviously had not.

Lynton's time, she thought, would have been better spent studying Jack Fitzhugh than her. The young man was too glib for Marissa's liking. He had agreed with every political point of view Tristan had expressed, and though the young man had managed to express his agreement thoughtfully enough not to seem to be a toady,, she'd have respected him a good deal more had he had found at least a point of disagreement.

"All right then." It was Adam Tresslick, Tremourne's younger groom, looking with bright eyes from Ben to Marissa and holding a white handkerchief aloft. "Get ye ready. And set . . . and go!"

Tristan made his way slowly through the orange trees. It seemed a mountain of work had amassed in his absence. Nothing insurmountable, mostly niggling questions to be settled, such as who was responsible for not having done the ditching in the fields to the northwest and what was to be done now that there was water standing in them. Still, it was a pleasure to see his gamble on the orange trees was paying off nicely. They were healthy, and he needed every penny he would earn from their first crop.

He came out of the orchard near a gazebo. Erected when the Lodge had been built for his great grandmother, it stood now by his mother's rose garden. She often took tea there in the afternoon, but it was early afternoon, and he was mildly surprised to see Tory sitting in the fanciful little structure.

"Tristan, this is unexpected," Tory called out as he dismounted. "I thought you would stop off at the hunting box."

"I've too many more immediate concerns pressing for my attention, but not so many that I may not take a moment with you." Taking the two steps up to the gazebo in a single bound, he smiled at his sister. "I am not trespassing, am I?"

"Oh, no!"

If Tory spoke a little too fervently, Tristan put it down to the fact that her sketch pad had slipped off her lap. "I didn't mean to upset you," he said, grinning as he seated himself next to her.

"You didn't upset me," she protested, sweeping up the sketch pad and a pencil that had gone down with it. "I am glad to see you. I missed you while you were away more than I can tell you without swelling your head absurdly."

That sounded so precisely like Tory that Tristan's smile widened and he leaned over to tweak one of her curls. "I had some inkling that you were at least not displeased to see me when you nearly knocked me over in greeting."

"I did no such thing! I am seventeen now and know very much better than to nearly knock you over in greeting. I am sure I recall curtsying demurely."

Despite her protest, Tory's eyes were dancing, and when Tristan laughed so did she. Having shared much tribulation from the tragedy of their father's death to the financial ruin he had bequeathed them, they were close despite the eleven years between them.

"Was I gone so long?" He gestured to the sketch pad, half smiling. "When I left you could not write legibly."

Tory made a play of hitting him with the sketch pad. "You wretch. And no, my penmanship is not improved! Lud, Tristan! The truth is I cannot seem to draw a straight line. It's Rissa who draws. Quite well. Her likenesses are amazing, and she is trying, despite all odds, to teach me."

Tristan did not remark aloud that Marissa would have had the benefit of the best tutors. For all he knew, she actually had a talent for something other than scandal. "Where is our guest, Tory?" he asked, hearing the coolness in his tone, but unable to moderate it.

Tory did not appear to notice. "Marissa?" she asked, as if they'd another guest. When Tristan did not answer the obvious, she flicked him a glance, only to look away again almost as soon as their eyes met. She had never avoided his gaze before. Tristan knew whom to blame, and it was oddly satisfying.

"Yes. Lady Marissa Portemaine. Where is she, Tory, or did she bid you not to tell me?" When Tory flushed guiltily, Tristan swore angrily.

Tory had only heard Tristan swear on rare and exceedingly difficult occasions, and her hazel eyes went wide. "Oh, my! Rissa said you did not care for her, but I thought there surely had been some misunderstanding. Do you truly not like Marissa, Tristan? I thought you would! She is more beautiful than Celia. That is"—Tory rushed to address a flash she caught in her brother's eyes—"Celia is very pretty, but Marissa is more . . . umm . . . interesting to look at. Don't you think so?" she asked, then rushed on before he could answer. "I mean, there is her coloring; her hair is such a shining black while her eyes are such a rare shade of silver and blue, and her features are so perfect and refined."

"Perhaps they are, though, for my part, I have always thought of her features as sharp." Tristan gave his astonished sister a wry look. "You needn't be quite so amazed, Tory. Most of the world would agree with you. She is accounted an exceptional beauty in town, but she was right. I don't care for her. She's a spoiled, wayward girl who has wanted for discipline all her life as far as I am concerned. Be wary of her, Tory. She never considers anyone but herself."

"She gave me two of her dresses," Tory pointed out, but her voice was small, for she could not remember ever disagreeing with her elder brother.

Nor was Tristan much persuaded by that line of defense. "Did she? How generous of her when I daresay she has hundreds of them and giving away two dresses would mean nothing to her, particularly if she thought she could win herself an ally." Tristan believed he spoke no more than the truth, but Tory looked so stricken that he felt a sudden reluctance for what he did. The feeling was not one he liked, and he irritably raked his hand through his hair. "Perhaps I was harsh," Tristan allowed on a sigh after a moment. "Perhaps Marissa wished you to have the dresses because they suit you. But if she is not quite a Machiavelli, she is still not to be trusted far. I have known her for five years, and I do not think I ever visited her brother that she was not embroiled in some difficulty or scandal. Will you promise me, Tory, that at the least you will think carefully before you do anything she suggests?"

It did not seem an insupportable request. Tory believed

in her heart that either Tristan was mistaken about Marissa, or that Marissa had changed. "Yes, of course, Tristan."

Tristan sat forward in his chair and chucked his sister under the chin. "Good, girl. Now, where is she? Or did she order you not to tell?"

"No! Of course not. That is . . ." Tory bit her lip. She had never seen her generally good-humored brother look as hard as he did then, yet she admired Marissa Portemaine as much as any young, uncertain girl would admire an elegant sophisticated young woman a little older and seemingly leagues wiser than she. "She did ask me not to divulge her whereabouts if I did not have to, but truly, Tristan, she told me not to lie to you, if you asked after her outright."

"Which I am now doing."

Tristan's gaze was steady but unrelenting, and Tory threw up her hands. "Oh, Tristan! She is not doing anything dreadful. She is riding with Ben Hawkes."

Ben was personable, Tristan knew, and not ill-favored, either. Half to himself he growled, "And I was surprised that she did not argue about taking a groom with her."

Tristan's exact point eluded Tory, yet she knew he meant some criticism. "But Rissa does not take Ben with her all the time," she said, though hesitantly, for she was uncertain whether she defended or damned Marissa. "I mean, she does not take any groom at all. She rides too well, except for Ben, of course."

"Of course," Tristan murmured, the irony in his tone as thick as pitch.

More confused and increasingly anxious, Tory hurried to say, "But Ben is a far better rider than Adam, and the two of them race! That is what they are doing now. Rissa is riding her mare, Circe, against Stockings."

"Where are she and Hawkes to race?"

It never occurred to Tory that Tristan might mean to jerk Marissa off her horse and read her a lecture about using her wiles to distract a groom from his legitimate chores. She thought he meant to watch the race. "They have begun already, actually, on St. Mawes Hill. Ah, here comes Dorcas,

now! She was to watch for them from Mama's window.
They must be nearing the woods. After they cross the drive,
they will ride for the river."

Tory stood and waved to Dorcas, who had seen Tristan
and abruptly slowed her pace. He thought the chambermaid
was displaying the best judgment of her day, as she surely
had better things to do than run about the house and yard
following a horse race.

"Could you see anything, Dorcas?"

"Aye, miss. 'Twere neck and neck down St. Mawes Hill,
but her ladyship shot ahead into the woods."

Tristan wondered if Dorcas' mournful tone could be put
down to jealousy of another, and he admitted, far more
beautiful woman. But then Dorcas was forgotten when
Tory wailed, "Oh, no! Tristan, look. Here comes a curricle!" Following his sister's agitated gaze, Tristan saw that,
indeed, a bright, shining curricle had just emerged from the
wooded section of the long drive that wound back to the
Lodge. "They can't have seen them!" Tory cried. "It is
Elise and Gerald! And of all the ill luck! Elise has chosen
now to ape Rissa and try her hands with the reins."

Already on his feet, Tristan leapt from the gazebo. Elise
Kendall could not even ride well, and she was fast approaching the place where the path from St. Mawes Hill
and through the woods opened onto the drive. Sprinting as
hard as he could, he waved urgently, but the pair in the curricle never saw him, and then suddenly, just as he had
feared, a horse and rider burst from the woods.

The Kendalls' carriage horse reared in fright, its large
eyes rolling in its head. Miss Kendall screamed, a high,
panicked sound, and flinging her hands up to her face,
dropped the reins. When her horse felt the slack, it bolted,
racing forward, dragging the light, swaying curricle behind
it.

Marissa was equally as startled as the pair in the curricle,
but when Circe reared, she managed to control her mare
and then did the only thing she could think to do as the curricle tilted precariously. Digging her heels into Circe, she

leaned over to catch the bridle of the runaway horse. The girl in the curricle was screaming, but Marissa concentrated upon the thin bit of leather she must grab. Leaning out dangerously, she shut her mind to the thundering sound of the horses' hooves, and the dust that filled her nose. She'd only a little further to reach, but it seemed impossible until something gave near the shoulder of her coat, and she was freed to extend her arm an inch further and catch the bridle. The horse jerked against her, nearly pulling her off Circe, but Marissa tightened her thighs about her mare, and yanked at the curricle horse's bridle as forcefully as he had pulled against her. By God, he would not pull her to her doom, silly, frightened thing! And he did not. He did her bidding, slowing. Heaving for breath, Marissa clung to the bridle until the horse stopped still.

"By Jove! You saved us, Lady Marissa! You saved us!"

Marissa looked back to find Gerald Kendall rather pale of countenance, but regarding her with dazzled, grateful admiration. Miss Kendall did not speak at all. Slumped against the seat, she still held her hands over her mouth. Marissa was just going to inquire whether she was hurt, when Ben Hawkes rode up behind her.

"Cor, m'lady! I ne'er saw anyone ride better! Cor!" He repeated in the same awed tones. "I thought you'd fall to yer death."

"It was nothing, Ben. I used to perform that trick every day as a child."

Her voice shook as she said it, and Marissa felt a surge of uncontrollable laughter well up in her. Almost as giddy with relief as she, Ben Hawkes began to laugh then, too.

That was how Tristan came upon them: Marissa and his groom, who together had very nearly caused the death or the maiming of his neighbors, laughing witlessly.

"Are you hurt? Miss Kendall? Gerald?"

The moment she heard Tristan, Miss Kendall began to sob. He held out his hands and she nearly fell into them, allowing him to lift her down bodily from the curricle. Mr. Kendall was able to descend without assistance, but his legs

were shaky, and he gave an uncertain laugh. "We suffered a
scare," he said, "but I think we are whole. Jove, I thought
we were done for when I saw that Ellie had dropped the
reins! If not for Lady Marissa . . ."

"I didn't know what to do!" his sister wailed in protest.
"I was frightened! And Dobbin reared, and, and I did not
want to look!"

"Of course you did not," Tristan said steadily. "You
thought you were about to overturn and likely meet your
end. Here is Tory, Miss Kendall. You and Gerald go with
her to the house. Hobbes will bring some brandy and tea,
and you will soon be right as rain."

"But, but aren't you coming, too, Lord Lynton?" Miss
Kendall, a not unattractive girl with auburn hair and brown
eyes, settled back into the crook of Tristan's arm. "I feel so
safe now," she sighed, fluttering her eyelashes.

"I'll be along shortly. By the time you've put your
clothes and hair to rights . . ."

Marissa awarded Tristan a point. Smoothly reminded of
her mussed appearance, Miss Kendall found the strength to
move on her own. Gerald Kendall went, too, perhaps
prompted by some of the same vanity that had spurred his
sister, but he looked back over his shoulder to Marissa, as if
he wished to say something. She was not aware of him,
though. By then Tristan had turned his attention to her.

Chapter 6

Tristan did no more than turn slowly and lift those eyes the color of topazes up to her, where she sat still on Circe, but had she had less control of herself, Marissa would have given a cry of alarm. He had lulled her, dealing efficiently and capably with the Kendalls and ignoring her. But now that he had rid himself of most of their audience, his golden eyes blazed.

He did not address her, though. They'd an audience still, and if Marissa had wondered whether he had the respect of his staff, she'd have had her answer when cocky Ben Hawkes burst into rushed speech. "I'm that sorry this happened, m'lord! I'd no thought there'd be company this soon after luncheon. The curricle must'a come just after we rode into the woods."

"Which is why I trust that path will never be used for racing again," the viscount said in a voice that prompted Ben to nod vigorously enough to hurt his neck. "You may take your horse and Lady Marissa's to the stables now, Ben. I shall speak to you later."

Ben Hawkes did not protest that the challenge to race had come from Marissa. A servant, he did not even think to try to divert the blame to a noblewoman. With a hasty nod of his head, he spurred Stockings and extended his hand for Marissa's reins.

Marissa, however, was not a servant, and she did not wish to remain alone with Tristan. "I shall ride Circe to the stables myself, thank you," she announced.

Tristan never argued. He was tall and powerfully built. It was nothing for him to reach up, encircle her waist with his hands, and lift her out of the saddle. She gave a cry, but it rang more with shock than outrage. Outrage would come later. But not then.

With all that had occurred, Marissa had not spared a thought for how her coat had seemed to give, when she had reached for the bridle of the runaway horse. But now she was fully reminded of it. When Tristan encircled her waist, one hand pressed on her coat, the other, however, met nothing more substantial than the fine lawn of her brother's old shirt. Nothing more. The coat had split at the seam, and she wore nothing, not even a shift beneath the thin shirt, for she'd not thought she would need anything, given that she had been covered by the coat. Tristan's hand might almost have touched her bare flesh. She saw his eyes flare, knew he felt the heat of her body as she felt the warmth of his hand. Then his thumb grazed the underside of her firm breast.

And she was set down upon the ground and released so abruptly, she staggered. Tristan made no move to steady her. To the contrary, he pulled his hands away from her.

With another man, Marissa might have been amused by such haste to release her. She might even have smirked, thinking his embarrassment just reward for having dragged her out of the saddle as if she were little more than a sack of potatoes.

But not even later did she smirk to herself about Tristan's discomfort. She scarcely noticed it, in truth, for a rush of warmth had streaked through her, swelling in her breasts, centering at the point his thumb had touched.

With a part of her mind, Marissa was aware that Ben had caught Circe's reins and was leading the mare away, unaware of anything but his own desire to escape from the vicinity of his displeased employer, but most of her energies were concentrated upon willing the heat from her face and denying that she felt anything warm and quickening anywhere else. Jaw clenched, she stared tight-lipped at Tristan.

"Damn it!" he swore, though she didn't know what—or whom—precisely he damned. She could only stand there and wonder why her heart was racing so wildly. A year before she had allowed a rakish boy who had been pursuing her to touch her breast. It had been an experiment. She had wanted to know what men lusted for, but the experiment had told her little. She had felt only a faint distaste and a desire to slap his hand away. Yet now, when Tristan scarcely brushed her breast, she'd a charged response that might have been pleasurable, had it not been so bewildering.

"I have not been home a week and already you have unthinkingly put the lives of two young, perfectly innocent people at risk."

Marissa blinked. Almost . . . almost she had forgotten the race and the curricle. But not the honey man. If touching her breast had surprised him, it had not moved him otherwise. Marissa felt her cheeks cool.

"I should say I saved the lives of those young people!" She flung up her chin, adding derisively, "Though one of them was witless enough to relinquish the means by which she could have controlled matters from the beginning."

"I see." Tristan snapped out his words quite as sharply as Marissa had. "And what should I do for the future? Slap a victory laurel on your brow, and give examinations for cold-bloodedness as well as quick thinking at the gate? That way, we'll have only those people who can survive you to visit. Of course some of mother's contemporaries will not pass muster, but she can go . . ."

"Stop it!" Marissa stamped her foot. "You are raging like this only because you have been waiting for years to give me a dressing down. If I were anyone else, you would be applauding that I stopped the curricle before it overturned."

"After you were the one that nearly caused it to overturn?"

Tristan looked thunderous, but Marissa had withstood a

good deal of anger in her life and replied wihout hesitation. "Yes! From the instant you first saw me, you took me into dislike. Admit it! Admit that even today, five years later, you do not know—because you never bothered to learn— that Billy and I grew up together, that he was like a brother to me, that he was not even kissing me that day in the stable, only playing as if he were in order to shock Durston into turning his blasted sheep's eyes on someone else!"

"If you think you will persuade me to applaud your actions today by bringing up your behavior in the stables at Penhurst that day, then you are, indeed, a fool, Marissa." Tristan's voice had calmed, but to a pitch that somehow lifted the hairs on the back of Marissa's neck. "What you did then was inexcusable for a goodly number of reasons, not the least of which was that you put at risk the livelihood of the very servant you say was such a fast friend. Perhaps you did grow up with him, perhaps it was a scheme you concocted with him, but had your mother or another guest come upon you, the boy would have been turned off without a reference to his name. As it was, I believe Kit only had him sent to another of your father's estates, a mild punishment, indeed, and one he deserved for the poor judgment he displayed. You, Kit admitted later, got around him and escaped scot free, but I am not Kit, Marissa. You will suffer the consequences of your reckless actions here at Tremourne, particularly when you entice another astray with you. In this case, you will be denied the privilege of riding for a full week."

"What?" Marissa stared, dumbfounded.

"You heard me very well," Tristan informed her grimly. "As you demonstrated the poorest judgment possible while riding, you will be forbidden riding for a week. Hopefully after that time, you will demonstrate that you have the capacity to learn."

Marissa could scarce breathe for her anger. The petty tyrant! No one had ever spoken to her so. He had all but called her a witless child. As to keeping her from riding, he would not succeed there . . . .

"There will be a cost to defiance, Marissa, never doubt it," Tristan warned, reading her thoughts easily. "For every ride you attempt, I shall forbid you an additional fortnight."

Marissa curled her hands into fists. She had called him the honey man, but she had gotten it wrong. Perhaps to others he was good as honey, but toward her he was like a light-haired Viking, eager to exert his dominion over a captive.

Well, she had no intention of being bullied by any man, nor of allowing him to bully any whom he associated with her. "Listen to me, Viscount Lynton." Marissa mockingly emphasized Tristan's title, making certain he understood in what little regard she, a duke's daughter, held it. "I have no intention of surrendering to your petty tyrannies. I did nothing more heinous than ride a race, and by the same token I shall not allow you to let loose the anger you harbor against me upon another. You said that I have dragged Ben into trouble, but you have no reason to punish him!"

"Do I not? I wonder why as I pay his salary? Will you plead that he is another childhood friend, or merely that any young, rough-hewn lad should be left to dally with you as you like?" Marissa gasped as if he had struck her. "No?" Tristan pushed, mocking her.

Marissa ached to hit him. Her hand came up even, yet in the end, she clenched her fingers over her palm. Tristan had not moved, but there was a tension in him that almost begged her to strike him, giving him the excuse to retaliate in kind. She was not such a fool and dropped her hand as her nails scored a mark on the palm of her gloves.

"The idea for the race was mine," Marissa said in a low voice that vibrated with tension, "not Ben's, and I made the wager one I knew he could not refuse."

"Ah. A wager he could not refuse. I wonder if it was anything like the one you made with your old childhood friend?"

"Oh!" Marissa was shaking. "You are a bloody righteous prig, my Lord Lynton, with an ugly mind and deaf ears! I made no wager with Billy. And he was not kissing me, only looked to be. As for Ben Hawkes, he wishes, as you should know for yourself, to marry Dorcas, your chambermaid. To marry her, he needs money. That was why he was willing to race me and no other reason. And as the challenge and wager were my doing, he deserves no censure from you!"

Whether Tristan believed her as to the limit of the groom's interest in her, Marissa could not tell. His face was set too grimly to read. "I am not in the habit of repeating myself, Marissa, but I shall make an exception this once, because I know that you have never been made to understand the consequences of your actions. Once more then, I pay Ben to perform duties he neglected while he chose instead to race Stockings for money and a lark. If he is a child still, he will quit in anger. If he is a man, as his interest in marriage suggests he may be, then he will accept the consequences of his actions and perform the extra duties he is given. If that upsets you, so much the better. Perhaps you will think more carefully the next time you've an impulse to involve someone else in one of your reckless larks."

Marissa felt like a tiger that has found itself suddenly caged. Her hand shot out before she could think better of what she wanted to do. Tristan caught her, not by the hand, but easily avoiding her slap, by the upper arm, and taking the excuse she had so foolishly given him, he shook her hard. "Stop!" she cried, nothing cool about her eyes now. The silver that had so often been likened to ice, fairly sizzled. "You would never punish anyone else like this! You hate me!"

"I wish to God I did thoroughly detest you, but evidently I do not sufficiently!" Tristan heard the rage in his voice and he let go of her abruptly, but his blazing eyes held her as surely as his hand had. "I went through hell watching you risk your life, Marissa. An inch more, and I would be writing to inform your mother and father that you had been mangled beyond recognition beneath a horse's hooves. If you want applause for the risk you took, I am afraid you chose the wrong audience. Now," he went on, a muscle in his jaw working as if he had to fight for control, "you and

Ben will suffer the consequences of your ill-considered challenge. You've only a week to suffer. You may put the time to good use, or you may rebel and lengthen the time of your punishment. The choice is yours. Try to choose wisely, and get yourself out of those absurd, ragged clothes!"

He left her then, with one last contemptuous, blazing look at her boy's breeches and ripped jacket. Marissa ground her teeth together, watching him disappear, honey gold head and broad shoulders, into the Lodge. Even if it had been frightening to watch her lean out between two racing horses, he had no right to punish her. She had not been at *such* great risk. He ought to have known that. He had seen her ride before, and everyone knew she had a superb seat.

Oh, he didn't care! Not that he wanted to see her dead. Doubtless he had been truthful when he said he would not relish informing her parents that she had died while under his so-righteous protection. But she knew the source of his fury. It was the same as her mother's always was. She had embarrassed him before his guests. Well, she'd not pay him any more mind than she did her mother. He had less authority over her.

Chapter 7

"It's beastly annoying my friend Mr. Restwick could not come!" Gerald Kendall looked glumly about at the small group he and his sister had gathered for a picnic. Extending invitations for the small affair had been the purpose of their nearly disastrous visit to Tremourne Lodge. "He was to have accompanied me to a prime cockfight in Penryn tomorrow night. Now I shan't have any company, and I am certain as well that you would have enjoyed Restwick greatly, Lady Marissa. He's a trump! Would do anything, don't you know."

"Oh?" Marissa said, slanting an encouraging look at the young man.

Mr. Kendall's chest expanded before that single, silver blue look. "Indeed, yes! Restwick's a dab hand at fun. Used to get up to some devilish tricks at school, I can tell you. We almost got sent down more than once. Why one time, we put powder in the master's snuffbox!"

Marissa thought if she'd been the master, she'd have made the little scoundrels do their sums until their hands fell off for wasting snuff. She did not say so, however. Instead, she flicked Mr. Kendall another look, half smiling now, and was satisfied when he launched off into another tale of schoolboy derring-do, for she was prepared to allow Mr. Kendall to go on in that vein as long as it took him to be firmly committed to the idea of himself as a hellion.

That did not mean, however, that Marissa felt any obligation to listen to the young man. For her purposes, she needed only to pretend to listen, and so her eyes strayed to the site the Kendalls had chosen, and the smile she then gave her companion was honestly approving.

Mrs. Kendall had had her servants set out the several rugs, chairs, and assorted hampers a picnic requires beside a small stream that tumbled over rocks and boulders down the thickly forested hill rising behind them. Glancing at the clear, cool water, Marissa entertained herself by imagining how it would feel to wade in the water. Her feet, stuck in stockings and tight shoes, were sticky and hot. It was a warm day, and she had played croquet for a little.

Elise Kendall and Tory were playing now as partners against Mr. Fitzgerald and the local doctor's son, Mr. Richards. Tory looked the picture of a young, green girl reveling in the pleasure of her first admirer's smiles and flattery. Her cheeks were flushed and her eyes sparkled. Marissa's eyes narrowed as she flicked her gaze to the admirer in question. Mr. Fitzhugh, predictably, was all light-hearted smiles and teasing flattery. Marissa heard him call out, "Good shot, Miss St. Aubyns! I can't think how I allowed myself to agree not to have you on my team." Tory blushed, but replied with some self-deprecatory remark to which Mr. Fitzhugh replied with more flattery and a deliberate miss on his next shot.

At least his miss seemed deliberate to Marissa's eyes, but she knew that she was inclined to mistrust young men as a rule, particularly ones who smiled a great deal and were unfailingly accommodating and flattering. Perhaps Mr. Fitzhugh meant every word he said and was not deliberately trying to overwhelm Tory. Perhaps.

Marissa knew she would keep a cool eye on the young man, though, at the same time, she told herself that if she meant to be such a broody hen, she ought to go and sit with the dowagers. Lady Lynton had not felt up to a picnic, but it was not as if Tory were not watched. The Tregaron ladies could always be trusted to keep an observant eye out for everyone, as could Mrs. Kendall when it came to it, and Mrs. Richards, the doctor's wife, was certainly not napping.

But Tory had no one from her own family to look after her. Tristan was not such a diligent guardian as he really ought to have been. Marissa smiled, taking Mr. Kendall so by surprise he stammered, and she was obliged to encourage him with a "Do tell me more," before he relaunched himself on whatever his story was.

Tristan was to come, but late, having made the excuse to the Kendalls that a great deal of work had accumulated for him at Tremourne during his absence. Marissa doubted the excuse. He had spent almost all of the several days since he'd returned immersed in estate affairs. Her father devoted perhaps half of a day out of every quarter to his several estates, and though Tristan would naturally be more conscientious than Exeter, she thought his excuse merely a means to avoid her company.

He had taken her by surprise in that regard. She had feared he might think it his duty to dog her heels, but he must have thought he had enough people to report to him on her activities, because he had gone to quite the other extreme, riding out on the estate or sequestering himself in his study for such long periods each day that she had scarcely seen him.

She had thought of him, of course, whenever she'd thought of riding. Her blood boiled afresh every time she thought how, merely because he'd been embarrassed before his guests and dismayed that he'd have to account to Exeter for any harm that befell her, he had forbidden her one of her greatest pleasures in life.

She could hardly bring herself to speak to him, though she did when his mother was present, out of respect for Lady Lynton. Indeed, it seemed Tristan was operating on much the same principle, for the only time he initiated conversation with her was at dinner, when his mother and sister were looking on.

That he cared for his mother was obvious, for he had told her only the vaguest story about the contretemps with the Kendalls, mentioning only poor timing and a frightened horse Marissa had quieted, and nothing at all about disciplining Marissa. Nor had Marissa been any more enlightening. She did not wish to cause Lady Lynton anxiety about anything, whether her riding or her relations with the viscount.

". . . and we all had a great laugh, I can tell you."

Marissa allowed her mouth to curve when she turned to Mr. Kendall. "You are a game 'un, as my brother would say, Mr. Kendall." He flushed and began to stammer again, but Marissa continued pleasantly, "And being so game, you are a man after my own heart. La, I've just had an idea, Mr. Kendall! What a lark it would be if I replaced Mr. Restwick as your companion at the cockfight!" For a half moment, until she regained control of herself, Marissa's mouth twitched in earnest. Mr. Kendall suddenly resembled nothing so much as a codfish hauled out of water. "I would go in male costume, of course. I've the very thing, an old pair of breeches and a jacket a footman left behind at Exeter House." Mr. Kendall could not seem to gain control of himself. He continued to gape at Marissa and never more than when, at the mention of Exeter House, he was reminded just who she was. "I have worn the costume before, and I assure you, Mr. Kendall, that no one guessed who I was— or what." Marissa chuckled. When she was genuinely amused, she had a rich laugh. Mr. Kendall's throat worked as if he found it difficult to swallow, though whether it was Marissa's laugh or her plan that undid him would have been difficult to say. "You will have to bring a horse for me, as of course, I cannot ask Lynton for the loan of one of his. Now, where shall we meet? I know! There is a great rowan tree on the path that winds through the woods from the Lodge to St. Mawes Hill. I shan't have far to walk to it, and you'll not have to chance the drive to the Lodge. But what time, Mr. Kendall? When shall you be going?"

Mr. Kendall stared at her still as if she had sprouted a second head. But Marissa was accustomed to bringing reluctant young men around to her bidding. She smiled again. "Will it be after dark? I know I shan't have to be afraid with you on hand. Ah!" she said then, a pair of approaching riders distracting her. Tristan she recognized from afar. She knew the easy way he sat a horse and the broad-shouldered outline of his figure too well to mistake him. Until the riders came closer, she could not identify his companion with such certainty. Then she saw the woman was the widow, Mrs. Lowell, riding free as she pleased beside the viscount.

"Come, Mr. Kendall, quickly! The viscount approaches, and I would not have him see us together. He might guess our business."

Marissa's eyes were alight with a devilish gleam that spoke to young Mr. Kendall of exciting, forbidden fun such as he had never had. But he thought it must be normal to her and the pinks of the ton with whom she associated and like whom he desperately wished to be.

"Eight o'clock, then!" he exclaimed, his voice squeaking slightly.

She grinned, and he thought he had never seen a more enchanting sight. "Excellent, Mr. Kendall! We'll have had dinner by then. And now, I think I shall just explore the hill and stream a bit. If anyone asks, you may tell them I shall return in a little."

Pivoting on her bottom, Marissa slipped off the boulder on the stream side, and lifting her skirts, climbed nimbly out of sight.

Tristan knew she was missing from the gathering in the glade before he drew rein. He looked for her before he looked for his sister, but he made no apologies. He knew both young ladies, too well, and proving his point: Marissa was not where she was supposed to be, while Tory was playing croquet with three other young people in plain sight of her hostess, not to mention the keenest, most inquisitive pair of spinsters in the kingdom.

The Tregaron sisters' attention to the affairs of others was famous in the parish, and they did not disappoint anyone that afternoon. When Tristan greeted then, Miss Hester inquired, her eyebrows lifted as if in disapproval, whether he had escorted Mrs. Lowell to the picnic.

Tristan did not resent the question, for he was not at all sorry to establish publicly that he and the comely widow had met by chance on the way. He half thought it a pity that he could not go on to say, as the Tregaron ladies would have liked so much to know, that Mrs. Lowell was not his mistress. He thought her a trifle too accommodating, and in all, she bored him. Perhaps she had disagreed with him once. Perhaps, but he couldn't recall the occasion. And she was the kind of woman who would hold tight once she got a purchase. Were they to have an affair, he imagined she would begin to drop hints about marriage after the second, or perhaps the third tryst, and worst of all, would remain a neighbor, when the affair had run its course. For he'd never marry her. He would not care to wonder with every man he met, if his wife had accommodated the other man, too.

But alas, Tristan thought, smiling to himself, he could not simply be over and done with Barbara Lowell by publicly satisfying the Tregarons' avid curiosity. He had to be more subtle, and so he left the widow to Gerald Kendall, and greeted Elise Kendall with as much warmth as he had accorded Mrs. Lowell when she had "happened" to cross his path.

Miss Kendall wore a silk dress, festooned with yards of heavy lace and wide, thick bows. The effect was pretty enough, but the costume looked hot, given the day, and despite himself, Tristan glanced to his sister. She wore a muslin dress that Marissa, Tristan knew from Tory, had chosen for her. Not only was the material cool, he saw, but the dress relied solely on a stylish cut for appeal. There was not one fussy bow weighing down the hem, only a thin rouleau of satin that set it off nicely and coolly.

"Lord Lynton," Miss Kendall began, hurrying over to him from the croquet game. "I wish to thank you again for how kindly you treated me the other day! Mama says I was only displaying proper sensibility when I dropped the reins out of fear, but Gerry has done nothing but deride me as dreadfully missish!"

The girl fluttered her lashes effectively. Tristan had not

noticed before how long and curling they were, but Miss Kendall did not want him merely to approve of her pretty eyelashes. She wished him to say he approved her tossing away the real—and only means—she'd had to save herself and her brother.

He did manage a smile for her. "I am glad to see you suffered no lasting harm, Miss Kendall," he said. Of course the Tregaron ladies were listening, openly, and of course they had heard all about the horse race and Marissa's quick action. Tristan heard Miss Hester sniff disdainfully and had to bite his own lip against a smile. Miss Kendall looked very uncertain. Which was just as well. She had no business even touching a set of reins again.

Tory had come from the croquet area, but she stopped with Mr. Fitzhugh and Mr. Richards to speak to Mr. Kendall and Mrs. Lowell. All the young men seemed attentive to Tory, Tristan noted with pleasure, as well as a pang for how grown she seemed. Still, Marissa was nowhere in sight, and directing Miss Kendall to her mother, who had gotten up to call to the servants for the refreshments, Tristan turned toward the most knowledgeable source present to ask, as casually as he could, if the Tregaron ladies knew Lady Marissa's whereabouts.

Miss Millie spoke up at once. "Yes, indeed, Lord Lynton! Lady Marissa is such a bright flame of a girl, remarkably, really, that I readily admit I can scarce keep my eyes off her. She began following the stream up the hill, just as you arrived."

Miss Millie spoke as if Marissa were alone, but not certain what she might be doing. Tristan thought it advisable not to take witnesses along with him, and slipped away, telling only the two spinsters that he would fetch his mother's guest for the refreshments.

Taking a path through the woods that was an easier walk than clambering along the rocks that bordered the stream, Tristan came out of the woods above Marissa. She sat on a large boulder, unaware of him, gazing through the trees down to the slate roofs of Penryn village, an unexceptional activity except that her shoes and stockings lay discarded on the bank, and she sat with her skirts pulled up to her knees, dangling her bare feet in the stream's cool water.

Had she planned for Gerald Kendall to come and see her thus? Had she hoped to entrance the pup with the sight of her half bared for his pleasure? And pleasure it would have been. Tristan admitted it. Her feet were as delicately boned as her face, her ankles trim, and her calves finely curved. Perhaps she'd have allowed Kendall to kneel in front of her and dry her pretty feet.

"Marissa."

At the growl, Marissa started so, she half slipped into the water. Finding a footing and grabbing up her skirts, she whirled about to face Tristan, her blue eyes flashing.

"You frightened me!" she accused. Then she added sharply, "I suppose it was deliberate."

"No." She looked unexpectedly young, standing barefoot in the stream, the skirt of her dress at midcalf, and almost trailing in the water. Of course, she was young, just twenty, but she did not usually seem young. "I am not in the habit of trying to frighten women or children."

A slim, soot-black eyebrow shot up at that, managing to convey to Tristan both that Marissa questioned in which group he put her and at the same time that she did not give tuppence for his opinion.

"Well, you did frighten me," she retorted waspishly, and lifting her skirts to her knees, retraced her steps across the stream.

"I had no idea you were so lost in your thoughts," Tristan said, propping himself against a tree, as she did not appear to need any assistance.

Gaining the bank, Marissa shot him a dark look, but was more immediately concerned with her feet. To dry them, she began wiping them on the grassy bank. "I would lend you my handkerchief," Tristan remarked, "but I don't think it's large enough to do much good."

"They'll dry," she muttered, shrugging.

He studied her a long minute, the tone of her voice making

him question whether she did, in fact, have any idea how provocative the sight of her daintily arched feet and bare ankles was. Ordinarily he'd have said she understood to an inch, but not only did he know how much she disliked him, she sounded too disgruntled to be thinking of teasing him.

"Well?" she said, casting him a look as disgruntled as her tone, and rather settling his question. "What have you come to castigate me for now? Or did you come only in the hopes of finding a reason?" She tossed her head and pointedly did not wait for an answer. No sooner were the words out of her mouth, than she flounced over to the shoes and stockings she'd dropped haphazardly on the ground, and sitting down on a rock, her back turned to him, proceeded to don them.

As she had not walked out of his line of vision, Tristan could see her lift her skirt, and he could imagine easily enough what she did as she bent her knee and began smoothing the stocking over the calf he'd studied a few moments before. Swearing under his breath, Tristan looked away, but Penryn village lacked the power to block his imagination, and he found himself thinking that perhaps he'd gotten his first question all wrong. Perhaps she had not thought to tease him merely because he was male and present, but to tease him in order to punish him for scaring her. Or for coming after her at all. She was a witch and might well flaunt herself, even disgruntled.

"Actually," Tristan said, his tone distinctly harder, "I came to fetch you because your hostess is having the refreshments served. But now that I have found you, I see no reason not to remind you that is simple courtesy to remain with your hostess and her guests. As well, of course, as it is correct, albeit tediously so, I'm sure, to remain fully clothed when in a public place."

"And what do you intend to do?" Marissa demanded. Tristan heard her stand, but saw no reason to treat her with any more ceremony than she had treated him. A boat was being rowed into the Penryn estuary below them, and he spared a moment to hope that the man's catch had been good. Lord knew there was not enough work on the estates in the area for all the men who needed it. "Well?" she demanded, her ire evidently kindling when he kept his back to her. "Do you mean to forbid me clothes, my lord? I am following your reasoning in the matter of riding, you understand."

He could see her naked. It was tantalizingly easy. He had only to recall how she had looked with the Grecian gown clinging to her body. Could she possibly not know what she did? Tristan turned abruptly. "You speak brazenly, Marissa. Are you practicing to enthrall Gerald Kendall?"

Marissa lifted her haughty chin. "Yes, my lord," she answered without hesitation. "I wish very much to practice my wiles, for I long for Gerald Kendall to be my slave, and you make an excellent stand-in for him, don't you think?"

The last thrust almost made him smile and for more than one reason. From her sarcasm it was obvious she had not thought either to entice or to punish him earlier. She thought him utterly immune to her. And being immune to everything but her looks, for he was male, after all, he was in essence immune to her . . . but Gerald Kendall was very young. "I think," he said, regarding her steadily, "that you would have the impressionable Mr. Kendall do your bidding."

She did not blink an eye. Tristan gave her that. If she was planning to use Kendall in some way, she did not give herself away.

"Well, whatever your plans in relation to the pup," he said, putting her on notice that he was not taken in, "Mrs. Kendall's repast awaits. And it wouldn't do to be late for it. You might disappoint Miss Millie and Miss Hester, who have likely penned you into their next Minerva Press attempt. They think you a bright flame, you see."

Marissa had an expressive mouth. Tristan had noted the attribute before when he had seen her mouth set mulishly or lift sardonically. Now the corners twitched, as if she could not control them. But if her eyes betrayed amusement as well, she didn't allow him to see it. Before he could, she turned toward the path he had used.

Chapter 8

"Good morning, Marissa. What a pleasure it is to have you to look at every morning."

Marissa gave Lady Lynton a self-amused smile. "I suspect most people would say that looking at me is the only pleasure to be derived from my acquaintance. No, I know you are not one of them, and I do thank you for the compliment. But are you ill, ma'am? Is that why you are lying down?"

As Lady Lynton lay in her bed, a stack of pillows behind her, Marissa had reason for frowning, but the elder woman shook her head. "No, no, my dear, I am not ill at all, only fatigued. It is my gardening. There is so much to do at this time of year, and my heart does not want me to do so much as I wish I could."

Marissa gave her hostess a level look. "I would not say that your gardening has been the only or even the major cause of activity for you. Though I may be fairly accused of self-absorption, even I can guess that I am the one taxing you. You needn't keep me to the detriment of your health, you know, Lady Lynton. I can serve out my sentence of exile at Mama's sister's home. Aunt Vi would have to take me. She depends upon Mother for funds, you see."

"But I do not wish you to go away!" Lady Lynton exclaimed, rising slightly from her pillows. "I should miss you, Marissa. I look forward to these early morning cozes of ours."

"I enjoy them, too, my lady, but I'd not have you made ill."

"It is my gardening making me weary—not ill—my dear. And you, I hope, are going to be a help to me."

"Certainly, I shall do anything you wish," Marissa answered with a touch of surprise.

Lady Lynton smiled. She had eyes more Tory's hazel than Tristan's golden brown, but when she smiled the resemblance between her and Lynton was more obvious, for they'd both smiles that went bone deep and suffused their faces with warmth. Not that Marissa had experienced Lynton's smile herself, of course. But she had seen him bestow it upon others, the widow Lowell, for example, at the picnic the day before.

"I knew I could count on you, my dear!" Lady Lynton fell back as if vastly relieved. "You see, I act as Tristan's secretary. The work does not involve much. For the most part, I write letters for him and keep his appointment book current. It is the former responsibility I wish you to carry out for me. I have neglected my duties for him in favor of my gardens, and I am afraid a daunting stack of notes has accumulated. Tory could write them, of course, but you have seen her hand. It is nearly impossible to read. She will keep up Tristan's personal correspondence, as hopefully his close friends will feel generously enough toward him that they will not quibble over having to guess at every word, but I do not think we can require such forbearance from strangers."

Normally Marissa would have chuckled at least. Tory's handwriting was a family joke, and the younger girl had even begged for sketching lessons in the hopes that her penmanship would improve as a result.

Marissa frowned then, though. "Have you spoken to Lord Lynton about what you wish me to do?"

"No, my dear," Lady Lynton replied, with supreme unconcern. "I have not seen Tristan yet this morning, but he will not object. Though he must have the letters written, he would not wish me to overtax myself."

"No, of course not, but I think he might prefer to write his letters himself."

"He would protest to me that he could write them himself," Lady Lynton responded agreeably. "But in truth he would be sorely pressed for the time. He has been away two months, and there is a great deal for Tristan to do, you see." Marissa truly did not see. Her father and elder brother relied on their stewards, bailiffs, and agents to manage their estates. But as she took a breath to object again, Lady Lynton gave a tired sigh and laid her head back upon her pillows. "Lud, but I resent this weariness! Please, my dear? You may do the work when you wish, and I should be so relieved."   .

When Lady Lynton closed her eyes for a moment, as if she lacked the strength to continue, Marissa knew her answer. She had never forgotten the day Lady Lynton had come into the music room at Penhurst and seeing Marissa there reading, had asked her if she would bother her with her playing. It was a small gesture, surely, but not to Marissa. She had known almost since she could reason that her mother cared nothing at all about her wishes; that, indeed, simply to counter what she could of Exeter's influence, Her Grace was more likely than not to demand that Marissa do the opposite of what she wished. But the truly painful realization that had come to her more gradually was that her father, her champion in her mind at least, cared as little about what she wished as did Lady Catherine. One too many times, when she had begged him not to leave her to her mother, he had merely chucked her under the chin and told her that as a Portemaine, she'd the spirit to successfully defy anyone, alone.

An hour later Marissa sat in Tristan's study at the small desk Lady Lynton used. Not eight feet away was the viscount's desk. Positioned to receive the best light from the windows, they stood at an angle, half facing each other. His was larger and not particularly tidy. There were several ledgers upon it and papers stacked in two or three piles. Her own desk was neater, but the stack of papers she was to transcribe into letters was higher than either of his. Though Lady Lynton had given her a hint, Marissa had not realized there would be so many letters, or that she could not possibly finish before Tristan came to the study that day.

She did not want to work shut up in the same room with him. She did not want to work with him at all.

He might easily have sent Tory to look for her at the picnic. But no, he must come himself to see how depraved she was, and he had found her barefooted! Horror of horrors. Not that he himself had been even mildly unsettled by the sight of her bared feet. Oh, no. As far as he was concerned, her charms could affect only impressionable, immature pups like Gerald Kendall.

At the thought of that young man, Marissa rolled her eyes. She had warned Mr. Kendall that she did not want Lynton to associate them too closely in his mind, and yet, halfway down the hill, whom should they meet but Gerald Kendall ascending. She had not had to look to know precisely how sardonic Tristan's expression would be. And it was. He'd even smiled, if something that caustic could be called a smile. She'd wanted to box Gerald's pink ears, but had been obliged, instead, to be relatively pleasant to him, just to spite Tristan.

She had had, too, the less than exalting experience of being in company with Mrs. Barbara Lowell. Just as she had come out of the woods, Marissa had chanced to see Mrs. Lowell and Mr. Fitzhugh exchange a look. It had seemed somehow intimate, but the pair had not looked at one another again that afternoon, and it was not upon Mr. Fitzhugh that Mrs. Lowell had publicly set her sights.

Had Marissa behaved as the widow had, Tristan would have shut her in her room for a month, but he only smiled at Mrs. Lowell when she sat close enough to him to feed him by hand, or managed to brush her cowlike bosom across the hand he offered to her to help her rise. Marissa knew the woman's type, for London was filled to the brim every Season with lushly formed, sultry women looking at the least to have an affair with the highest-ranking, most presentable man in sight, and at the most to marry him, and it made her blood sizzle that Lynton should consider her more reprehensible than such a calculating witch.

Marissa picked up a second sheet of vellum and slapped it down on the desk before her just as the study door swung open without warning. Tristan stood there, his hand on the door fastener, but he was turned, speaking to someone behind him. Marissa felt the beat of her heart. Not that it pounded. Her heart would not pound, but she was aware of it; and aware, too, that he seemed to fill the doorway. The honey man was not slight.

Not that she was physically afraid of him. Tristan would never lay a hand on her. Indeed, why her heart should be beating so hard, she could not fathom. He was only the honey man, always good, always purposeful. When an issue interested him, he made influential speeches in the House of Lords. Kit praised him ad nauseum, said he was an excellent leader, demanding but fair, intelligent . . . and a prig, given to snap, if permanent, judgments. Kit had left that last out but Marissa was happy to supply it.

He turned. He was frowning slightly, looking abstracted. A lock of honey gold hair had fallen onto his brow. Absently, he raked it out of his way with his fingers as he shut the door behind him.

As if on cue, when the door clicked closed, he looked up. His gaze, still abstracted, roved by the windows, passed Marissa at her desk, then jerked back to fix on her incredulously.

"What in the devil's name are you doing at Mother's desk?" he demanded.

His mouth, the mouth that had curved so readily for the widow, and even silly Elise Kendall, was a straight, taut line.

"My being here has nothing to do with the devil or my own choice." When Tristan grunted, Marissa took the equivocal sound to mean he could not see much difference between her and the devil. Her silver blue eyes narrowed. "Your mother asked me to come."

"That is absurd."

He was standing before her desk, looking very tall and powerful as he locked eyes with her. Marissa considered pushing her chair back, for the desk was a small, feminine thing that seemed no barrier against him. She wanted distance, walls, doors between them. But she would have died before she betrayed to Tristan in even the slightest way that he had the power to discomfit her.

Accordingly, she made herself actually lean forward. The morning sun streaming in the window behind her lit his face. It ought to have illuminated at least one flaw. One flaw was not so much to ask, but she got the Greek ideal, strong, well made, arresting. Even to small details. She had not noted his lashes before, but the light streaming in the window behind her played on his face, revealing the unexpected, hedonistic length of them.

Marissa dropped her gaze from those lashes, thrown off balance by having noted such a small thing. All men had eyelashes, after all. And she was certain she had seen other men with lashes as long.

"You may tell Lady Lynton her request is absurd, if you wish, but you needn't expend your ill humor on me, my lord," Marissa said, and then loftily swept her slender hand over the pile of papers she was to transcribe. "Lady Lynton asked me to write these letters for you, and I came down dutifully to do so."

Pleased to be, and so clearly, too, in the right, Marissa lifted a face smug with self-satisfaction to Tristan. He did not scowl or flare. He gave her a flat, steady look and said in similar flat, unequivocal tones, "You have never been dutiful in your life."

Had she thought she could escape without retribution, she'd have slapped him. As it was, Marissa closed her fingers tightly around the pen she held and snapped thinly, "Well, I am being dutiful now. Perhaps you should congratulate yourself for your effect upon me. But, if you care to dispute with your mother, be my guest. She told me that she was tired. Perhaps you can convince her otherwise."

That gave him pause. With a great deal of satisfaction, Marissa watched as Tristan frowned. And raked his hand through his hair again. It seemed to be a habit, when he was distracted. "She said she lacked the strength to write these letters?"

His eyes were dark as he indicated the pile of paper beside Marissa, but she realized that for once he was not angry with her. "Yes, but she swore she was not ill, merely fatigued from working overlong in her garden." When Tristan's expression did not lighten, she added quietly, "Truly, she did not look ill."

"When did you see her?"

"This morning. We take our chocolate together sometimes." He nodded absently, as if he knew of their custom. Marissa watched him a moment then asked, "Does this happen often? I mean that Lady Lynton takes to her bed for a day?"

"On rare occasions, and I cannot say I am astonished that she should tire now."

Marissa's chin shot up. "Lady Lynton professes to enjoy my company, and I do not believe she is a liar. But perhaps you have been fatiguing her with disparaging tales, my lord. Is that the case?"

"Oh, indeed. I came straight back from the Kendalls' picnic and advised her that you had half stripped for your host."

"I did not half strip!" Something heated flashed at the back of Tristan's eyes. Of course it was anger. She had roused that emotion in him, and that one, alone, from the first.

"You may have stripped off no more than your shoes and stockings, Lady Marissa,"—he all but sneered her title—"but for Gerald Kendall, you'd have been as good as half naked. Great God! He hasn't ever seen so much as an ankle before."

"You are being disingenuous!" Marissa flung back. "He is older than I."

Tristan leaned down, fisting his hands upon the desk and

bringing his face not a half foot from Marissa. "Very well then," he said with lethal softness. "Gerald Kendall has likely been to a whore. Is that what you aspire to be to . . ."

It was the second time he had all but called her a whore. And he cut her. Cut her enough that she flew to her feet, meaning to quit the room and him altogether. But she did not get so far. Her hand caught the three letters she had painstakingly completed, knocking them to the floor, after they hit the bottle of ink she'd used. It was unstoppered and wobbled. Afraid the ink was about to spill across Lady Lynton's elegant little writing desk, Marissa moaned and dove for the bottle. It slipped through her fingers, teetering dangerously, making her dart for it again. She caught it then, spilling only a few drops of black ink on her hand.

Feeling a bumbling fool, Marissa refused to look up as she blotted the ink from her fingers with her handkerchief. "I warned Lady Lynton that this arrangement would not work, and as it clearly will not, you will have to find someone else to write your letters, my lord."

Tristan did not say anything. Nor did he move away. Marissa was intensely aware of him standing there, watching her blot the miserable ink from her hand as if she were a child too stupid to be trusted to do it properly by herself. Finally, when she could not bear the scrutiny any longer, she flung him a fulminating look.

She had expected he would be scowling, half angry still over her behavior at the picnic and half derisive at the mess she'd made. But he wasn't scowling or derisive. He was watching her with an unexpected look in his eyes. It was not soft, exactly, but neither was it hard.

"Here."

He held out his own handkerchief, but Marissa shook her head. "I'll only stain it."

"I see." Marissa had the oddest impression he meant to smile. She tensed, scarcely breathing for some reason. But he didn't. He returned the handkerchief to his pocket, then bent to retrieve the letters she'd knocked onto the floor.

"Are they ruined?" Marissa demanded, frowning. She had spent a full hour on them.

Lynton scanned them, then shook his head. "No, they are fine. You've done very well, actually, filling in all the etceteras nicely. Thank you." He looked up from the last letter to meet her eyes. "I did not mean to say that I believe you are a light-skirt, Marissa, but that you will confuse a young man like Gerald Kendall should you act in ways that are fast in his eyes. For him, there are only two sorts of women: the kind one treats gently, and the kind one does not but does gossip about."

"Thank you for that insight, my lord." Marissa moved with stiff dignity from behind the desk. She hated being lectured like a child by him, and she hated almost as much having been a bumble-fingered fool in front of him. "At the admitted risk of wasting my breath, I shall repeat that I did not intend for Gerald Kendall to find me with my feet dangling bare in his stream, nor I might add, did he find me so. Only you crept up on me and I do not expect you will gossip about me. Now if you will excuse me, I wish you luck with your letters."

She was pleased to think she had stung him just a little by neglecting to say she expected him to treat her gently, for he frowned, but then, as she made to pass him, he seemed to be reminded of his letter, and glanced down at the ones he held again.

"I'll need luck with them, actually," he said slowly. "There is no one else to do them. My penmanship is as deplorable as Tory's, and I cannot imagine that Hobbes would do any better. Certainly I don't expect he could write so perfectly as this." Tristan held out the letter. Marissa ignored it in favor of studying his face. He looked decidedly wry. She could understand perfectly why.

"I am gratified that you have found something I do commendably."

He actually smiled a little. "Do you mean to make me beg, Marissa? I'll concede that I concluded on thin evidence that you knew Gerald Kendall would be sent out to look for you, if you wish."

"That is a thin concession, sir, as you do not concede that you judged me wrongly, nor even that you judged me on no evidence at all," Marissa said. "But I won't even take it amiss that you call me a liar at nearly every turn, and I will write all the rest of your letters, if you will send word to Tibbs that I may ride."

The slight softening of Tristan's expression vanished. "I see. Then, I shall write them, for I cannot bend the rule I made simply for the sake of convenience. You would never believe my word in the future."

Marissa wanted to lash out, to kick him, to kick the desk even. Lud, but he was a despot. He would not take her word for anything; and then, having insulted her as deeply as anyone ever had, but for her mother, he would not make a reasonable trade. Well, he could write his own letters then. And she hoped his hand cramped.

Marissa brushed past him, stalking to the door. Lady Lynton needn't know. She wouldn't tell her . . . "Oh! Damn and damn! And I hope your honey ears are burning!" Marissa raged, spinning about at the door.

At any other time she'd have laughed at Tristan's startled look. "I beg your pardon?"

"You needn't," she snapped. "Simply forget what I said. It was an absurd fancy, but I shall write those letters. Not for you—never for you—but for your mother. I told her I would do it, and contrary to your impression, I keep my word."

Chapter 9

"Lady Marissa? Lady Marissa, are you there?"

Marissa stepped out of the shadow of the great rowan tree, confirmed in her opinion that Gerald Kendall would make a poor conspirator in any serious plot. He sounded as nervous as if they were defying Napoleon, himself.

"Yes, Mr. Kendall, I am here."

"Oh!"

It was late evening, but still she could see the whites of Mr. Kendall's eyes widen. Did he not recall that she'd said she would wear boy's clothes? Or that she'd worn breeches the day she'd raced Ben Hawkes? Perhaps he had been more distraught that day than he'd let on, but what had he imagined she would wear to a cockfight? An evening dress?

Ignoring Gerald's shock at her boy's breeches and jacket, Marissa looked over the mare he'd brought for her. The animal was somewhat leggy but Marissa did not mean to ride her the night long. "She is fine-looking, Mr. Kendall. What is her name?"

"Ah, Dilly. Oh, Lady Marissa, allow me to help you!"

Gerald nearly tumbled from his horse in his haste to get to Marissa, but she had already swung up on the mare, unaided. "Leave off, Mr. Kendall. Please," she added, taking some pity on him. "If you act the chivalrous gentleman tonight, everyone will know I am a female."

There was quite ample light for Marissa to read young Mr. Kendall's expression then. He did not believe anyone would take her for anything other than a female. "You needn't worry, Mr. Kendall. I've done this sort of thing before," she assured him, and withdrawing something thin and fuzzy from her pocket, applied it to her upper lip. When Gerald gaped, Marissa laughed aloud. "You see? The scraggly mustache of a youth. One of our housemaids in London had a sister who worked as a wardrobe mistress for a theater in London." So saying, Marissa also removed a pair of spectacles from her pocket. The glass in them was clear, but the frames were thick. Wearing them and with her large, floppy hat pulled low, she hid most of her face, and she knew from experience that with her oversized jacket, rather baggy trousers, and scraggly mustache, she would draw little if any attention.

"Shall we go?" she asked, and gave Mr. Kendall a grin.

Marissa couldn't know her grin was cocky and charming at once, but she could see the effect it had on her companion. He grinned back. "You're a bang-up girl, Lady Marissa! I never thought to meet anyone like you. Aye, let's be gone!"

There was just enough light to canter, and though Gerald's mare did not have a gait so smooth as Circe's, Marissa was in alt. Her mind and body, both had seemed to become cramped with only trudging about the small park at Tremourne for exercise. Now the soft evening air flew by her cheeks as the horse moved powerfully beneath her. There was simply nothing like the feeling. Everything seemed to slip away, even . . .

But he did not slip away so smoothly as all else. Predictably, for she had spent an hour the day before and two that morning shut up with him, not all else.

Yesterday, after her furious announcement that she would do his letters, on his mother's account, Marissa had fallen to her task with such intensity that not one word had passed between them.

Nor one glance, either, for while Marissa felt Tristan's presence so keenly that she had found it difficult to concentrate on what she must write, he had immersed himself in some large books and seemed to forget her completely. Glancing through her lashes to discover what absorbed him so, she came to the conclusion that Tristan was making numerical entries in ledgers, and therefore was acting as his own clerk. She was not so astonished as she might have been before learning that Lady Lynton served as her son's secretary, but still, she was surprised. Obviously Tristan was either an eccentric or strapped for funds. She wanted to incline toward the first explanation, but it was so patently untrue that she realized her question as to why he had not rebuilt his family's seat was answered. He hadn't the funds.

Yet, if it was necessity that prompted him to attend as closely as he did to his estate, he had developed an interest in what he did. She did not imagine that her father's bailiff kept up as extensive a correspondence on agriculture as did Lynton. He wrote to others asking questions, or in his turn, answered theirs on crop rotation, crop succession, seed maturities, soil composition, climate requirements, and so on. He inquired about a mechanical thresher powered by water; recounted his experience with olive trees (they grew well in Cornwall's mild climate, but he did not think they would thrive elsewhere in England), and explained why he had resisted expanding the sheep herds that were the traditional livestock in his area of the country.

Marissa conceded that she would never admit as much to Tristan, but she found the letters rather interesting, and had he been anyone else, she might have asked him to explain further one thing or another. But he was not anyone else. He was the man who had forbidden her to ride, told her she behaved like a light skirt on the one hand, and on the other, treated her like a child. "I see no reason not to remind you that simple courtesy requires you . . ." Lud, but he sounded like her mother!

And she would spend more time still shut up in his study with him! Oh, it did not bear thinking on. She had gone early to his study that morning, hoping to avoid him, but he was there already, and looking up from his ledgers, said, "Good morning, Marissa." In her turn, Marissa had inclined her head and said, as effusively, "Good morning, Tristan." And that had been the extent of their conversation.

Marissa might have gnashed her teeth, had she been given to such behavior. It was the most absurd and untenable situation she had ever encountered: being shut up in a room with a man who did not want her there any more than she wanted to intrude. And yet there was no other room in his doll's house where a proper desk and writing materials could be found, and worst of all, she, who held few people in real esteem, both respected Lady Lynton and had an abiding fondness for her. Marissa would sit in the study again tomorrow.

She briefly closed her eyes. She had come riding with Gerald not for the cockfight ahead but for the ride she was all but ignoring in favor of dwelling on Tristan. Devil it! Forcing herself to take a breath, she looked around at the night. The moon was a beautiful, blade-thin crescent, shedding only just enough light for them to see the road and the occasional house they passed. The air was soft as a caress on her skin. Then she and Gerald Kendall were riding through a creek, sending water splashing up to sparkle in the moon's light, and Marissa was so glad to be out, so glad she had not allowed Tristan to dictate to her, that she wanted to toss her hat in the air.

It was not the time to reveal the thick plait pinned up under her hat, however. There were other riders ahead, and some men behind them in a cart. They were nearing Penryn village. The cockfight was a local affair. Mr. Kendall had told her that the winning cocks would go on to fight in Falmouth, after they had proven themselves in the stables of the inn, the largest enclosed public space in the small village.

And even then it was a small enclosed public space, Marissa thought, looking around from beneath the brim of her hat with a faint smile. The "arena" had been set up in the place where two of the stables' aisles intersected. On three sides, bales of hay had been arranged to form graduated benches, while some of the younger men had hoisted themselves onto the surrounding stall partitions. Gerald Kendall had, and Marissa credited him for the foresight, considered where it would be best for her to sit, and with a motion of his head, gestured to the partition of the stall nearest them and not so incidentally nearest to the main doors of the stables. Using an unoccupied bale of hay, Marissa climbed nimbly into position, and realized after a few minutes that Mr. Kendall had found her the safest spot in the stables, for she was so close to the doors that the men coming inside didn't look up until they had already passed her, and then they were so intent on the cocks in their cages that not one in the crowd of fifty or so men looked back to the inconspicuous lad in the shadows by the door.

Nor did Gerald Kendall betray her in any way. After he scrambled into place in front of her, she whispered that he should ignore her, and he did, talking exclusively with the young man in front of him.

Marissa's baggy brown clothes were not at all out of place, she was glad to see. Most of the men were dressed similarly in rough, bulky clothes of either brown or dark gray. Most were drinking, many out of tankards of ale supplied by the inn, but a few from bottles they'd brought themselves. Hardworking fishermen and farm laborers for the most part, they were intent upon making the most of a night of excitement, hailing one another with boisterous shouts as they reckoned the worth of the various cocks and made their wagers. The excitement in the air grew thicker along with the smoke from the many pipes, as it came time to set the first two cocks against each other.

One had a bright reddish cast to its feathers, the other was greener-looking. Both were proud, strutting arrogantly about as the men called out, "Red!" or "Green!" depending upon where they had put their money.

Marissa realized the fault was hers and foolish in the extreme, but she had not once considered what a cockfight would entail. She'd thought of the ride and even of the strong, weathered faces she'd study for a subsequent sketch, but no more. When the green cock flew at the red, spurs glinting in the lantern light, she caught her breath at the sudden violence. It was a bold move. As she watched, unable to look away, a crimson jet of blood spurted suddenly from the red cock's neck.

The crowd gave a great cry, but Marissa could not have said if it was a pleased roar. She scarcely heard it. Sounds had receded, and she felt hot and cold at once. With a sense of panic, she fought the not unfamiliar feeling. Adrian, her eldest brother, had hurt himself once and come running to their governess with blood dripping from his hand. Marissa had taken one look, gone hot and cold, and then fainted dead away.

Without a word to Mr. Kendall, who was exclaiming over the brevity of the fight with the lad in front of him, Marissa dropped down from her seat and slipped out the door. The air was not cool, but it was fresh, and forcing herself to stagger around the corner of the stables out of the light, she sank against the wall and tried to will the light-headedness to pass.

"Shall I burn a feather under your nose, Marissa?"

Marissa's eyes flew open, and the blood surged back into her head so hard she felt dizzy again. His hands on his hips, Tristan glowered at her pitilessly, standing so close and so tall and large, he blotted out the moon.

"Didn't the cockfight suit you? You look a trifle peaked. And what in the bloody hell is that on your lip?"

Trying to straighten, Marissa swayed. "My mustache, of course," she said, but her voice was a mere thread of sound.

Tristan did not extend a hand to steady her, but instead reached out his hand to rip the sticky, false mustache from her lip. He hurt her, and she gave a yip. He was not apologetic. "Did I hurt you, Marissa?" he demanded sarcastically even as he roughly unburdened her of her false spectacles, too. "Do you not care for pain? I thought perhaps you would, given the pain you invited by going into those stables."

"I only felt light-headed for a moment," she muttered, though in fact she still felt unsteady.

"I did not refer to your reaction to watching two animals maul each other for the amusement of a pack of bloodthirsty gamesters. I was referring to the pain those same bloodthirsty gamesters would have inflicted had they discovered a disguised female in their midst. God hear me, you are the stupidest person it has ever been my misfortune to meet!"

That righted Marissa's bearing. Scandalous or reckless she might be. She was a Portemaine, but she was not stupid. Tristan gave her no time to shout what she thought of him, however, he grabbed her wrist and summarily dragged her away from the stables. "Let me go! Stop! Where are you taking me?"

"Home."

Had she not known with utter certainty that Tristan would not do her physical harm, Marissa might have flinched at the way he snarled the word. As it was, she fought against his hold. "But my . . ." Her voice trailed off when she realized that if Tristan were to take her to the mare, he would learn the identity of her coconspirator.

"We shall leave young Gerald to discover you missing and his horse unridden," Tristan retorted, snarling still, as he informed her that he had either learned or guessed with whom she'd come. "The worry he'll suffer should be some recompense for agreeing to bring you along on this idiotic expedition."

"But I did not want to come to a cockfight!" Marissa hissed, pulling against Tristan with no success. He continued to all but drag her to the front of the inn yard where he had left his gelding. "I came to ride!"

"Recompense for helping you to break my rule before bringing you to a cockfight, then." When they reached Stockings, he jerked her in front of him. In the light of a nearby lantern, she could see that white lines of fury bracketed his mouth. "You little fool! I gave you my word that if you tried to ride, you would earn a full fortnight on foot. Did you think I would forget?"

In truth, Marissa had not considered Tristan's threat, for she had not imagined that he would catch her. A fortnight more, beyond the three days she had yet to go on the first week. It seemed to Marissa that she would not ride for an eternity, and suddenly she could not bear any of it, not that he had found her nearly fainting away like a fool, not the punishing grip he had on her wrist even then, not the way he had dragged her like a ragamuffin across the inn yard, and most certainly not that he would keep her off a horse for almost a month altogether.

Shrieking in anger, Marissa lashed out, hitting him as hard as she could. "You cannot do it! You are not my jailer! I would rather be confined in the Tower. At least there is honor there. Let me go!"

Tristan swore harshly, and catching her other wrist shook Marissa until her hat fell off and her braid tumbled down her back. Her breast heaved as she fought for breath, and yet she gazed up at him as furiously as she had when she began her futile struggles. Tristan returned the look with interest.

"Through no desire of my own, Marissa, you have fallen into my keeping, and while I have responsibility for you, I'll not allow you to put yourself or any other into harm's way. You will learn not to be so heedless and reckless while you are at Tremourne at least. That means you will suffer the consequences I have promised. Now, do you mount Stockings and ride before me, or do I throw you over my saddle like a sack of potatoes?"

He had handled her as easily as if she were a kitten, dragging her about, shaking her at will. Marissa believed not only that he would throw her over his saddle to ride with her derriere in the air, but that he might enjoy it.

"I hate you!"

"We make a matched pair, then," he shot back and summarily lifting her by the waist, threw her onto the gelding hard enough that her teeth rattled. Marissa had no time to contemplate some vengeful escape. Tristan swung up be-

hind her in the next moment, enclosing her in the prison of
his arms, and kicking Stockings once, set off fast enough
that Marissa had to cling to the horse's mane to keep herself from falling back against him, the infuriating tyrant
whom she detested.

Chapter 10

Marissa waited until teatime to work in Tristan's study the next day. She left only an hour later, one letter completed and a dozen efforts crumpled and thrown in the paper bin, all casualties of a distracted mind. She had been listening warily for Tristan's footfall, though she knew he was to take tea with his mother.

But not dinner. He was not to dine at the Lodge. His friend Mr. Haydon had returned from Italy in a display, as far as Marissa was concerned, of providential timing. Else she'd have had to fabricate an excuse to take dinner in her room. She could not possibly do anything so civil as sit down to dinner with a man who had shaken her until her teeth rattled.

The next day, however, Tristan took Marissa by surprise. She entered the study to find him already sitting at his desk, though she had thought he would still be with Mr. Haydon. Pinning her gaze upon her desk, she in no way acknowledged his presence, and for the next hour worked with her head down, never lifting it. Finally, as her neck began to ache unbearably, he did her the favor of removing himself from the room, one of the ubiquitous ledgers dangling from his fingers. The moment the door clicked shut behind him, Marissa threw up her head and breathed deeply. The crackling silence in the room had been nearly unbearable. But never would she have left the room first and have him think she fled either the tension or him.

The next day was much the same. Tristan was at his desk

first, and again Marissa never glanced at him and so had no idea whether he looked up, prepared to acknowledge her. She did not care, if he was. She would be damned if she would go through the motions of courtesy after the insufferable way he had treated her.

But it was not easy to ignore Tristan completely. He sat only ten feet away. If he moved to lay his pen aside, she knew it. If he stretched his legs, she heard him. If he shifted, she could glance through her lashes and see the sun shining in the window behind him turn the light streaks of his hair to wheat gold.

Mercifully he continued to dine at Mr. Haydon's. As Lady Lynton was fully prepared to receive the man, Marissa believed that Tristan had not invited his friend to the Lodge for dinner only because he feared that she, with her dubious reputation, would compromise Haydon's effort to restore his own. She did not believe she was quite so notorious as that, but the important point to her was that she did not have to see Tristan when Lady Lynton's presence would force her to pretend to be on at least even terms.

On the next day, Marissa went with Tory and Lady Lynton to Falmouth to shop. They were gone until almost nightfall and had a very pleasant outing, during the whole of which Marissa fought not to think about the viscount.

She failed. She conceded it the next day, as once again she entered the study to find him present and ignored him as completely as if he did not exist. Seated at her desk, her head bent, but her eyes lifted, looking through her lashes, studying him as he bent over a ledger, she admitted she had wondered if he worked any more efficiently when she was not there. Studying him, she could find no evidence that she affected him. Or that the silence did.

But the silence affected her. Broken only by the sound of their pens scratching across the vellum, the silence grew, paradoxically, louder, whenever Tristan was in the room, and continued to intensify until Marissa half wanted to scream. Or until he left, which he did then, even as she was thinking the thought.

Marissa thrust her eyes down as Tristan pushed back his chair from the desk. He rose. She had no idea what she was writing as he walked around his desk. It seemed to her that he slowed as he neared her. She never looked up, but she had to hold so tightly to her pen, her fingers cramped around it. She could feel his presence. She could smell his scent. He was that close. She stared at the paper before her, forming the word she wrote as carefully as she had done anything in her life, though she could not have said on pain of death what the word was.

If he had slowed, he did not stop at her desk, but finally passed by her and left the room. When the door clicked, Marissa let her head sink down on her hand. She could not go on behaving as she was. She had missed tea so regularly that week that Lady Lynton had inquired only that morning if Marissa had taken offense at the tea she served. The elder woman had smiled as she asked, but nonetheless Marissa had been obliged to make up a lie about how interesting she found the shadows in the late afternoon.

As to ignoring Tristan in his study, she was, she admitted, finding that to be as great a strain upon her as it could ever be a cut to him. He was probably glad of the shrill silence between them.

Marissa lifted her head and smacked a fist against the desk. Damn the man! He had probably not felt anything that night. He'd have been too angry. As she should have been! Great God! He'd not have treated a servant the way he had treated her, hauling her about, manhandling her, calling her stupid, stupid!, and throwing her up onto his horse as if she were a sack.

Oh, but then the rub really came! Literally. She grimaced, finding no humor in the pun. She had sat in the cradle of his thighs. His arms, snug at her waist, had kept her from slipping sideways, while his chest had been there, hard and warm, to lean against each time she forgot herself. Even now, days later, in the bright light of day, she felt the heat charge through her. No creeping here, no subtlety. She felt aflame, even her breasts, which he surely had not touched, though that night the balance of her awareness had seemed to pool there at her bottom, where his thighs held her. He was strong . . . no, no! She could not go on thinking how his thighs had felt against her, every shift of every hard muscle. Dear God. She had leaned forward once to get away from him only to bring her belly against his hands.

Marissa got up and left the room abruptly. She would go outside and sketch. She had discovered the burned ruins of Tremourne Abbey. No one mentioned them, neither Lady Lynton, Tory, nor Tristan, and so she did not broadcast that she found them interesting. High on a cliff facing the Channel, they seemed almost as old as the stones standing in a ring on the cliff across the Penryn estuary. Some days before she had seen two riders investigating those old, pagan stones. They had ridden off as she approached the Abbey's ruins, and Marissa had not been able to identify either person conclusively, but she rather thought, from the woman's general build and the way she sat in the saddle, that the woman might have been Mrs. Lowell. Her companion had worn a hat, but he had not, she thought, been so tall as Tristan, nor had it seemed, after only a glimpse at a goodly distance, she admitted, that he'd had light hair.

The couple might never investigate the stones again. Or, if they did, they might be too far away to identify. Still, for Tory's sake, she would keep a watchful eye out to see if Mr. Fitzhugh was taking his pleasure of the widow in between bouts of professing to admire Tory.

Marissa did not see anyone at all on the bluffs that day, though she did make some satisfying sketches of the ruined Abbey. But the next day, she could not escape outside. It rained.

Marissa marched into the study with her chin at a militant angle. But he was not there. She felt . . . let down, which was so absurd she called herself the idiot he had all but called her and sitting briskly down at the desk, polished off more letters than she had managed in several days. Then he came.

She had thought she was prepared to speak, but just

glimpsing him reminded her how beastly he'd been. And of the ride he'd made her endure. That last memory particularly tilted her head down before their eyes met.

He did not speak, either, or slow at her desk to see if she would. In the pulsing silence, he sat down at his desk and buried himself again in the ledgers. Marissa studied him through her lashes, unafraid he would look up and catch her. He worked hard, rarely looking up at all as far as she could tell. Monkish honey man.

But he was not monkish. Her response that night on his horse was, perhaps, upon consideration, not so surprising, even though she had been so angry. He was not a pale, slight, tight-lipped man.

His lightly tanned coloring, in addition to setting off his honey brown eyes and hair, was that of a man of action. As to slight, he was certainly not that. He was hard, lean, tall, and broad-shouldered. Well made to put it simply. As to tight-lipped . . . The rain thrummed steadily on the windows, and her gaze slid to his mouth.

Even if she had not seen for herself his effect upon women, and there had been women in London who had given him the same inviting sort of looks as did the widow Lowell—Kit had even let slip the name of one, a widow, too, now Marissa thought of it in relation to Tristan—but even had she not known all of that, she'd not have judged his mouth a monkish mouth. It was well defined, but it was not tight and thin as she imagined an austere monk's mouth would be.

Of all the times that Tristan should finally choose to look up from his so-mesmerizing ledgers, he chose then, when Marissa was studying his mouth, half wondering if he met Mrs. Lowell at the hunting box in the woods. If he noticed the direction of her gaze, however, his eyes did not betray the knowledge. They were cool and veiled.

"Have you a question? Or are you done with the letters?" he asked.

"Neither. I was wondering whether we would exchange

another word before the powers-that-be deem that the Home Counties will not be scandalized by my return."

His brow lifted so that his eyebrows nearly touched the lock of hair that he had knocked down onto his forehead earlier, when he'd been calculating and absently raking his hand through his hair. There was nothing boyish or endearing about the look in his eyes, however. Hard, they held Marissa's unflinchingly.

"You made it very clear you were too furious to exchange a word with me."

"You dragged me around an inn yard as if I were a child!"

"You were dressed as a laborer's son! I treated you accordingly. Except for the spanking you deserved, and I longed to administer it, never think that I did not! Great God, I have never been so furious myself!"

"All right!"

She had shouted. Marissa could hear her own voice, could feel herself shaking. And Tristan's eyes were blazing, for all that his voice was more controlled.

She had not known the anger was still there, fresh and blistering for all they'd waited days to discuss that night. Marissa jerked her gaze from Tristan's. There was no point in talking to him. He despised her. And she didn't care for him very much either. So. They would just sit in this throbbing silence. She could not even gather herself to lift her pen, not with him watching her, burning a hole in the top of her head with those censuring eyes.

"Damn it, Marissa!"

She looked up without a thought for the decision she had just made never to look at him again for the rest of her life. She met the honey man's eyes, although they were not so honey-colored then. They were dark. And fiery, too, somehow.

"I am in the awkward position," he said, enunciating every word, "of being unable to carry on a civil conversation with you and yet at the same time of owing you the greatest thanks for the time and effort you have given me. I know it is for my mother's sake that you have sat at that desk working day after day, but the benefit of your labor falls primarily to me. And I am deeply grateful for it."

She thought he was sincerely grateful. He looked wooden enough at having to thank her.

"You are right," she said as stiffly. "I do it for your mother. The work she does in her garden is good for her, but you are welcome for the benefit I've done you."

Marissa inclined her head, more to break the contact of their eyes than anything, and then taking up her pen pretended to resume her writing. After a moment, she heard Tristan return to his work as well.

It was over, then, that silence that had stretched so tensely between them it had seemed tangible. They had even touched on her offense and knew better than to return to it. She ought to feel relieved. They could return to their previous pattern, nodding in greeting and exchanging only so much conversation in company as was necessary to keep up the appearance that they were not at each other's throats.

Marissa briefly closed her eyes. She felt nothing like relief. She felt dissatisfied and let down. Why? What had she expected? That they would make up and dance a jig in the middle of the room?

When she opened her eyes, she looked at Tristan, as if his face or shoulder, perhaps, could provide her some answer. She had misinterpreted his movements, however. He had not returned to his ledgers. He was studying her, his handsome face sober, but not conveying anger any longer, or scathing contempt, or a grudging, dragged-out-of-him thanks.

"In truth, I have not minded writing your letters," Marissa said before she thought better of it. "They have given me something to do, and they are not uninteresting in their way."

"Letters about crop rotation?" He tilted his head slightly as if to study her from a different angle. "You have not been bored to tears writing about it and soil composition and whatever else?"

Marissa shrugged a little diffidently. "As I know nothing about agricultural matters, I could not help but be curious."

"And it is not trying to write letter after letter about such unfamiliar subjects?" He was frowning now, as if the thought had just occurred to him.

She smiled a little. What a slowtop the honey man could be. But handsome. He was definitely that, with his honey gold hair and honey gold eyes that seemed keener than was comfortable. "Lady Lynton has explained a little of what she knows, and I met your Mr. Thompkins one day when I was walking, and he was very kind."

"What did you ask him?" Tristan regarded her curiously, trying to imagine his ill-educated, laconic bailiff conversing with Exeter's elegant daughter.

"Well, I was curious about crop rotation, you've written about it so often, and Thompkins made an effort to answer."

At that, taking them both by surprise, Tristan laughed aloud. Marissa's heart seemed to jump in her chest. She put the response down to astonishment at his sudden good humor, as well as a start of recognition of how similar his smile was to his mother's. As Marissa had noted before, when he smiled his entire face seemed to come warmly alive, from the flashing white of his teeth to the lights glinting in his eyes.

"Thompkins is a man of few words. Did he make you any answer at all?"

"I know that this year you have planted oats in the fields nearest the river, but next year you will plant rye there. As a result your crops will 'make better,' which I translated to mean will yield more abundantly."

Perhaps she had taken *him* by surprise. Marissa couldn't be certain from his expression, only knew that Tristan said slowly at last, "You surmised correctly. Would you like to know more?" He leaned back in his chair as if preparing himself to answer her as fully as she wished.

"Yes." Marissa nodded, for in fact she did. "Why does it

matter if you grow oats one year in a field and rye the next? The soil is the same."

This time she knew she had surprised him. His brow lifted. The glint in his eye, however, was amused. Marissa summoned patience, never an easy task for her, but after all, she herself was half bemused that she had spared a thought for soil—or dirt.

"The soil is the same," Tristan said, answering her steadily enough after a moment, "but the nutrients that crops absorb from the soil in order to grow will vary according to each crop. The difficulty comes when one crop is planted repeatedly year after year. Gradually the soil becomes depleted of the nutrients required to sustain that particular crop, and the yields become less and less, until eventually, there is no yield at all."

Marissa tapped the end of her pen against her lips, considering. "And rotation?"

"When a different crop is planted, the soil is given a respite from the previous crop and allowed to rebuild whatever it used. In addition there are crops that actually restore certain nutrients to the soil."

She frowned a little. "From your letters I thought rotation a novel notion, but what you say appears to be the merest common sense."

Tristan smiled lopsidedly. He looked almost boyish and entirely charming. She hoped he could not discern the sudden catch in her breathing. "I am pleased to know I am so persuasive, but in fact, the theory that crops are best rotated is quite new. And soil depletion is a gradual process not easily proven."

Marissa had other questions, specifically about the man to whom she was writing even then. Mr. Mansfield, it seemed, had theories on which crops should succeed which crops. She could not but note, as they spoke, how knowledgeable Tristan was on the subject of agriculture, and it was equally impossible not to compare him again to the men she knew. Perhaps Exeter or her elder brother Adrian, Exeter's heir, had heard of crop rotation, but only if the subject had been discussed over one of the gaming tables in town, something she thoroughly doubted.

The next day, Tristan caught her studying him again, and Marissa did ask him another question, but this one was a trifle rushed, as she was embarrassed. Not that she had been criticizing him. Actually Marissa was stung to realize she had been doing the opposite again. She blamed her artist's eye. It had prompted her to try and determine what exactly made Tristan so handsome. She had been considering the clean planes of his face, from the strong line of his jaw, to the straight line of his nose and the firm, if more curved, one of his mouth, when he lifted his head, and she found herself suddenly looking into the golden depths of his eyes, seeing surprise there.

Immediately, she asked, "What is it you pore over so assiduously every day?" The very brow she'd just studied lifted slightly, prompting Marissa to regret the question she had not planned to ask in the first place. "Oh, never mind." She waved a slender hand in the air. "I can see those books are ledgers."

She couldn't be certain, but it seemed to her that one corner of his decidedly unmonkish mouth quirked upward, as if he were . . . amused. "They are ledgers," he said, his amber eyes holding her blue ones. "I am recording debits and credits in them, and attempting to reconcile the two."

Marissa considered Tristan a moment, but in the end saw no reason not to admit her ignorance. "And, what, precisely, does reconcile mean in this context?"

The suspicion of a smile became a decidedly drier look. "It means to enter all the credits and the debits in order to discover that there are, indeed, sufficient credits to pay the debits."

"And if there are not?"

Tristan shrugged those well made shoulders. "Then something must be sold to raise the money to pay the debit or the money must be borrowed. You cannot sustain an enterprise on losses."

"No," she agreed, and then because she really had been

curious about what absorbed him so, Marissa asked, without much thought, "May I see?"

A moment's silence ensued. Tristan's expression changed subtly, hardening at the edges. "Are you being rude or heedless or both?" he asked. "One doesn't ask to see the statement of another person's finances."

Nettled, Marissa was sarcastic. "Why? For fear I might sink myself beyond redemption in your eyes?" She gave him a withering look. "Or because I might learn something of your finances I have not learned already simply by living in your home? Lud, I was merely curious about what has kept you utterly absorbed! My apologies. Oh!" she cried suddenly, a new and infuriating thought overtaking her. "Or do you believe I am common enough to gossip about the figures I read?"

Tristan ignored the flashing look she gave him. Studying her impassively a long minute, he finally allowed evenly, "No, actually. One thing I have never known you to do is gossip."

"Well then," she said, firmly ignoring the start his remark gave her. He had not praised her, after all. Grudging honey man. He could have said, "You are too honorable to gossip" or something to that effect, but he hadn't. He'd only neglected to criticize her. "Why should I not ask to see something that appears to be amazingly interesting, if I know I cannot sink myself lower in your eyes or when I know the gist of the information I would see?"

By then Marissa cared less about seeing the ledgers than she did arguing the criticism he'd made of her, and perhaps Tristan guessed that, for his tone was surprisingly level as he replied, "You don't ask to see another person's financial records, because such information is private. If the person wishes you to see it, then he will show it to you of his own accord."

As they were obviously at an impasse, Marissa tossed her head and returned her attention to the dratted letters she wished she had never seen.

But Tristan's voice caught her in midarrogant head toss.

"I suppose you may as well see," he said consideringly, and then when she made no effort to hide her surprise, shrugged lightly. "As you say, you've already committed the indiscretion of asking. That can't be changed, and who am I to say your interest in bookkeeping should be denied? Who knows? Perhaps you'll learn something interesting."

With that somewhat grimly stated reasoning, Tristan swung about in his chair and lifted forward a light, straight-backed chair that stood against the wall. Marissa watched him, not moving until he cocked a quizzical brow at her. "Why do you hesitate, Marissa? Are you afraid you'll be overcome with embarrassment by the figures you'll see?"

"The thought never crossed my mind," Marissa muttered, rising immediately. Not having intended to make him laugh, she eyed him suspiciously, when he did just that. "Why are you laughing?"

"Because I should have known it would never occur to you to consider how it might affect me, and then you, to have to see the state of my finances."

He was faulting her, and as he had done that from the first, Marissa ought not, perhaps, to have felt the odd stab of something like hurt. Disconcerted by it, she replied to Tristan in her loftiest tones, "As I am never affected by the opinion of a person I despise, I could not imagine that you would be affected by my opinion of you and your finances."

It took him a moment to work out what she meant, but when he did, there was a flashing change in Tristan's expression. Marissa might have thought he was startled, but she couldn't think why he would be startled and so she assumed he was recalling how little he did care for her and her opinion, and she suddenly wanted no part of him.

But even as her steps across the room slowed, Tristan said quietly, "I think 'despise' is a little strong, Marissa. I don't despise you."

Precisely because she felt her face go warm, Marissa stated shortly and unequivocally, "But you don't like me,

Tristan. The point's the same. Now, shall I look at your ledgers?"

He did not protest her analysis of his regard for her. Though his amber eyes remained locked with hers for a long minute, at the end of it, he said merely, "Of course. Please be seated."

Chapter 11

Marissa had lost all interest in the ledgers. She wanted out of the room, but she would not allow him to see that her own plain speaking had affected her. As she knew full well he did not care for her, she wasn't even certain why it had, and so she did the opposite of what she wished. With every evidence of satisfaction, Marissa sat in the proffered chair and leaned forward a little to look at the dog-eared ledger Tristan put before her.

To her surprise, when she did finally look at the page she found it an aesthetic pleasure. "How neat it all is," she murmured, half to herself. "These are things you have bought then?" she asked, a tapered finger skimming a column which included an entry for lemon tree seedlings. The lot had cost forty pounds and was written in a dark black ink.

Tristan told her those were his expenditures for a fortnight, the approximate time each page represented. Running his hand through his hair, he admitted his system of accounting might not win him a position in a banking house. He showed her where several entries had had to be added late, because someone or other had not given him the information he needed in a timely fashion.

"Why is the color of the ink different?" Marissa asked, pointing to the light ink on one page and the darker ink on another.

Tristan half laughed. "I am reluctant to admit it, but more than once I entered individual debits and credits in the wrong column." When Marissa whistled low, Tristan laughed wryly again. "Yes, they were nearly disastrous errors and took forever to uncover, and so half in desperation I experimented with using different inks for the two."

"But that is clever," Marissa said, giving Tristan a swift glance. He was very close beside her, his arm all but brushing her shoulder. She leafed through several more pages of the ledger. "And this light figure?" she asked, pointing to a figure set apart in a box.

"It is the total I have left after paying the fortnight's debits with the credits I either earned or carried over." Flipping back a page, Tristan explained how and why he carried a sum from one page to the next.

His fingers were long but his wrists strong. In town Marissa had known men who prided themselves on having wrists as delicate as a woman's. She decided their pride had been misplaced, and moved her eyes from Tristan's hand to the figures he was explaining. "But have you not added these sums before?" she asked, distinctly remembering the forty pounds for lemon trees.

"Yes, in fact, I have." Tristan slanted her a look that she thought held more surprise than approval. "I entered those sums in the ledger that covers a fortnight. This ledger is for the quarter, and in it I enter the same sums in order to check my mathematics. It's a tedious process but prevents mistakes. I do the same with the expenditures for household expenses," he said, gesturing to a page on which debits for everything from candlesticks to lye soap had been recorded, "except that I am checking Tory's addition, for Hobbes records the daily entries in a ledger that Tory completes before she gives it to me."

His butler recorded the household accounts, his sister finished them, and his mother acted as his secretary. No, he did not live in a grand style. Her mother kept a full orchestra permanently installed at Penhurst. But Tristan did appear to have a sense of purpose in his life, and surely, a sense of shared effort as well.

When Marissa glanced at him, wondering what that last, particularly, would be like, she found him leaning back in his chair, observing her thoughtfully. She gave him a look of inquiry that was somewhat defensive, but she could not help herself. "You've an eye for numbers, Marissa," he said, smiling a little on account of her lifted chin. "Will I insult you if I admit I'm surprised?"

She was surprised, certainly, that he would decide she'd a second redeeming quality after her penmanship, but Marissa dismissed his compliment and her start of pleasure, too. "I have always found numbers pleasing. They don't equivocate."

She could not guess why the obvious remark should make his brow knit. Or why he should pursue it. "Have you worked with them much?"

"No," she said firmly, lest he consider her for the position of clerk. "Kit's tutor taught me a little, but . . ." She ended her remarks with a lift of her elegant shoulders.

"But what?"

Her eyes narrowed on him, and she considered observing that a gentleman did not press a lady. To which he would likely reply that she was no lady. Marissa's eyes flashed at the thought. She would not, did not, care what he thought, and so she gave him his answer, albeit flippantly. "But, my lord, Her Grace did not wish her daughter to study a subject that was, it seems, a favorite of her husband's. And so, is that all there is to your ledgers?"

For a moment, Marissa thought Tristan might not leave off looking at her in that steady, seeming-to-see-too-dratted-much way. But he finally glanced down to push away the two ledgers they had been studying in favor of another smaller one.

"Here is the final set of numbers," he said, and Marissa marked that he spoke in a new, unexpectedly sardonic tone. "In this column I enter the sum of the revenues from Tremourne after all the expenses have been deducted." The ink in that column was light. But it was the next column, in which each figure was written in the blackest ink, that Tristan stabbed with his finger. "And in this column I enter the payments I must make to the moneylender in London from

whom I borrowed to keep Tremourne afloat. And here"—
he drew a long finger down the page, passing line upon line
recording payments of a staggering one thousand pounds
quarterly—"is the final figure unequivocally describing
what is left yet to pay." It was written in the boldest ink.
Marissa stared at the number, thirty thousand and some
pounds, and felt something tighten in her chest. "I could
lose Tremourne, indeed all I own," Tristan went on,
"should I miss more than two of the accountings I owe Mr.
Hieronymus Greeley. One or two poor harvests . . ." He
shrugged, then closed the ledger with a snap. "So there you
have it, Marissa. The unequivocal truth." Unbelievably, he
laughed. "I live with the threat of debtors' prison every
day."

Despite the laugh, there was a challenging gleam in his
eye. Marissa did not think it had much to do with debtors'
prison, but rather with the fact that she was Exeter's daughter and His Grace was the single wealthiest man in England. As she had often been called to account for the purely
chance circumstances of her birth, she disregarded that
somewhat defiant look, and said instead, "You are not
afraid."

She caught Tristan off guard. His brow lifted. "No," he
said. "Once Tory is married, I could always make a life in
the army. I would earn enough to support Mama and at
least one garden. But in fact, I've no intention of losing
Tremourne."

There was still a gleam in his eyes, lighting the amber,
making it dance, but the gleam was not quite the same as it
had been. Marissa considered him thoughtfully. "You like
this challenge," she said slowly. And then she heard herself
add, "You are brave, just as Kit has always said."

The grin with which Tristan had begun to react to the
first of her remarks got lost in a start of surprise. But he
could not have been more surprised than Marissa was to
hear herself blurt such flattery. Or to realize that she had
meant it. Before he could say a word in response, Marissa
rose to her feet. "Sitting too long at a stretch always drives

me a little mad. Well, thank you very much, my lord, for the ledger lesson, but I must go and stretch my legs now. I shall finish your other letters tomorrow. The ones I've completed are there on the desk, awaiting your frank."

She heard Tristan rise, but was out the door of the study before he had an opportunity to reply. Which was just as well. What could he have said to her idiotic remark? That he was a craven coward? And though Kit had said he was brave, her brother had been referring to no more than Tristan's demeanor as a schoolboy. He had never, it seemed, bowed to the inevitable bullies.

"Rissa! Oh, good! I have found you!"

Marissa shut her sketchbook before Tory could see that rather than the roses before her, she'd made a sketch of Tory's brother. Cornwall was making her maudlin. The sketch was too flattering, and all because she was still half caught in the same absurd mood she'd been in the day before when she'd told him he was brave, as if she were some starry-eyed country maid.

With the sketch pad safely closed, she found a smile for Tory, whose bright eyes and flushed cheeks suggested that Mr. Fitzhugh was not far away. Marissa tried to be glad.

"Hail and well met to you, too, Tory. I thought you were to practice your piano. Did the day prove too pretty?"

"No, Mr. Fitzhugh has come!" she exclaimed, rather as Marissa had expected.

"Ah."

Tory giggled. "Yes, 'ah,' but Mrs. Lowell has come, too, and having noticed that you have a way of becoming invisible when she visits, I have come out to beg you to join Mama and me, for I invariably feel as awkward and graceless as a new colt, when I am in Mrs. Lowell's company."

"New colts are charming, actually," Marissa remarked in the offhand way that, oddly, carried weight with Tory simply because it was so casual. "But what does Mr. Fitzhugh have to say when you tell him Mrs. Lowell causes you to feel at a disadvantage?"

"But I have never mentioned Mrs. Lowell to him, Rissa! Lud, I would feel a complete fool, if I did."

Marissa rose, and looking into Tory's open, generous, hopeful countenance, as they walked toward the house, found she simply could not say more than, "You are no fool, Tory, and you may be assured that I know, for society is positively filled with them. As to Mrs. Lowell, she condescends so insufferably to you, because there is no woman more desperate to proclaim age a virtue than an aging strumpet."

"Rissa! Mrs. Lowell is no strumpet!"

"Perhaps the definition of strumpet is different here in kindly Penryn," Marissa replied, cool despite the grin dawning upon Tory's pretty face. "I shall not debate with you, but I do notice you did not dispute she is aged."

Tory crowed delightedly. "You see! I was right to fetch you! I'll need only to look at you and remember what you've said to be reassured that Mr. Fitzhugh is not privately thinking what a child I am compared to her sophistication."

Recalling the look she'd seen Mr. Fitzhugh and Mrs. Lowell exchange at the Kendalls' picnic and recalling not only the pair of riders she'd seen on the cliffs overlooking the Channel but that Mrs. Lowell's property marched with Mr. Fitzhugh's, Marissa thought there was good reason to wonder what the Irishman did, exactly, think of the widow. Her suspicions were too vague to voice, particularly in view of Tory's pleasure in Fitzhugh's attentions, but Marissa would not forget them.

Not surprisingly, therefore, Marissa's greeting for the voluptuous widow, draped decoratively upon Lady Lynton's couch, was cool and the look she gave Mr. Fitzhugh more assessing than cordial. Tristan, it seemed, was out with Mr. Thompkins, but to Marissa's pleasure she found that the Tregaron ladies had taken advantage of the pretty day to drive their little trap up to the Lodge. She knew she could count on them for a distraction from the other two guests.

As it happened, though, Miss Hester plunged directly and briskly into Marissa's very line of thought, the dear. After everyone was seated, and Tory had passed around the tea, Miss Hester fixed Mr. Fitzhugh with a no-nonsense look and asked without hesitation, though he had taken a seat beside Tory, "Do you and Mrs. Lowell ride together often, Mr. Fitzhugh?"

Marissa took a sip of her tea, though it was steaming hot, for fear she would smile broadly otherwise. However, Mr. Fitzhugh extricated himself from the pointed question with ease. "Alas, I am too new to land owning to have the time to ride solely for pleasure. Mrs. Lowell and I met by chance at Tremourne's very gates, for I came from the village. Did you not see me pass by Rose Cottage?"

Miss Hester said she had not, adding that it was her custom to write for a few hours each day after luncheon, and Miss Millie's to nap. "But tell us how you are taking to Penryn, Mr. Fitzhugh. I hope it is not too dull here for a young man of your energies."

"Dull?" He smiled charmingly and glanced to Tory, who blushed, though his dark gaze could not have rested on her longer than the blink of an eye. "To the contrary, I have found Penryn delightful. Indeed, I find I like Cornwall in general. The countryside is wonderfully picturesque and the more I know of them, the more I find the customs here interesting, indeed. As you were born and bred in Cornwall, Miss Hester, can you tell me anything of Lammas Night? I gather the day is observed rather differently here than in the rest of England."

To Marissa's interest, Miss Millie, who had chosen sherry over tea, twittered as if Mr. Fitzhugh had mentioned something slightly outré, but Miss Hester did not hesitate to nod approvingly. "Indeed, Lammas Night is a most interesting celebration, Mr. Fitzhugh. Officially Lammas is a Christian day, but in Cornwall there were celebrations on the night of the first of August long before Christianity was brought here. Millie, there, is blushing, because our father, the vicar, you know, would not speak of the revels of Lammas Night, as they are said to be quite abandoned. For my part, I am not sure. I think, from what Tilda says, that there is just a good deal of vigorous dancing around a bonfire, as well as much drinking, of course."

"Of course," Mr. Fitzhugh said, and Marissa did not fault him for the fact that his mouth twitched. She was smiling herself.

"Whatever may occur on Lammas Night," Miss Millie said, darting an uncertain glance at her sister, "Parish Day falls sooner and we did come to the Lodge to discuss it."

"Parish Day?" Mr. Fitzhugh inquired.

Miss Millie gave him a pleased little smile for taking her cue. "Yes, Mr. Fitzhugh. A week from tomorrow is Parish Day, when we have a little fair in Penryn to raise funds for the church and the parish for the coming year. There are the usual booths with games and various items for sale, but we've a unique feature to our fair that I must say does draw people. You see, traditionally the most important ladies of the parish have been the hostesses in the booths, but this year, alas, there had been some controversy and scarcely anyone has volunteered."

"And why should we?" Mrs. Lowell cast a defiant look at Miss Millie. "In the past the monies we raised on Parish Day were used for the lower orders we already have the misfortune to have in our parish, but this year this new curate, Seaton, with all of his Wesleyan notions, wants to import an entirely new and even dangerous group of miscreants for us to support."

"Import miscreants?" Marissa echoed. "What an odd curate to be sure. Will they come from France or perhaps Ireland. There are always miscreants there, I believe?"

She shot a neutral look at Mr. Fitzhugh and found that for once he looked less than amiable. Indeed, with his eyes narrowed so, he looked rather forbidding. "You prove you are very English by saying so, Lady Marissa."

"Actually, my paternal grandmother was an O'Neill, Mr. Fitzhugh," Marissa said, and saw he realized his mistake immediately. Had he had no fear of being thought a miscreant, he would have bantered with her, but she gave him no time to recover himself. She looked to the widow. "But I did not mean to interrupt, Mrs. Lowell. You were saying about miscreants?"

Mrs. Lowell's eyes had narrowed. "I did not mean import in the sense you took it, Lady Marissa. I meant that Seaton would bring into our parish ne'er-do-wells we shall have to support for the rest of our lives."

"Oh, come, Mrs. Lowell!" coaxed Miss Millie. "Surely Mr. Seaton's plans are not quite so bad as that."

"They are!" the widow insisted. "And the Comptons quite agree with me. I have never heard Mr. Compton so opposed to anything as he was when he heard of Seaton's plan, and he's more money than I to throw away. Of course, Mrs. Compton knew she would be in London on Parish Day, but she told me that she had warned Seaton that most of the ladies of the parish would fail to support him, and as it happens, she was right. Most of us will not turn our hands in order to cosset these shiftless rogues let loose on us by the army."

"Your Mr. Seaton wishes to build a home for men who served in the army?" Marissa queried, at that juncture simply trying to comprehend why Mrs. Lowell was so exercised.

"He is not my anything," Mrs. Lowell returned, seeing affront where none had in fact been intended. "And he wishes to build a home for men, who, when discharged from the army, turned not to labor to improve their fortunes but to drink to forget them. It is unconscionable to reward such."

"It is my understanding," Tory spoke up rather breathlessly to say, "that there is no sufficient work for the many men let go by the army now the war with Napoleon is truly over."

Mrs. Lowell gave her a condescending, almost pitying smile. "You are young, my dear, and naive. There is always work for those willing."

Perhaps courtesy dictated that she allow the subject to

drop, as it was obviously a contentious one, but after that smile and remark Marissa would not have denied herself an answer had Tristan threatened her with another month of no riding.

"Perhaps it is you who are the naive one, Mrs. Lowell," she said in her cool way. "My brother, who is in the army, is forever being approached when he is home on leave by men who served ably under him on the Peninsula and at Waterloo, risking their lives on our behalf, but who, now that we have no use for them, cannot find employment. The sight of them more often than not sends him into a rage, for they are almost invariably gaunt, and from Kit's report not from drink but from lack of that most basic necessity, food." Younger than Mrs. Lowell, Marissa certainly was, but she spoke with the assurance of a young woman whose father was the twelfth duke of his line. And dismissing Mrs. Lowell as surely as if she were a vassal whose petition had been denied, she turned smoothly to her hostess. "Would you object, Lady Lynton, if I worked at one of the booths this Parish Day? I don't think I could face Kit, did I not."

Lady Lynton was smiling faintly. "Far from objecting, Lady Marissa, I approve wholeheartedly. I fear I lack the strength to do more than visit the fair this year, but I, too, consider the reception we have given these men shabby, indeed."

"Well, I insist upon working with Rissa! Surely I may, Mother?"

"Surely you may do what with Lady Marissa, Tory?"

Tristan strode into the room, and though his hair was windblown and his riding coat, buff breeches, and riding boots all showed evidence of wear, he looked as handsome as any man Marissa had ever seen. He greeted his mother's guests upon seeing them, smiling nicely, but Mrs. Lowell's husky invitation to sit by her did not prompt him to forget his question.

He repeated it, though this time he looked to Marissa. "You and Tory wished to do something, Lady Marissa?"

The last they had seen of each other, he had opened his

ledgers to her, and she had made him that absurd, girlish compliment. She had not known how things would be the next time they met, had even been slightly unsettled about it. But now Marissa realized she had been a fool to worry. Nothing had changed. Nothing. To the others, all attending closely, too, Marissa thought, Tristan's expression might be neutral, but she was looking directly into his eyes. He mistrusted her. Completely.

Her blue, almond-shaped eyes never left his as her mouth took on a faintly mocking slant. "Why, my lord, Tory and I mean to set an example. To broadcast the benefits of exercise we intend to ride our horses down to the commons on Parish Day and work in one of the booths."

Lady Lynton caused an interruption at that moment, for she experienced a bout of coughing, which sent Mrs. Lowell scurrying to clap her on the back, while Tory rang for water, and the Tregaron ladies offered to send up to the Lodge an herbal concoction for coughs when they returned to Rose Cottage. Marissa sat where she was. She suspected the rather shallow cough had been brought on by her assertion that she would ride to the commons, for though she had said nothing to Lady Lynton about Tristan's prohibition, she thought the elder lady surely knew of it through her maid, if not Tory. And so Marissa sat with her mocking look quite intact, enduring Tristan's coolly suspicious regard, all the while her hand lying tightly clenched in the folds of her skirt.

Only when his mother proclaimed herself recovered did Tristan deliver his verdict. "Working as a hostess at the fair is a commendable desire," he said, thus ensuring, Marissa knew, that Mrs. Lowell would soon sing a different tune about the issue, "but I wouldn't want you to tire yourself with too much goodness, Lady Marissa." He smiled, striking a blow, though he could not know how sharply she took the entirely sardonic smile. "As you will be on your feet the day long, you and Tory may drive down to the commons in the carriage."

"Oh, I am so glad you will come, Lady Marissa!" Miss

Millie actually clapped her hands. "Hester and I hoped you might, you see, for as soon as the other ladies learn that you approve Mr. Seaton's project, we are certain they will hurry to copy your example."

The dear. Marissa smiled fondly at both spinsters. "I am pleased that you believe I shall have a salutary effect on the parish, ladies. As you can perhaps imagine, it is a novel experience for me." She had thought she would flick a smug smile at Tristan then, but in the end, she found she hadn't, for one reason or another, the spirit to taunt him further.

Chapter 12

Rather to her surprise, Marissa found she enjoyed working in one of the booths on Penryn's commons. She and Tory, with Wren and Tory's maid Jenny watching over them, sold ladies' hair ornaments and their customers, common laboring folk for the most part, were unabashedly awed at having a duke's daughter serve them. Marissa had thought she might find the attention tedious, but she did not. Quite the opposite, in fact. Since she had done her paltry bit of work for Tristan, and watched him at work as well, she had become more aware of the amount of toil done by those not so fortunately born as she. Not that she was becoming a Wesleyan, she thought, smiling to herself as she watched Penryn's vigorous curate, Mr. Seaton, striding by her booth. She was not about to give all her wealth to the poor and retire to a small cottage, but nonetheless, she found she did not begrudge the pleasure she gave to people whose lives were defined by work and strain.

Not everyone who came to the booth was a fisherman's daughter with her swain in tow, of course. Gerald Kendall came, and while Elise, who was taking a rest from selling handkerchiefs with her mother, excitedly confided to Tory that she had persuaded her mother to have a supper dance in a few days, Gerald took advantage of a lull in Marissa's customers to murmur quietly, flushing to the tips of his ears, that he was deuced sorry she had fallen ill during the cockfight. "I wish I had known! Lord Lynton read me a lecture on the subject, you may be certain, but I had little need of it. I was most concerned about you."

"For which concern I am grateful, Mr. Kendall." Marissa said, and with a sincerity that caused the boy's ears to flame again. "I regretted that Lord Lynton would not allow me to advise you that I was leaving. He thought it best that I not risk being noticed. And . . . his point of view prevailed, but I thought it a shabby way to treat you."

"Nonsense! Not shabby at all!" Gerald sputtered, gratified and beside himself all at once. "Lord Lynton brought me to see how dangerous taking you to the stables was. He said nothing to either my mother or my father, you understand, and he told me in the most adamant way that if word got out in any way at all of what we'd done, he would hold me responsible, as I am the only person aside from the two of you, of course, to know."

"How fearsome of him," Marissa mused, rearranging the little display of combs so that one with a tortoise shell handle was in front.

"Lord Lynton was most fearsome, indeed!" Gerald Kendall agreed, having completely missed the irony in Marissa's tone. "I did not mistake that he would call me out if I breathed so much as a word. Not that I would!"

"No, of course not." Marissa studied him briefly through her lashes. She realized, however, that had Tristan not taken it as his duty—or right—to interfere in her affairs, Gerald might well have boasted about his night ride with Lady Marissa Portemaine, had he enough to drink and a receptive audience. To emphasize the desirability of restraint, she added flatteringly, "I am persuaded, Mr. Kendall, that you are too much the gentleman to tell tales out of school."

The young man flushed proudly at being called a gentleman by her, and assured her that he would never do anything to cause her harm. He was not a bad sort, really. Marissa fully believed that he would not want to cause her harm, and yet for no reason at all an image of Tristan flashed through her mind. At twenty-and-eight, he could not have been much more than five or six years older than

Mr. Kendall, and yet the latter was a boy, while the former
. . . well, he had had adversity to overcome. And she had
new customers, Ben Hawkes and Dorcas as it turned out.
But even as she bid Mr. Kendall adieu, Marissa was, for
she'd an honest streak, conceding that even had Tristan
never seen a ledger in his life, he'd never have been the
slightly foolish, if well-intentioned, fellow Mr. Kendall
was.

Not well pleased to have had to concede so much to Tristan, Marissa declined the Kendalls' invitation to take luncheon with them. Sending Tory off for more discussion of
the supper dance, she told the three young people she
would stay and mind the booth. "If I've only one day to be
a shopkeeper, I wish to make the most of it," she said, earn-
ing bemused looks from the Kendalls and a laugh from
Tory.

Marissa was still smiling to herself, and thinking what a
gem Tory was, when she glanced idly along the thorough-
fare created by the two rows of booths facing each other.
Tory and her friends had already disappeared into the
throng, but by pure chance the crowd parted slightly, and
Marissa saw another familiar face, Mr. Fitzhugh, emerging
from a curtained area between two booths, one of which
was the booth at which Mrs. Lowell had agreed to work,
after all.

As Marissa watched, eyes narrowing, Mr. Fitzhugh lifted
a hand to his cravat, and finding the knot at his throat half
undone, darted glances to his right and left as he attempted
oh-so-casually to restore the thing, using one hand. To
Marissa it was incriminating enough that the Irishman
should emerge from a private nook by Mrs. Lowell's booth
sporting a disheveled cravat, but then a gloved hand snaked
out from behind the curtain and languidly caressed the
Irishman's neck. He half jumped at the touch, turned,
smiled, darted another pair of looks left and right along the
concourse between the booths, and then slipped back behind the curtain.

Had Marissa thought Wren could manage the booth

alone, she'd have gone then to confront the pair hidden in the curtained space between the booths. She knew to whom the glove belonged, for it was dyed a distinctive shade of canary yellow, the very shade Mrs. Lowell had worn on more than one of the occasions she had visited Tremourne.

But Marissa was not obliged in the end to go to Mr. Fitzhugh, at least. He, secure in his ignorance, came fresh from Mrs. Lowell to Marissa, a cheerful smile on his face as he greeted her and announced he wished to buy a ribbon for Tory. "I think Miss St. Aubyns will not be offended by so small a token of my esteem, do you agree, Lady Marissa?"

More than one buck in town had noted that a certain look from Lady Marissa Portemaine could literally freeze a fellow. In Mr. Fitzhugh's case, it was his smile that froze.

"If you wish to buy trinkets for females, Mr. Fitzhugh, confine yourself to ladies of your own ilk, to whit, Mrs. Lowell. And do not, pray, bother to disclaim any interest in the widow." Mr. Fitzhugh shut his mouth with a snap, and Marissa nodded, approvingly. "Good. You see, I saw you and her beside her booth just now. A cozy pair you are, and by the by, your cravat still bears her mark." Unthinking, he reached up to touch the cravat to assure himself the knot was properly retied. Marissa smiled unpleasantly. "You give yourself away, Mr. Fitzhugh, but it is just as well you reveal yourself for the base cad you are. What do you believe Miss St. Aubyns' response would be should she learn that you have repeatedly brought her into company with a woman you are bedding even as you profess the greatest devotion to Miss St. Aubyns?" Could a look kill, Marissa thought she'd have been dead, but as she wished more than anything in the world at that moment that she were a man and could call out the Irishman and inflict bodily harm upon him, she only further narrowed her eyes before his seething look. "You may look as furious as you like, Mr. Fitzhugh, the answer is the same. You would cause Tory the greatest hurt. And I'll not have it! For once, I am pleased to be Exeter's daughter, for I've both the influence and the will to see you are known in the circles that count as unworthy of any powerful man's influence. Do you understand? I will do it, if you press your attentions on Tory ever again. Indeed, I think it would be in order for you to leave Cornwall for a little so that you are not tempted by your ambitions."

All around them were the sounds of the crowd, laughter, loud calls, and the high, squealing, excited cries of children, but between Marissa and Fitzhugh there was absolute silence as they regarded each other, bitter anger flowing from him and determination from her, and in the end, it was Marissa who prevailed. Without speaking a word, Fitzhugh spun on his heel and stalked away into the crowd.

Having flayed the young man with her tongue, Marissa understood that she had done the easy part. Now she must decide whether to tell Tory.

As it happened, however, the younger girl decided Marissa's question when she returned from her luncheon with the Kendalls. "I saw Mr. Fitzhugh, Marissa just a moment ago." Marissa looked at her sharply to find that Tory did appear to be distressed. "He gave the Kendalls and me unhappy news! He must go back to Ireland for a time and will not be here for the Kendalls' entertainment."

It surprised Marissa that Mr. Fitzhugh should succumb to her demands so readily. From the look on his face she'd thought he might resist, but as he had, she could see no reason to tell Tory the truth. Better to have Tory think that her first admirer had forgotten her upon his return to his native land, than to think that he had deceived her with another woman from the first. Mr. Fitzhugh's prompt departure from the scene settled another question as well. Marissa had questioned whether she should speak to Tristan, but hadn't wanted to involve Tory's brother without Tory's permission. Smiling dryly to herself, she decided that Mr. Fitzhugh had proven far more commendable upon his departure than she had ever thought him while he was present.

Tory had other news besides that involving Mr.

Fitzhugh, and recalled it after a little, when she had pushed her unhappiness over Mr. Fitzhugh's departure to the back of her mind. "I forgot to tell you, Rissa, but Tris has come without Mama."

"Has something happened to Lady Lynton?" Marissa asked, her brow creasing.

"She twisted her ankle in her herb garden," Tory said, hurrying to add when Marissa exclaimed with concern, "It is not serious. Truly. Dr. Richards has visited and said she only needed to rest with it wrapped for a few days, but the annoying aspect of it all is that Mama had meant to acknowledge Mr. Haydon publicly today."

Marissa had not known. Lady Lynton never mentioned Mr. Haydon when they took their chocolate together in the mornings, most likely, given Lady Lynton's nature, because she had not wanted Marissa to think she was under any obligation to recognize Mr. Haydon herself. As Exeter's daughter, her recognition might influence others in Penryn to do the same, but in all, she appreciated that Lady Lynton did not think to use her to reinstate a man Marissa did not know.

Tory went on musing about other things Lady Lynton might do to show her neighbors she considered Mr. Haydon worthy of esteem, but Marissa scarcely listened, for the simple, if prosaic reason that she had become ravenously hungry. Tory might have eaten, but Marissa's only sustenance had been the aroma of the meat pasties being sold in a booth just down the way. At the next lull in customers she made her excuses to her friend and after Wren had made the necessary purchases adjourned to the shade of an oak tree across from the commons to enjoy one of the pasties that had tantalized her.

Marissa had finished her pasty, though Wren had not, when a gaily colored ball just a little smaller than the width of her palm came rolling down the hill behind her to bounce against her. Hefting the errant ball in her hand, Marissa turned to find a small boy regarding her with unusually solemn, wide, wide brown eyes. He said nothing, but he held against his chest two other balls that matched the one she was tossing in the air.

"Have you ever juggled?" she asked the boy. He did not blink at the odd question, but after a long drawn-out moment slowly shook his head from side to side. "Have you ever seen anyone juggle?" Again, the little boy, four or five years of age, shook his head very slowly. "Well then, I shall juggle for you. When I tell you to do it, toss me your other balls one at a time." The little boy never changed expression, but when Marissa stood, tossed her ball in the air, and said, "Now, toss me another one," he did it. "And the last," she instructed, grinning as she caught it and at the same time kept the other two balls aloft. When she was smoothly juggling all three, Marissa glanced at the little boy and smiled again. He did not look so solemn now. Wonder had made his eyes wide, and if he was not smiling, Marissa thought it was because he could not with his jaw dropped like that.

When Tristan met Matthew Haydon and gave him the news about Lady Lynton, Matt was keenly disappointed. None of his neighbors, most of them people he had known all his life, had called upon him but for Tristan, of course, and feeling shunned for the crime of saving a woman's life, albeit the woman he had loved, he was questioning his decision to return to England. But if he thought of returning to Italy, there was no thought of returning that day to Twyckham Hall. Escorted by his Italian nurse, Will, his young son, had already disappeared into the throng on the commons.

Besides, Tristan had made the imminently pleasant suggestion that they adjourn to the Sea Maid for ale. Chairs had been set up outside the inn, and they could watch the doings on the commons, if they wished.

As they sipped their ale and idly watched the passing throng, Matt related what he had found upon his latest examination of his agent's ledgers. Tristan was interested. He knew the agent was a rascal and wanted to see him receive justice, but nonetheless his mind wandered.

He had not ridden straight down to the commons from Tremourne. He had turned off on a small path that climbed the hill behind the commons. From a vantage point midway along the path, he had been able to watch Marissa, to spy on her in effect, though he made no apologies. Her history, he thought, made it his duty to be certain that her sudden interest in playing shopkeeper at the parish fair was not part of some grander, reckless, even dangerous scheme.

She had done nothing untoward, however. True, she had spoken to Gerald Kendall, but for a very short time only, and in all, she had looked more thoughtful in relation to the pup than coaxing or cajoling. In the end, too, Tory had been the one to leave with him and his sister, not Marissa.

As to her behavior aside from Gerald Kendall, it had been, Tristan admitted with a reluctant smile, surprising, for though Marissa had elected quite on her own to work on Parish Day, Tristan had expected her, even had she not had some ulterior motive, to fulfill her duties as tradeswoman-for-a-day reluctantly, even grudgingly. But she had laughed and chatted easily with the couples and the pairs of girls who had thronged her booth. They had come to her in part because she was Exeter's daughter, and they'd not soon have another chance to be served by someone so well born, but had she been haughty and arrogant, they'd not have lingered or given up their hard-earned pennies. Watching Ben Hawkes and Dorcas, Tristan had thought they would stay the day with Marissa, they had enjoyed themselves so.

But then Ben and Tibbs were firmly in her pocket. Tristan took a swallow of ale, nodded at something Matt said that he thought made sense, and all the while considered, with half of his mind anyway, why the two men, one old and one young and both at bottom sensible, were devoted to her. Of course she rode as if she'd been born in the saddle, but there was more to it. When she'd gotten Ben in trouble with the challenge to race, she had not only pleaded his case with Tristan, she had gone to the stables and offered to help Ben muck out the horse stalls, for his punishment for dereliction of duty had been to clean them without assistance for a week. Tristan took another swallow of ale. Tibbs had related the incident in tones of awe likely similar to those a pilgrim to Lourdes might have used, had the man been miraculously healed.

Tristan understood the astonishment. A duke's daughter offering, seriously, to clean out horses' stalls was not the rule, and given the particular duke's daughter in question . . . indeed, he shared Tibbs' amazement.

Nor was he done listing all the surprises Marissa had given him, Tristan admitted. Her interest in agricultural terms had been so unexpected, he had thought she meant to sweeten him up in order to wheedle something out of him, likely to do with riding. But she had not asked for anything, except to give her time at Parish Day, and he was not quite certain what to think, except that she'd a broader range of interests than he had ever suspected.

It was not entirely surprising that he would not know more of her mind. Since he had dragged her to her brother to report her behavior with the groom at Penhurst, she had avoided him as assiduously as possible, whenever he'd visited Kit. If he had entered a room, she had left as soon as she could. If he dined at the duchess's table, she rearranged the name cards to be certain he was not beside her. And the few times fate had forced them together, some misdeed or other of Marissa's had generally dominated the moment. So, he had not known she could interest herself in anything other than defiance, scandal, or judging from her generally impeccable clothes, style.

As to his books . . . the only curious thing there was his own action, to whit showing her the last ledger, the one so starkly describing the extent of his indebtedness. Even Matt did not know how much he owed Greeley, and yet he had made it a point to show Marissa. And Tristan acknowledged, drawing on his ale again, that he could not say exactly why he had done it, except that it had seemed a point of honor that he not hide anything, lest she—or he—think he was ashamed.

She had not reacted as he'd expected then, either. Tristan studied his ale, not even hearing Matt any longer. Those blue eyes, thoughtful and in all, approving, she'd said he was brave. Brave. He had more than half expected her to say something slighting.

Not that relations between them had changed entirely. No sooner did he question her motive about Parish Day than she flung up her chin, gave him a mocking look, and said something deliberately provoking. No, she'd not suddenly become as cloyingly admiring as Barbara Lowell, nor as ubiquitous. Indeed, he'd scarcely seen her since the exchange at tea that day. He did not think she had urged his mother to resume her secretarial duties for him, but he doubted Marissa had protested when his mother had done so, saying she had less to do in her garden just now.

He thought his mother had noted the silent, more hostile than not, exchange between them and decided to spare them each the other's company, but whatever the reason, it was as well his mother had resumed her place in his study. He got more work done without Marissa there. He did not have to expend so much energy resisting the temptation to look at her. For as he'd noted before, whatever her behavior might be, she had ever been a pleasure for the eye.

"Dear God, look, Tris! Will's found a friend, and what taste he has!" Matt's exclamation pulled Tristan from his thoughts, and none too soon, he thought, realizing how Marissa had dominated them. Then he turned. "Do you know who the beauty is, Tristan? Surely not a traveling player. She may juggle those balls flawlessly, but she is dressed so finely . . . no, surely it cannot be."

"It is," replied Tristan. He had told Matt enough about Marissa to have his friend laugh aloud when he added wryly. "The duke's daughter who can juggle balls like a performer at Astley's."

"Well, Will is entranced," Matt observed, his eyes on his son. "And I am grateful to her. That is the first smile I have

seen on his face since we set sail for England. I cannot
thank her myself for entertaining him, but I trust you'll do
it for me, Tris. Oh, Lud, no, here comes Maria, his nurse!
From the look on her face, she must have lost him and is
now furious with both Will and Lady Marissa."

The nurse was, indeed, in a frenzy. Matt sprang up to in-
tercept her, but did not reach her before she roughly jerked
Will from the circle of children who had gathered about
Marissa. Will set up a wail, but angry with him for having
wandered away from her, the Italian woman ignored her
charge and shouted at Marissa in broken English, "The
balls! The bambino's balls! Give!"

Tristan, following in Matt's wake, feared Marissa might
box the woman's ears, but she did nothing of the sort. Ex-
hibiting a tact that surprised him as much as anything else
had, she said merely, "Of course," and stooping down,
tucked the balls between Will's arm and chest, saying to
him with a smile, "Thank you for the use of them, young
man."

Had Will cooperated with his nurse, nothing else might
have happened, but he dug in his heels and began to cry as
Maria tried to drag him away. Marissa frowned and looked
about to interfere when Matt reached his son and nurse and
Tristan got to Marissa.

She gave him a swift look, and having seen the men ap-
proach together, drew the correct conclusion. "Are they Mr.
Haydon and his son?"

When Tristan nodded, Marissa reacted unexpectedly.
Her eyes sparkled. "I see! After you identified me, he sent
the nurse to all but drag the boy away from such a perni-
cious influence. Thank you very much for the character reference, my lord. I hope you are satisfied. Making a child
cry just to save him from my clutches is surely a grand ac-
complishment."

They stood in full view of every booth in the commons,
and Tristan knew without looking that half the people at the
fair were watching them, for if Marissa had not already
drawn their interest with her juggling, of all the unlikely

things, then they'd have looked when Will began shrieking volubly in Italian as he was dragged away from her. And still, despite their audience, he almost grasped her arm and shook it.

To control himself he clenched his jaw and informed her tightly, "You have leapt to a most incorrect conclusion. The maid acted on her own. I imagine she must have lost the boy in the crowd. That would explain her anger, and as to her haste to take him from you, perhaps she believes you are a traveling player. Matt, for his part, asked me to thank you for entertaining his son. He would thank you himself, but you see, he fears, as do I, that given the state of his reputation, he would compromise yours beyond redemption, if that is possible."

Why Tristan added that last, he would never know, except that she could provoke him as no one else could, and as they were standing now twenty feet from the Sea Maid he had suddenly thought of her stumbling out of the stables dressed in the boy's breeches that had disguised nothing of the softly rounded bottom he had had to cup between his thighs for the nearly half hour it had taken them to return home.

Marissa held Tristan's blistering gaze a half moment, but no more before she stalked away toward Will, who was tugging at his father's hand as tears streamed down his face.

"Marissa," Tristan warned, catching her in one long stride, "the very last thing in the world that Matt needs now is more gossip. When Mama has recognized him and one or two of the other dowagers, then you may juggle for Will all you like."

She flicked him a set, stubborn look. "I do not believe, my lord, that I am inclined to make the child wait that long."

Despite the onlookers, Tristan would have caught her before she took another step, for he truly believed that Matt's reinstatement would be hindered by Marissa's interference, but Marissa swerved suddenly and instead of making for

Matt and little Will, proceeded across the commons to the
booths. Will's cries growing louder rather than softer, Tristan watched Marissa go straight to Mrs. Kendall, who was,
he saw, observing Will with a distinctly sympathetic expression.

What Marissa said to the woman, Tristan never learned,
but it was effective, for Mrs. Kendall left her booth and ac-
companying Marissa across the commons, not only greeted
Matthew Haydon but presented Marissa to him and his son.
Matt said something to her and made a rather helpless gesture, which caused Mrs. Kendall to laugh in a rather mater-
nal way, and her expression warming even further, she
gestured toward the booth with the meat pasties. She must
have invited Will to go to it, for after looking at his father
and then to Marissa, the boy nodded slowly, whereupon
Mrs. Kendall, Will, and Matt started toward the booth.
Marissa did not join them immediately. She scooped up the
balls that lay forgotten on the ground, and looking directly
at Tristan, began to juggle them, a distinct smirk curling her
expressive mouth.

Chapter 13

Marissa floated down the back stairs. Wren had been too efficient. Lady Lynton and Tory both were notoriously slow at dressing. They'd not be in the drawing room yet, but Lynton might be. Marissa's net frock, worn over a blue satin slip, swirled around her ankles. The décolletage of the dress was low. As she moved, she could feel the air brush the swell, albeit small, of her breasts. Not that the dress was beyond the bounds. It was not. Wren had chosen it, not she, after all, but still she was aware how tiny the bodice was, and she had decided when she left her room that she'd prefer to while away the time before the Kendalls' supper dance alone in Lady Lynton's herb garden, particularly as the alternative was to sit in the drawing room alone with Tristan.

The door to the small, walled garden, Lady Lynton's pride after her children and her roses, lay just to the left of the last step of the servants' stair. Without anyone the wiser, Marissa let herself out the door.

It closed with a click behind her, and when she stepped forward, looking across the garden, she looked directly into Tristan's golden brown eyes. He was not fifteen feet away, half resting on his heels, inspecting a bed of tall, fragrant lavender spikes.

Her eyes locked with his. She had seen little of him since Parish Day. Lady Lynton had resumed her duties as his secretary, and he had spent more time than ever at Twyckham Hall, as Matt Haydon had fired his agent and desperately needed seasoned advice. Still, Tristan did not seem surprised to see her. Instead, she thought she detected the faintest spark of humor in his amber eyes, as if he knew she had intended to avoid him. And perhaps had been, in his turn, thinking to avoid her.

He did not refer to their thwarted efforts, however, as he regarded her over the purple shafts of lavender. As if she had questioned his intent, he said, "I am thinking of growing lavender."

No longer surprised by Tristan's interest in agriculture, Marissa nodded. "Would you make a profit?"

He smiled. As they had not been on good terms since he had questioned her motives about Parish Day, if they had been on good terms before then, his smile caught her off guard. "That is the question I was asking myself," he said, explaining the friendly expression. "And I think so," he went on more thoughtfully.

He brushed his hand across the heads of the stalks, sending the scent of lavender into the air. "It is a pleasant scent, don't you think?" he asked, rising to his full height. "And now the wars with the French are over, I believe people here and on the Continent will want more luxuries, such as perfumes and soaps and the like. On my way home from Italy, I stopped off at an estate in France where lavender is grown for sale. The climate and soil are much like that here at Tremourne, and so I think I will give it a try."

So. He had not stopped off in France to visit a woman. Or at least not only to visit a woman. He had stopped to investigate the feasibility of growing lavender, a rather mundane matter in all. But it interested Marissa, too, she acknowledged, primarily because she realized how much Tristan's every experiment meant to him. And to Tory and Lady Lynton, of course.

She was not interested, certainly, simply because he was handsome, though he was that in the black evening clothes that set off his sun-streaked hair and amber eyes.

"I think it is an excellent idea. I have always liked the scent," Marissa began to walk toward the bed, deciding that if she stayed by the door she would look a fearful fool, and she did not think herself as either. "If you grow it, I shall have Father's steward buy it to use on the sheets at Penhurst. That should assure you some return."

Perhaps the suggestion reeked of largesse to him. Marissa had really meant it as a joke, though the idea of lavender-scented sheets did appeal, but even as she thought to tell him, she saw Tristan flick his gaze over her, and she leapt to the conclusion that it was her appearance that had brought on his cooler expression. Because she would never allow him to see that she was not entirely confident of what she wore, she naturally attacked.

Allowing her chin to float up so that she was all but looking down her slender nose at him, though he stood a head taller, she said coolly, "You look as if you disapprove my looks, my lord. If so, you will have to take up the matter with Wren. She selected the dress, and I have not dampened even a flounce on my shift, either."

Marissa did not know what she expected from Tristan then, perhaps a lecture on small bodices, but she got a long, somehow unnervingly intense moment of silence before he spoke, that gaze of his steady yet unreadable as usual. "Whatever criticism I have made of your behavior from time to time, Marissa, I have never disapproved of your looks. You are beautiful tonight, but then you always are."

She turned away so abruptly, the curls spilling artlessly from the Grecian knot into which Wren had fashioned her hair, fanned out around her face. Putting Tristan out of her sight did not, however, put him from her mind. She was acutely, exquisitely aware of his gaze, and felt all the more foolish for not having been able to hold it. For something to do, she snapped the head off a dill plant.

Tristan watched her pluck the dead umbrel head. Her gloved fingers were slender and elegant and graceful, and in the next moment he heard himself say, "That Grecian dress and the dampened underclothes that went with it were objectionable in and of themselves, but I think what I objected to most about the costume was that it cheapened your beauty. Were you to paint your cheeks or your lips, it would be the same."

A second dill head went with a snap. Marissa leaned forward, bending her head over the two fragrant heads to inhale their scent. Her neck made a long, graceful white curve, and admiring it, Tristan almost missed what she said. "Happily, Leicester never again pressed me to marry him after he saw me at that ball.'

It took him a moment to absorb the remark, her voice had been so low and another moment to comprehend fully what she meant. "Could you not simply have told the earl no?" Tristan watched as her hand reached for another dill head, and a trace of wryness to be heard in his voice, he warned, "Have a care, Marissa. That one is green, yet."

She pivoted away from the dill and in the end turned all the way about, the two brown heads of dill cradled in one palm. Her eyes met Tristan's. "I did tell him no. Repeatedly. He would not believe we were ill suited until I proved it." She seemed to be half smiling, but he could not be certain because she lifted the dry dill heads and softly blew them into the air. When she dusted her hands a trifle more vigorously than necessary, he had the sense she was thinking still of Leicester and how she had managed finally to dispatch the wealthy and famously punctilious earl, whose suit, Tristan guessed, her mother would have vigorously promoted.

In the evening light, the white of her net frock seemed to glow, setting off the pearly white of her satin smooth skin. Exeter's daughter, who could exert such an attraction that by her word at least two men, Durston and Leicester, had refused to accept her rejection of them, even when it was repeated. And Tristan believed her.

"You've made a new conquest," he said, smiling faintly. "Will Haydon has not stopped speaking about you all week. Where did you learn to juggle?"

He had drifted closer to her, for it was time they went inside. His mother and sister would soon come down to the drawing room, and closer to her, Tristan saw the smile that teased the corners of Marissa's mouth, just lifting it. "From an underfootman whom I caught juggling apples in the dining room at Exeter House. He hopes to get on at Astley's."

"Will was much impressed."

Marissa smiled outright at that. The smile transformed her face; lighting it; making him want to smile with her. "He's a charming little boy with a very appealing smile."

She was looking up at Tristan, her neck arched so that she could meet his eyes. There seemed to be odd lights in those eyes. Marissa knew the effect was only a trick of the twilight's reflection, but as the faintest scent of sandalwood drifted to her, her heart began to beat faster.

"I have not seen you to commend you as I should have for persuading Mrs. Kendall to acknowledge Matthew. In one stroke you made him more accepted than not in Penryn. Mrs. Kendall has even invited him to the Grange this evening."

Marissa resisted the temptation to bend low over the lavender. She could not avoid Tristan's gaze every time they broached something difficult, or he would learn to read her even more easily than he already did. "I thought you were angry with me," she said, her gaze quite steady.

He smiled lopsidedly, the expression causing Marissa much the same catch in her breathing that it had before. "No doubt that is why you all but juggled those balls in my face."

Marissa thought she ought to have looked away when she first had the impulse. Not having done so, she ought now to return his smile, for he was only teasing her, and gently at that, but somehow she couldn't. He had faulted her too often for her to find the subject amusing. And so she stood, rooted to the spot, regarding Tristan too gravely.

His smile faded before her look, and then he did a most unexpected thing. Lifting his hand, he touched the corner of her mouth, where the fullness of her mouth became the line that could curve and bring her face alive when it lifted. Marissa could not move even enough to draw breath. "I was angry," Tristan admitted, as solemn now as she. "I thought you would prompt the people who have accepted you here in Cornwall to recall that there has been scandal attached to your name. But I underestimated you, Marissa. Appealing to Agatha Kendall was a master stroke."

"Ahem, my lord?"

Tristan looked up, and Marissa all but fell back a step, as color rose in her cheeks.

"Yes, Hobbes?"

"Lady Lynton and Miss Tory are waiting in the drawing room, my lord."

"Thank you, Hobbes."

Marissa was already walking to the door, briskly. She had not realized how close they stood. She had not heard Hobbes come into the garden. And why? To hear Tristan tell her he had underestimated her? He had done that often enough, and he had not been moved by his gratitude, on his friend's behalf of course, to allow her to ride again.

Unsettled by the entire scene, she avoided Tristan the rest of the night, and when he asked her to dance, as he had politely asked every lady present at the Kendalls' to do, she refused him, saying she had already promised to talk to the Tregaron spinsters just then. He did not ask again, and Miss Hester and Miss Millie were giddy with pleasure when, uninvited, she spent the quarter hour with them.

Chapter 14

" 'T is nearly Lammas Day already, is it? Jove, but August has come quickly this year!" Matthew Haydon shook his head. "It seems as if only yesterday the month was June and I was in Italy."

"You have had a great deal to do," Tristan observed, studying his friend. Matt had come to Tremourne to consult with him on a number of matters, and had stayed on afterward to share a glass or two of port. "Are you glad to have returned, Matt? Or did I pull you back ill-advisedly?"

"You were not the least ill-advised to warn me that I would either have to sell Twyckham or return. Not one of the agents I employed appears to have been entirely honest and the last one was the worst of the lot. But truth to tell, for a time there, I was seriously considering selling and raising Will in some other part of England. Jove! Bessborough nearly killed her, Tris, and yet even Barbara Lowell, who is no better than she should be, would not nod in greeting." Matt shook his head again, but after a little, a smile began to curve his mouth. "Now, however, all is different. Squire Kendall and his wife have even had me to dinner at the Grange." He slanted his oldest friend a dancing look. Tristan held it, though he knew what was coming. "Lady Marissa is the one responsible, you know."

Tristan nodded. "I do. And she is."

He took a swallow of his port, apparently uninterested in discussing Marissa further, but after a moment, swirling the ruby liquid in his glass, Matt asked, "Why did she do it, Tris? Did she defy you?"

"She knew it wasn't my wish that she risk reminding everyone in the neighborhood of her propensity for scandal," Tristan admitted. "But in truth, I don't believe either of us figured much in her calculations. She took a liking to Will, and all but dragged Agatha Kendall into the fray, so to speak, on his account."

"Yes, that is what I thought. And I suspect as well that there would have been no stopping her. Had she not gotten Mrs. Kendall to present her to me and Will, I'd the distinct impression Lady Marissa might have dragged Prinny down from Brighton to do the honors. She's spirit. Lud, but she's as much spirit and determination as she's beauty!"

If Matt had been hoping to provoke his friend into an intemperate response, and the twinkle in his eye suggested as much, he did not get his wish. Tristan only murmured, "Hmm, all true," as he levered himself out of his chair and went to collect the decanter of port that Hobbes had brought. "Well, what do you say, Matt?" he asked as he freshened the other's glass. "Shall we go to Penryn on Lammas Night?"

"Jove, but I would like to! It seems ages since I really enjoyed myself, and as to Lammas Night, I can remember revels that should likely be forgotten."

Tristan remembered them, too, and laughed. "Those were our salad days, Matt-o, but I see no reason why we can't have a pint or two of Treginnis' stout ale at the Sea Maid and reminisce with the other old dogs."

"Old dogs?" Matt laughed uproariously. "Well, then, I suppose there are times I feel like a deuced old dog, but I cannot go, Tris. Ever since Carlotta's death, Will has become distraught if I leave him at night. Though I gave him every assurance I could, when I returned from the Kendalls' supper dance, he was wide awake, sobbing disconsolately."

"Devil it, Matt. I am sorry to hear that." Tristan frowned sympathetically. "His nurse cannot comfort him?"

Mr. Haydon shook his head. "He doesn't believe her when she tells him I will return, though he did say," Matt continued slowly, "that if I must go out at night, he would not mind so much if he could stay with . . ." Abruptly he shook his head. "No. It is too preposterous. She would not do it. But can you guess who it was he wanted?"

A particular face did flash into Tristan's mind, but for one reason or another he only shook his head. "Who is it?"

"Lady Marissa," Mr. Haydon responded, naming the very person Lynton had seen so clearly in his mind's eye. "Will has been entranced with her since Parish Day. She came to visit him, you know. Ah, I see you did not know," Matt exclaimed when Tristan looked at him in surprise. "She and Tory drove over in your gig. I was not at home, but Lady Marissa informed my butler that my absence did not signify as she had come to see Will. The three of them took tea together and then she gave him his first lesson in juggling. He was in alt and informed me when I returned that he intends to be a juggler when he is grown."

Tristan forbore to remark upon the lofty ambitions Marissa could inspire in a man. Instead, seeing a way to occupy both Will and Marissa on Lammas Night, he asked after a moment, "Do you suppose if I could persuade Lady Marissa to look after him that Will would like to come to the Lodge to spend the night? You could stay as well, after we return from Penryn. It would truly be like old times."

Mr. Haydon considered the suggestion, and the more he considered, the more boyish his expression became. "Do you know, I think that might just be the thing! If Lady Marissa invited him, I do believe Will would be persuaded."

"It's done then," Tristan said with a confidence that lifted his good friend's amiable brow. "I'll bring Lady Marissa to Twyckham tomorrow to speak to Will."

"You really think she'll agree? Somehow I find it difficult to imagine her playing nursemaid."

"Could you have imagined her expertly juggling a trio of

balls?" Tristan returned wryly. "Don't worry. She'll agree. I've the perfect carrot to use with her."

Tristan did not postpone putting into effect his plan to incarcerate Marissa on Lammas Night—and with her own agreement, yet. When Matt left, he rang for Hobbes, but his butler informed him that her ladyship had last been seen on her way to the stables.

Tristan displayed no sign of the anger that streaked through him other than that he wheeled away from his old retainer without another word and stalked to the stables. There, eyes narrowing dangerously, he observed that Circe's stall was empty.

When Tibbs entered the stables, Tristan swung around so abruptly the smaller man stumbled backed a step. "Yer lordship," he said in greeting, rough fingers going to his cap as he eyed his employer uncertainly.

"Where is she?"

It was all Tristan asked, but Tibbs' glance slid to the empty stall. "Her ladyship's walkin' the mare, m'lord. I swear that's all. She gave me her word."

"My God, man!" Tristan swore, though even he could not have said, perhaps, whether he was angry with Tibbs for allowing Marissa near a horse or merely astonished that the man would risk his employment on Lady Marissa Portemaine's word of honor.

"She'd not break her word, m'lord!" Tibbs exclaimed, addressing the latter point, at least. "You've only to see for yourself. She walks the mare to the ruins."

The ruins. His jaw hard, Tristan stared a moment, thrown off stride by the thought of Marissa frolicking at the charred ruins where the worst had happened. "Saddle Stockings, Tibbs."

He'd have wagered every valuable he did still own on the proposition that she was riding free as the breeze to the ruins, and so it was lucky that Tristan had given up serious gaming on the day his father died. When he topped the ridge that sloped to the bluffs overlooking the Channel, he saw Marissa walking down the slope to the promontory upon which stood the charred stones that were all that was left of Tremourne Abbey.

She heard him unlatch the gate in the briar hedge that kept the few sheep he did have from trotting over the bluff's edge, and she turned to look up from under the flat brim of her straw cottage bonnet. Tristan told himself it was absurd that he should feel at a disadvantage for having doubted Marissa would keep her word to Tibbs. God knew she had done enough ill-advised things to give him reason to doubt her. But she knew he had mistrusted her. The knowledge gleamed in those large, thickly lashed, clear, silver blue eyes of hers.

"Well, my lord, as I have not seen you ride here before, I take it you have come to assure yourself that I did not secret a saddle somewhere and slap it on Circe the moment I was out of sight of the Lodge."

"I came for several reasons, actually," he said, swinging down from Stockings. "That was only one."

"You have learned something then." She turned to continue her walk. Gulls wheeled about overhead, screaming shrilly. In comparison her voice was low, but equally fierce. "I keep my word when I give it."

"I'll remember that," he said, falling into step beside her. "Just as I shan't forget the converse: that you won't give your word unless you mean to keep it."

That earned him a flashing look. But no more. No agreement, no argument, only a look that left him musing, irrelevantly, that Miss Millie had been right as rain when she'd said Marissa's beauty was vivid as a flame. And it was her eyes, shimmering silver blue, surrounded by eyelashes black as soot and thick as the grass through which they walked, that were the spark of that flame.

When they reached the cliff's edge, Tristan looked out over the choppy waters of the Channel. From where he stood, he could look back to his right toward the estuary of the Penryn River and its fertile valley, where the Lodge was safely tucked away.

Watching him sidelong, Marissa noticed that Tristan did not so much as glance to his left to the jutting promontory on which stood the stones, some charred, some bleached by the sun and the wind, that were all that remained of the St. Aubyns' home. It was a dramatic spot—the Abbey must have seemed to stand guard on the bluff, protecting Penryn and the rich valley behind. And though loss and sadness were surely a part of the place, still Marissa found it curious that there was such a pall over it that no one spoke of the Abbey, much less came, and now Tristan did even not look to it.

Nonetheless, she removed her sketch pad from a pack Tibbs had fastened on Circe's back. There was no chain on Tristan's leg, shackling him to her. He could leave if he wanted. She wished he would. She'd not be able to sketch much with him all but looking over her shoulder.

"It seems a morbid thing for you to draw."

His voice was almost harsh and certainly censorious, and ordinarily Marissa would have answered in kind, but they spoke of his home.

"I understand that the fire must have been wrenching for you and your sister and mother," she began more carefully than was her custom. "But I only know the promontory as it is, and to me the stone arches and walls have a stark beauty silhouetted against the sky and the sea, and played upon by the shifting light and shadows."

"And God knows there are enough of those."

He was looking at the ruins at last, his hands curled into fists at his side. Marissa observed him, astonished but uncertain as well. He was not the honey man now at all. He looked like one of the Viking ancestors he had surely had, fierce and furious over his loss. And bitter, too.

"Come." Tristan jerked around abruptly. His eyes were dark, unyielding. "Walk with me. I wish to talk to you."

The honey man would never be so curt. What had happened to him here? She did not ask. She couldn't abide people who pried, but the intensity of her desire to know took Marissa aback. She looked away from him and tossed her sketch pad on the rock where she meant to sit later.

They walked so long in silence, Marissa half thought he had forgotten her. If he had, he was reminded of her presence when she began to untie the ribbons of her bonnet. She glanced at Tristan, half expecting him to object that ladies did not expose their faces to the sun, but though he was watching her, he said nothing. Marissa's fingers became oddly clumsy when she found his eyes on her and not so dark as they had been. Then the bonnet came off, and the thick braid Wren had made of her hair spilled over her shoulder.

Tristan's eyes followed the plait's progress, coming to rest where it did, upon her breast. Unthinking, Marissa took a breath, and was exquisitely aware how her breast lifted, swelled even, as if it had some desire of its own to rivet him.

Would he think she puffed herself out for him? "So?" she snapped in as curt a voice as she had ever used.

"Your ribbon is coming undone."

It was. Marissa felt a fool. He'd only been looking at her straggling ribbon. He likely thought her breasts too small, anyway. The widow Lowell was built like a cow. And what did she care anyway!

"Before I left for the Kendalls' picnic Wren bade me to make sure you wore your hat."

He spoke idly, and Marissa was grateful for the neutral subject. She had felt for just a moment as if her thoughts were spinning out of her control. "I don't doubt she did. She is forever cutting up at me for getting too much sun."

"And you don't listen to her."

"I must listen," Marissa disputed, making a rueful face. "Wren is not shy with her pet peeves."

"And you tolerate her?" Tristan regarded her curiously.

"What do you mean? I argue with her, though I suppose it's true I'll put the bonnet on again before I am ready, to avoid a full lecture on the subject."

Tristan was smiling at her honesty. "You could always turn Wren off and hire a more docile maid."

"Turn off Wren?" Marissa looked as well as sounded as if she couldn't conceive of the idea. But she couldn't put into words why the idea was so inconceivable. She'd have sounded too sentimental, and so she simply shrugged off the suggestion.

Tristan laughed but there was a warmth in his laughter that was reflected as well in the glint in his eyes. "You are loyal," he said.

And as quickly as that the neutral subject of Wren became fraught and uncertain for Marissa. Tristan's rare approval warmed her literally. Unsettled by that bloom of warmth inside her, she refused to acknowledge it.

And sought distraction. "I don't think you chased me out to the cliffs to discuss my relations with Wren, my lord. Why did you come? Aside from a desire to ride herd on me, that is?"

Perhaps it was because he had felt such dark emotions only moments before that Tristan seemed quick to laugh then, but he laughed again. "You are scarcely bovine, Marissa." She could have screamed with frustration, for her heart seemed to skip a beat when he did no more than tell her she did not resemble a cow. Honey-tongued honey man. And with a lazy gleam in his eye that, however, disappeared almost as quickly as it had leapt to life. "As to why I came . . . Have you heard anything of Lammas Night, Marissa, and how it is celebrated here in Cornwall?"

Marissa nodded and told him that Miss Hester had said Lammas Night was an old pagan holiday still celebrated in something of the same manner as it had been before Christianity had appropriated the day. She did not add that Tory had mentioned the night only a few days before, saying that in Cornwall it was deemed a night for lovers, and saying it almost defiantly. Marissa had thought Tory's manner a trifle odd, but had decided that Tory was feeling bitter against the Fates for taking Mr. Fitzhugh from her.

"And so I know," she said, putting thoughts of Mr.

Fitzhugh firmly from her mind, "that there is much drinking and dancing that night, and that the Tregaron ladies' father did not like to speak of the night and its customs."

Marissa cast Tristan a sidelong glance. "Mr. Tregaron was a very godly man," he said, but there was a twinkle in his eye.

"And Lammas Night is not godly?" she pressed, but she knew she had given herself away by smiling.

And Tristan took his cue from her smile. He laughed. "It is a night of celebration and revelry. Whether that is godly is for clerics, not a humble farmer, to say." Marissa rolled her eyes, and he laughed again. "I mention the revels because Matt, you understand he is the tempter here, I hope, wishes to go down to the village to see if the celebration is as he remembers it, but he is hesitant because Will refuses to stay with anyone but you."

"Me?"

"He likes you."

Tristan was smiling, amused, but he did not look so boyish any longer, for there was a hint of calculation about his expression.

Marissa studied him only a moment before she cocked her slender eyebrow at him and guessed coolly, "And if I agree to stay with Will, I shall be too occupied to run off and enjoy the revels myself?"

If her astute guess caught him by surprise, Tristan didn't show it. Indeed, he simply ignored the question. "I've a good reason for you to accept my proposal," Tristan said instead. "If you agree to look after Master Will, I shall rescind my order that you may not ride."

It was inexplicable, and Marissa admitted it, that she did not embrace Tristan's proposition with instant enthusiasm. But she did not care to have her best instincts used against herself.

"And this will teach me discipline?" she heard herself demand. "Bargaining my way out of punishment?"

Tristan had found a rock earlier and hefting it in his hand, he tossed it high in the air off the cliffs. "It is for a good cause," he said, turning back to her, seeming pleased with the arc of his shot. "And besides, I think you have learned that unpleasant consequences will follow when you act unwisely."

As he defined unwisely. Her eyes flashed, but she abruptly turned back toward Circe nibbling at the grass by her sketch pad. "Very well, I accept your bargain, my lord."

"Marissa." Marissa neither slowed nor turned. "Marissa," Tristan said again, and if he were not already raking his fingers through his hair, he sounded as if he might soon. What a pity that he should be frustrated, she thought nastily, but he caught her hand.

Her gloves were a fine, delicate kidskin and conveyed the warmth and strength of his hand as if she were touching his bare skin. "What?" she snapped, pulling her hand free of his immediately.

He did not look annoyed. The honey man looked calm and unruffled and forbearing, too. She glared into eyes that were the richest shade of amber.

"You are right, Marissa," he admitted on a long breath. "I do not want you to attend the revels in Penryn. But not, as I've a notion you believe, because I wish to deny you enjoyment." He had not gotten the immediate source of her pique quite right, but as he'd gotten the ultimate one, Marissa decided to give him a hearing, if an unsympathetic one. "Lammas Night is a night of revels, marked by drinking as well as a sense of license, and you are desirable. Do you understand that?" He was frowning at her. And what was she to say? That she thought she was a siren? "Devil it!" he swore, startling Marissa with the intensity of his oath. "I cannot say if you do understand. Or if you believe, perhaps, that being Exeter's daughter will protect you through anything. But it would not, Marissa. There are men who would not give a fig who your father was."

He raked his hand through his hair and looked off to stare, Marissa thought, at nothing, and then apparently having made some decision, he looked around again to address her intently. "I ought to have explained more fully the night of the cockfight or later in my study, but there was such anger between us . . . it seemed better to allow the matter to rest."

Again Tristan stopped to stare unseeing out to the Channel, as if he were gathering his thoughts. Dispassionately, Marissa acknowledged that he had made her curious, and so she waited patiently to see if he had had good reason for referring to the night of the cockfight.

"I had mistaken where Treginnis meant to hold the cockfight," Tristan said after a little. "Sometimes he makes use of his taproom, and looking in there first, I found a group of five or six strangers swilling ale while they waited for a particularly heralded cock to be brought out in a later match. They were hard men, and not simply by my accounting. Treginnis, who is no saint himself, feared them and their leering looks enough to send his serving girls home, and in comparison to you, Marissa, they are the merest drabs." In contrast to his words, the look in Tristan's eyes was uncompromising and unflattering. "Had those men found you before I did, seen that thick plait of silky hair or your butter-soft skin, they'd have dragged you off and used you—all of them."

It was Marissa's turn to half spin away and look at nothing in particular. She did not think, though, that Tristan was making up stories to frighten her. His voice had had a raw edge he could not have counterfeited.

"You flinch away, Marissa, and so perhaps you can understand that when I found you at the stable door, I was sick with worry. For all I knew, they had already stumbled upon you and Gerald. Then when I saw you . . ." He gave the faintest lift of his shoulders, not needing to say that his concern had transformed itself into a corresponding degree of anger when he found her safe. "I am not saying, by the by, that those particular men will be at the revels, but not all our local men are saints, particularly when they've drink in them and should a prize like you be set before them . . ."

Taking Marissa by complete surprise, Tristan reached out to draw his finger along the line of her cheek. And

withdrew it again almost before she had fully registered
that he had lightly caressed her. Nor did he say a word
more, but stood looking down at her, his hands resting now
in the pockets of his breeches.

If his stance was relaxed, though, his gaze was not.
Needing to escape the intensity of it, feeling as if she might
unravel if she did not, Marissa nodded curtly. "Very well!
You may be confident that you have convinced me. I will
not go to the revels. You have my word. I will look after
Will and be entirely amenable."

"And safe."

There was the faintest hint of a smile tugging at his
mouth. "And safe," she echoed, but grudgingly. He was
laughing at her while he regarded her . . . softly, for lack of
a better way to put it. She was not accustomed to such a
look from Tristan. But then, except for Wren, and Kit,
when he was home, she wasn't accustomed to having anyone worry themselves into a rage for fear she was lying
broken, or even dead, by the roadside.

"One more thing, Marissa."

She had started walking away from him again. "What?"

He ignored her ill-tempered tone. "I would like your
word that if you ride further than Tremourne's boundaries,
you will take Ben with you."

Their gazes met for a pregnant moment, but what could
she say: that she wanted to risk hurt? That she longed for
him to worry about her? "You have it."

Chapter 15

S he had not capitulated to Tristan St. Aubyns, Lord Lynton; she had merely, and wisely, agreed to have a care for herself, or so Marissa reasoned as she and Tristan made their way back to their horses. He had presented his case, and she was not an unreasonable person. In addition, he had not stipulated that she must be dressed in a habit to ride.

Wondering what he would say when she mounted Circe in a few moments, Marissa cast Tristan a glance, only to forget the reason she had looked at him. If her spirits had lightened suddenly, his had done the opposite. A muscle worked in his jaw, for he stared again, broodingly, out to the promontory.

Unwilling to challenge his taught silence, and yet oddly unwilling to leave him to it, Marissa caught up her sketch pad and turned to say something to Tristan, though what she had not decided. She'd not caught the sketch pad tightly, however, and it flew out of her fingers, falling open between them, laying bare two pages on which she'd roughly sketched how she imagined the Abbey might have looked.

He stared at them, and as he was closest, picked up the open pad. There was a tense silence, broken only by the gulls wheeling high overhead, and then Marissa could bear it no longer. "Was that how the house looked?" she asked.

Again there was silence. Tristan staring at the sketches so long that Marissa did not think he would answer her. But he did, finally, low and harsh. "The door and hall are wrong, but the cloisters are nearly exact."

Marissa seized the opening to ask one question about

which she had been curious a long while. "Will you rebuild there?"

"No," Tristan said shortly. He was looking to the ruins again, his profile as forbidding as his tone, but Marissa could not make herself let the subject lie now that it had been broached. Something was quite wrong, and without examining why she should want to expose whatever it was to discussion, she said, "It is a beautiful spot."

Tristan turned on her, sharply enough that had Marissa been of a fearful temperament, she'd have stumbled back a pace. As it was she had to tell herself not to flinch before the darkness of his expression. His hands were balled into fists, and she thought that if she could have called back her words, gone elsewhere for a walk even, she would have, for she had never seen, or even imagined Tristan, so . . . anguished.

When he had shown her the sum of his indebtedness, there had been challenge in his eyes, and a touch of defiance, perhaps, but nothing like the pain and anger that was in them now, and also, she thought, beneath them both, shame. Indeed, she did not think he would even hold her gaze much longer. And he did not. Tristan, tall and golden and brave, looked away from *her* eyes.

Only to look back again with an expression so intense Marissa did falter a step. "My father burned himself up in that house. Do you understand?" His voice was raw enough that Marissa's stomach knotted at the sound of it. "He deliberately set the blaze! And why did he do such a thing? Why did he put a period to himself? Why did he take the very roof from over Mother's head? He had learned by post that day that he had failed to break the entail and could not sell either the house or the land that had been in the St. Aubyns family for generations. Without the sale, he could not honor his gaming vowels, and when he realized he must live his life without his obsession, he chose to destroy himself as well as the house. So. Now you know."

Tristan wrenched his gaze from Marissa's. She did not know what he meant to do, launch her sketch pad over the cliff, perhaps. She'd have let him, but even as the realization startled her, she found his eyes on her again.

Had she been certain she would not offend him, Marissa would have touched Tristan in the hope that she could draw out some of the raw pain she saw in his eyes. Uncertain how he would receive such a gesture from her, however, she simply held his gaze as steadily as she could. "I am sorry for your father, Tristan," she said quietly, "and for the madness that drove him. He must have been quite wretched." Marissa paused a moment, considering what she would say next, then continued carefully, "But I do not see, whence your anguish and shame, too, I think, come. Your father's actions do not reflect upon you."

"Oh?" Tristan's mouth curled contemptuously. "You believe that, Exeter's daughter? I doubt it." This time he kicked a rock, sending it sailing over the cliff, saying to it as much as Marissa, "And Tory does not know he set the fire. I don't know why I have told you, but I would be grateful, if you would not enlighten her."

"Of course, I will not tell her, if you do not wish it. But I think Tory is wise enough to realize that she bears no responsibility for his madness. As she would understand equally well that you do not. You are his son, not his cipher. Am I a copy of my mother?" It was not necessary for Tristan to answer. The Duchess of Exeter was the most coldly formal woman he had ever known, and as little like her daughter as night is like day. "Or even my father?" Marissa went on, her eyes challenging him now.

He had called her Exeter's daughter. All of England did, and she promoted the comparison half the time. But Exeter would never have noticed a child's tears. He'd have been too absorbed in himself, in his pleasures and play.

"No," Tristan said finally. "You are not Exeter."

Marissa had not known what he would say, and her breath came out in a rush of relief. "Well then, there you are, you see," she said, brisk now. "We are none of us our parents, for better or worse. And as children can scarcely be called to account for their sins, I certainly have had nothing to do with the fact that mine have not spoken in nearly two decades. The fault lies with them. Both of them, I might add, but that is neither here nor there. And if all that is not enough to convince you how . . . .wrong it is that you feel shame on his account, just think how your father would have met the challenge he handed you. I don't think he would have considered growing lavender. Do you?"

But Marissa did not allow Tristan time to answer, if, indeed, he had any interest in doing so. It was a new role for her, delivering her opinions to him, and it went to her head. Her eyes narrowing thoughtfully, she went on almost at once. "In fact, I would say your father was the making of you."

"Oh?"

It was an odd, strangled sound that Marissa interpreted as a protest. "I did not mean to say I am not sorry for the pain of his loss! Of course I am, but you've purpose in your life, Tristan. You are not lost in London or Brighton or Bath with the other wastrels, exchanging one woman for another between bouts of gaming, empty of soul not to mention mind. Kit hasn't fallen into that pit, but only because he has remained in the army. All the others . . ." She shrugged, summarily dismissing most of the young men of their class. "You know them as well as I. They spend hours agonizing over their cravats or wagering which fly will cross the window first. But you were given a challenge, and you rose to it, Tristan! You are strong and capable and admirable."

Marissa rarely did things by halves. She had spoken feelingly, even fiercely, without considering how she would feel now, when she was done and looking into his eyes, with her words full of praise ringing in the silence between them. She felt naked.

And did not like feeling so exposed. And so began to feel angry with Tristan for not saying something. He could at least grunt noncommittally. Then she would not be waiting on tenterhooks for his response. But why was she waiting so? She had said her piece, and she had meant it. He could think what he jolly well pleased. Damn him.

"Hold there! Where are you going?"

Tristan caught her arm as she whirled to leave. Marissa glanced down at his hand, but he didn't release her. "You can't want me to stay and lecture you further, surely."

"Well, I admit it was a novel experience, being read a lecture by you."

He was smiling. Or close enough. His mouth had edged up on one side, and his eyes had gone warm in that way they could. He did not think her an utter fool, perhaps.

"And an instructive experience, I hope," Marissa said, prodding him now that she did not feel so absurd. She wanted to know that he would think on what she'd said, and her eyes held his, just as he held her arm. She knew the moment he thought again of his father, and she knew as well that he was considering at least some of her remarks.

"Yes," he allowed at last. "There was much in what you said."

Why she should go weak at the knees, Marissa could not fathom, or would not. But she did, and caught her breath, too. There was something in his eyes . . . but, of course, it was only the sun. She was Exeter's daughter, and if not a copy of the duke, then too much like him for Tristan.

She pulled away and went to catch up Circe's reins. Before Tristan could have guessed her intent, Marissa stepped up onto the nearest rock and swung nimbly onto the mare's back. Her skirts slid up, exposing her half boots, stockings, calves, and a froth of petticoat.

"I didn't want you to think I had transformed myself into a pattern card of wisdom and propriety." She cast him a half challenging, half mock-innocent look. "You might worry that the real Marissa had been stolen away by Cornish elves."

His hands were shoved deep into his pockets, and his hair lifted in the breeze, shining gold and brown as he looked up at her, a suggestion of a smile curving his mouth. "I suppose I should be grateful that you are so considerate."

Marissa had not really expected Tristan to fall in with her play so readily, and she grinned, an expression he had seldom seen. "You are not going to rail at me! And you are right not to. There is no one working in the fields between here and the stables. I know. I walked them. And so there is no one to see my legs sticking out of these stout half boots but you. And you won't look."

Some emotion flared in Tristan's eyes, but it was gone before Marissa could read it. She supposed that he had intended to say something about her admittedly improper appearance but had thought better of whatever he'd meant to say as she had already accepted more than one stricture that afternoon. What he did do was to hand her her sketch pad. "Can you manage it?"

"Yes, I've got my bonnet, too." She extended the hand holding the hat and took the pad between her fingers. "Thank you."

"Hmm. Oh, and, Marissa?"

She had already started away, but turned back. "You wish to race?" she teased with mock eagerness.

"No." His eyes held hers, and were more serious than not now. "I'll stay here awhile. I've a good deal of wisdom to consider, but you'll not forget your word?"

Even if he did not think what she'd said worthy of consideration, he would have her think he did. Marissa bit her lip, something she rarely, if ever, did and nodded. "I'll not forget. Good afternoon, then."

The scene with Tristan near the ruins did much to explain why Marissa was smiling wryly at about ten o'clock on Lammas Night. She had spent the evening entertaining Will Haydon by herself, for Tory, complaining of a deadly headache, had taken to her bed that afternoon. Having little experience with children, Marissa had simply done the things she liked to do. After taking an early dinner with Lady Lynton, she and Will had walked to the river and fed the ducks. They had practiced juggling, which had soon deteriorated into simply tossing and catching the balls, then Marissa had taught Will how to throw dice. As Will was a bright, receptive boy, it was a pleasant evening, but he was young and fell asleep before she had completed the first chapter of Captain Cook's adventure in the South Seas, as written for children, a book she'd found in the nursery.

And so, as she closed the nursery door softly behind her, Marissa smiled wryly to herself. If it had been Tristan's plan to occupy her for all of Lammas Night, he had failed. On the other hand, if keeping her at Tremourne and away from the revels in Penryn had been his goal, he had succeeded handily. She had given her word she would not ride so far without Ben Hawkes, and Ben and Dorcas, both, had left long since for the revels in Penryn.

She had learned a little more about Lammas Night, but not from Tory. The girl had been distant the last week or so, and thinking her blue-deviled on account of Mr. Fitzhugh's continued absence, Marissa had left her alone. Instead, she had returned to her original source, stopping in at Rose Cottage one day to learn more about what drew Tristan and Matthew Haydon to Penryn that night.

The Tregaron ladies had been beside themselves with delight to receive her, and Miss Hester, an avid gleam in her eye, had said the pagans in Cornwall had celebrated fertility on Lammas Night in order to assure fertile crops in the fall. Marissa had not needed to ask what, exactly, a celebration of fertility entailed, for Miss Hester had freely used the words "indiscriminate abandon" and "utter license," while Miss Millie had cried, "Shocking!" several times, and besides, Marissa had an excellent imagination.

Standing in her room on Lammas Night, all she had learned in her mind, something inside her quickened as she thought of what might be happening in Penryn. It was a night of license, and Marissa could not but wonder about Tristan. Tall, well built, handsome, honey gold, honey man at the revels. She couldn't quite imagine him drunkenly swinging a ripe maid about in a country dance. But she could imagine the maid eyeing him, swinging her ample hips, winking, as she all but begged him to invite her to dance or beyond into the woods and fields, where the evening, she had gathered, would end for most. Women's eyes followed Tristan. Marissa had seen it happen in so-phisticated London at the most exclusive balls, and in plain Penryn on Parish Day. He appeared oblivious to the inter-est, some covert, some not, that he excited, but would he not respond on Lammas Night, when the maid would surely make the most of her one chance to learn the feel of Tris-tan's arms? And the taste of his mouth.

Marissa closed the door to her room with a thump. She was, heaven help her, vividly imagining a buxom, broad-hipped lass rolling her eyes at Tristan and Tristan . . . This was what her mother did: this wretched imagining; this was how she had driven herself mad and her husband from her completely. Marissa had never sympathized before. Yet the images had been so vivid, and she did not love Tristan. Lud, she wasn't certain she even liked him.

Marissa walked forward into her room. Instead she would . . . read? It sounded such a dull choice she smiled to herself, though the smile was a trifle wan. It was not so easy as she'd expected to keep Tristan and the revels from her mind.

Would he tumble a maid in the fields? Two, perhaps? Adrian, her elder brother, had bragged once about taking two maids at once. But this *was* madness!

When there was a hurried knock upon her door, Marissa looked around in relief. She expected to see Tory, come to muse on the revels, but it was Tory's maid Jenny who rushed into the room, her face pale and a note in her hand.

"Beggin' yer pardon, m'lady, but I found this note and didn't know what else to do but bring it to you, his lordship bein' away and Lady Lynton fast asleep!"

Marissa took the note and read it. "I have returned as I promised, Tory, my darling, on this night for lovers. Meet me at the rowan tree, just after moonrise. Tell no one. They are against us, but all will be well. I shall make it so! I am desperate for you!"

Marissa did not need to read "Fitzhugh" scrawled at the bottom to know who had written the note. A glance outside the window showed her the moon had not yet risen. "I take it Miss Tory is not in her room?" Marissa asked, and when Jenny nodded frantically, she said, "Then we must hurry. Fetch a cloak for yourself, Jenny, and meet me in the library. We'll use the French doors. Now be quick, or we'll be too late!"

They were not too late. Running, holding up their skirts, trying to see by the bobbing light of the lantern Jenny carried, Marissa finally made out Tory's shape beside the great rowan tree.

Tory spun with a frightened cry when she heard them.

"It is only Jenny and I, Tory," Marissa called out. Tory drew up stiffly, though in a gesture that conveyed an underlying uncertainty, the hand that had flown to her throat fell to clench her other hand tightly at her waist. Marissa decided all she could do was to put the truth before the other girl. "Tory, you may hate me, for I've presumed dreadfully. I read Fitzhugh's note." Tory said nothing, only continued to regard Marissa with a mixture of defiance and uncertainty. It was not, Marissa thought, a good sign, but she continued as if there was no rift between them. "I know I am scarcely the person to warn you against a lark, but I must tell you something you should know before you meet Mr. Fitzhugh."

"Jack wrote me a letter and said you had developed a prejudice against him."

Marissa thought how different Tory had been in the last week and cursed herself for a fool. "I have taken him into dislike, I admit, but for good reason, at least in my opinion. I saw him on Parish Day with Mrs. Lowell."

"Jack said you misunderstood what you saw, Rissa," Tory responded solemnly. "He said Mrs. Lowell had torn the hem of her dress and needed his assistance to pin it up."

"And that is why he had to adjust his cravat?" Marissa asked, but with little hope of reaching Tory, for it was obvious to her that she had underestimated both Mr. Fitzhugh's and Tory's desire to believe in him.

And Tory did shake her head as if she were going to make little of Mr. Fitzhugh's disarranged cravat, but both girls had forgotten Jenny. "Beggin' yer pardon, Miss Tory?" The maid's voice sounded strained, and she peered hesitantly around the light of the lantern she held. "I couldn't help but overhear an' all, an' per'aps I ought to have told you before, but I didn't think ye was so lost over the gentleman as . . . as this."

She gestured to the dark woods around them and Tory gave a little half cry, as if she, too, were unsettled by where she had come all alone. "Yes, Jenny? Have you something to say against him, too?"

"Aye, miss, though it gives me no pleasure. You know my sister, Mary, works over to Mrs. Lowell's. She told me . . . she told me that Mr. Fitzhugh stays there most nights."

"No!" Tory clapped her hands over mouth. "It cannot be! He told me he loves me and that she is merely a helpful neighbor to him!" She looked from Jenny to Marissa. "He said he loves me!" she repeated.

Marissa bowed her head as the anguished cry rang in the night. But when she heard Tory's breath catch in a sob, she looked up with a gaze that gave no quarter, though she would have given a great deal not to be obliged to say what she would. "If Mr. Fitzhugh loved you, Tory, and if he was worthy of you, he would not arrange an assignation in the woods in the dark of night. He would come to the front door of the Lodge and look me in the eye, Mrs. Lowell with him, and tell me I had wronged him and the widow as well. Skulking about under cover of darkness and with the excuse of Lammas Night is the behavior of a guilty man who knows his sins will be exposed if he asks for your hand properly. Do you want to elope with such a man, Tory? That is surely what he wants you to do, for he knows that once he is married to you neither your brother nor I would take steps against him for fear we would hurt you."

Tory had no time to frame an answer. A horse approached down the path from St. Mawes Hill. Tory stood in front when they turned, Marissa behind her, and Jenny further back with the lantern. Fitzhugh pulled his horse up so hard that the mare half reared, and his dark eyes went from Tory to Marissa, where they lingered a long, tense moment before flicking to Jenny and then returned to settle intently upon Tory.

For a long, long moment, the only sound in the clearing was the hard breathing of Fitzhugh's horse. Marissa half feared Tory might still fly into the man's arms, but she did not. The younger girl stood very still, her chin up and her shoulders square. It was only her uneven breathing that betrayed she was fighting for control.

"You did not need to bring reinforcements, Tory," Fitzhugh said at last, an edge of bitterness in his voice. "I am not so dastardly that I would carry you off against your will." Tory said nothing, but the sniff she gave echoed in the silence. Fitzhugh's hand tightened on the reins they held so that the mare skittered sideways. "I never loved her, Tory! Believe it or not, but it is the truth."

Tory's head bobbed, as if she assented. "No," she said in a wavering voice, "I do not believe you. But neither, in truth, do I think you love me. Good-bye, Mr. Fitzhugh. Fare you well."

With that, Tory turned and fled, Jenny hurrying after her. They took the lantern with them, but Marissa stayed. For all that he had said he would not carry off Tory, she meant to make certain of it before she turned her back on him. He looked from Tory's retreating back to her. Marissa could not make out his expression and wondered if he hated her. She did not care if he did. He was a liar, unworthy of Tory; would have had her live under the shameful shadow of elopement. Marissa might have borne the gossip, but Tory, loved and cosseted all her life, never would.

Suddenly, Fitzhugh swept off his hat and bowed low. "The game is yours and the girl, Lady Marissa. Blast, but I wish I could hate you for it!"

Marissa watched him until he disappeared into the night. She suspected he had considered swooping down upon Tory, but in the end, he had not been so thoroughly dishonorable as perhaps even he had thought himself.

Chapter 16

In Penryn, Tristan and Matt Haydon went into the Sea Maid, where Treginnis, the innkeeper, was serving up frothy mugs of his potent ale. The taproom was crowded, but in one corner a table had been given over to several cardplayers who called out boisterous invitations to the new arrivals. It was Lammas Night, when highborn and low mingled, particularly if the nobleman were Tristan and his companion an object of intense curiosity to the local people, who remembered well enough that he'd run off with another man's wife to live in a foreign land for nearly a decade.

As is the way with cards, there was as much talk as play. The weather, a serious subject for farmers and fishermen, and the good fish catch that summer were discussed. But it was only when Matt confirmed that he had fired his unpopular agent and further announced that he would be hiring more laborers that the atmosphere truly warmed. One old tenant farmer, a pipe in his mouth, glanced slyly over at Tristan.

"I hear you've a new rider at Tremourne, m'lord, a lady, no less, that Tibbs says could win the Ten Thousand at Newmarket, if she cared to try."

Tristan looked up from the cards he'd been dealt and grinned lazily in the direction of the old farmer who had spoken. "Aye, Poldarne, the Lady Marissa is a rider. Why do you ask, though? You're not thinking of asking her to ride your Betsy in the Ten Thousand now are you?"

The other men roared. Betsy, a grizzled, ancient nag, was capable at best of a slow trot. Poldarne grinned in good humor. "Nay, I'm not so foolish as that, but surely you've raced her, m'lord. Did you prevail?"

All the men looked at Tristan, and seeing their good-humored but, in all, fascinated looks, he laughed. "And what do you want me to say, I wonder? That I bested a woman or that she took the victory?"

The question was taken under instant and noisy advisement. The answer, distilled from an hour's discussion, could be summed up in the words of Mr. Enoch Trellyan, an amiable, broad-shouldered fisherman who shook his large head and said simply, "But ye can't be havin' women bestin' their men! 'Tisn't the way o' things."

All the other men had spoken volubly by then, some recounting grim moments when they had been bested, others happier ones when they had bested, but when Enoch spoke his laconic piece, they all nodded sagely and "Oh, ayes" could be heard on all sides.

"Well, m'lord? Which was it then?" Poldarne had not forgotten the original question, and eyes twinkling, reminded Lynton of it.

"I'm afraid you'll be disappointed, Poldarne," Tristan remarked as he threw in a hand that was as poor as the others he'd been dealt that evening. "I haven't raced the lady. Ben Hawkes did, though, on Stockings, and Lady Marissa outrode him."

Interestingly, given that the men had been united in their opinion that the lady should not defeat the viscount, they all seemed more approving than not of her defeat of Ben Hawkes. He was only a boy, after all, and several murmured admiringly, "So, she did beat Ben, did she?" or "Well, the lass is a rider, then!"

Only Matt seemed to notice the apparent confusion of opinion, and he eyed his fellows around the table quizzically. "Here now, I've a question. Tell me why does it appear that we approve Lady Marissa outriding young Ben

Hawkes, and yet not one of us wished to hear she'd outridden Lynton?"

"Well, his lordship's here an' Ben's not," said one pragmatic soul. But another man shook his head. "Nay, 'tis like Enoch said. Ye can't have her beatin' her man. She'd run roughshod over him the rest o' her life, if she did."

Matt, who could, as Tristan was reminded then, be given to unwarranted starts of humor, laughed uproariously, and when he found his friend giving him a narrowed look, he only laughed harder.

Tristan could have corrected the impression of the local men. Marissa was not his. They were mistaken, and Matt had absolutely no reason to be bent nearly double with laughter, but he guessed it would be a great deal of trouble to convince the men they were wrong. What would he say? That she would laugh in astonishment—or derision—at the suggestion?

He thought of Marissa as she'd been that day on the bluffs, her heavy, ebony black braid swinging back and forth across her breast, and her eyes so light and silvery a blue as she assured him with all the considerable confidence she possessed that his father's tragic sins had saved him from a callow wastrel's life. In the very next moment, she had thrown her leg over Circe, exposing her long, lithe legs to him even as she informed him, in effect, and with that same assurance, that he would not be moved by the sight. Oh, aye, she might have learned, after a month of living in the same house with him, to tolerate him better, but she'd laugh at the thought that she was his.

He had not had one good hand that night, nor it seemed, one good breath of air. Tristan shook his head at Poldarne, who was dealing. "Count me out for this round, Martin. I must stretch my legs or lose the use of them."

While the others paid little attention, Matt glanced up, his eyes still alight with humor. "Would you accept company, Tris?"

Tristan feigned surprise. "When the alternative is to leave you undefended with these cardsharps?" The chorus of good-natured rebuttal his sally elicited quite drowned out, for all ears but Matt's, Tristan subsequent soft remark: "And she is not mine, by the by, Matt-o. Not mine at all."

Matt grinned as he followed Tristan out of the smoky, densely packed inn, but when they stood looking at the roaring bonfire that had been built on the commons, his expression was more chagrined than amused. "Lud, look at those dancers! It is nearly midnight and they are still kicking up their legs. They make me feel old. Stay and enjoy yourself, Tris, as your woman is not waiting for you at the Lodge. Ha!" He began to laugh again, reminded of the conversation around the card table. "Jove, but their reasoning was simplicity itself, wasn't it? If she is a lady and you are a lord, ergo, you are together. What a pair you would make, though, for my part, I do not think she is half so lost to hope as you say. Nay, we'll not discuss Lady Marissa now. We've tasted Treginnis' ale too thoroughly, and you are beginning to scowl. So, stay and enjoy the revels while I slip quietly away to look after my son. I cannot help but fear that he did not remain so happy with the not-to-be-mentioned-again Lady Marissa after I left, as he was before. Lud, I hope he has not cried all this while."

"I doubt Marissa would allow that."

It was said with humor, and both men entertained a vision of a slender, elegant girl gracefully juggling three colorful balls. Matt chuckled at the image. Tristan watched the dancers. They were shouting and laughing, cheeks flushed. One woman with sable hair flying caught his attention, but her eyes were dark as her hair, and when she smiled invitingly at him, he saw she was missing a front tooth.

"I think I am past Lammas Night revels, too, Matt." Tristan looked away from the abundantly blowzy, abundantly willing woman to add, "Though whether it's ale or age I've too much of, I can't say. Come. Shall we see if Will is sleeping soundly?"

"And if Lady Marissa is, indeed, at the Lodge?" Matt added with a grin.

Tristan did allow that Marissa's whereabouts were always a question, and even did so wryly enough that Matt laughed, but in truth he did not find the subject amusing. He told himself he found it a tedious subject, for she was not only an enormous responsibility but it was the very devil to keep up with her. He had guessed about the cockfight only because his old gamekeeper had hurried to the Lodge to report that he had seen one young gentleman enter the woods, but two leave. What if Marcher hadn't seen Gerald Kendall? It made Tristan's blood run cold all over again to think of, and suddenly he was imagining pulling Marissa into his arms and keeping her there, until he realized the direction of his thoughts. Then he smiled rather grimly to himself, and decided he had had more to drink than he'd realized.

Matt was talking about poachers, Tristan realized when he pushed Marissa where she should be, quite out of his thoughts. At first, he thought Matt was speaking about what he might do at Twyckham to discourage poachers, and then Tristan realized Matt was referring to his own woods, for they had passed Tremourne's gatehouse some time before.

"Forgive me, Matt-o, but I seem to have fallen asleep with my eyes open. Do you mean you heard poachers?"

"Devil it, you must be asleep, Tris! I said I thought I heard a horse off in the woods to the left there."

"Could it have been on the path to St. Mawes Hill?" Tristan asked, for it was the largest path through Tremourne's woods.

Matt thought so, though they both knew that sounds can be distorted in woods. "And I cannot even say I truly did hear a horse. It might have been a Lammas Night fancy."

Tristan thought immediately of the girl he'd thrust not so far as he'd wanted from his mind. But aloud he said, "I did give old Marcher and his grandson the evening off for the revels. Poachers would find the woods unprotected. I think I'll have a look. In truth"—he turned to grin at his friend, his smile flashing white in the dark—"I believe I need to clear my head with a walk before I meet you in my study for brandy."

Matt laughed. "I don't recall that we said we would meet in your study for brandy, but as we likely would, I quite understand. I'll just go along and look in on Will, though."

"Yes, do," Tristan said, waving his friend off as he dismounted. "I'll meet you in the study to report my findings."

Marissa had never been alone in a strange woods at night. Even at Penhurst, Kit had been with her or Billy, when she'd gone for a moonlight ride. And she was on foot now. She told herself not to be a fool and fear the woods. They were quite the same woods through which she had walked unhesitatingly when she had had the debatable protection of Jenny's company. And a lantern to light the way.

Lifting her skirts, she walked a little faster. It was summer. The thick leaves overhead blocked the moon's light, and all around her the woods were an impenetrable, mysterious black, while the path before her was frustratingly dark. Marissa walked off it and only realized what she had done when a branch brushed her face. Marissa was breathing a little harder then. There were noises she had never heard in the daytime, rustlings, twigs snapping.

She spun about, reasoning that the path must be directly behind her and trying to fight her growing fear. It was unreasonable. Even if there were poachers in the woods, they would not be interested in her. Of course, Tristan would warn her otherwise. Marissa could not help but remember what he'd said the men at the cockfight might have done to her, and she realized then that he had been right: she had always, in her heart of hearts, expected that her status as Exeter's daughter would keep her from harm. But why should a ruffian care? He could use her and kill her. No one would know.

She ran then, pushing low branches aside. She did not care if she was acting like a fool. She wanted out of the woods and desperately looked ahead through the dark for something familiar. A high, shrill inhuman scream rent the night just as Marissa bolted at last onto the path. Having never heard anything like it, unsure if it really had not been a human's cry, she ran as fast as her skirts and petticoat would allow.

Tristan recognized the shadowy form flying toward him as fast as if she feared the hounds of hell were on her heels. He had been half expecting her, but even had he not, there was a rent just there in the canopy of the woods, for an old oak, felled by a storm the year before, lay on its side, and moonlight flooded that one section of path.

By the moon's light, he could see Marissa did not wear breeches or any other riding costume, but was dressed still in the muslin she'd worn when he had left for Penryn, though she had taken down her hair. He braced himself to take her weight, but she sensed his presence at the last moment, and her head coming around to look ahead of her, she gave a wild cry. Oddly, though Marissa was in the woods on Lammas Night, when she could have no legitimate reason for being there, that cry of fear cut through Tristan.

He began to say her name, to reassure her that it was he, not someone who would do her harm, but she recognized him first. "Tristan!"

It was more sob than cry. And rang with a deep relief that might even have been gladness. He didn't quite know. His senses slowed by Treginnis' potent ale, Tristan had only registered that she was not infuriated by the sight of him when Marissa ran into his arms. Or rather, she flung herself at him, for his arms did not come up to hold her for a full, stunned moment.

She was trembling. With her forehead buried against his chest, Marissa was trembling and gasping for breath. Almost instinctively, Tristan caught her to him.

She felt very slender in his arms and vulnerable. "What frightened you so, Rissa?" he asked her softly, his arms tightening around her.

Marissa gave an unsteady, humorless laugh, muffled because she had not lifted her face from his chest. "I don't know. I thought I was lost in the woods, and then there was a shrill cry like a scream." She shivered, for all the world as if she could not help herself, and he smoothed his hand down the tumbling length of her hair. Perhaps it was the night, Lammas Night, when abandon was the order of things, perhaps only another instinctive gesture of reassurance, but Tristan brushed his lips against the crown of her head.

"Do you know what it was?" she asked in a small voice.

Later he would think how he ought to have been thrusting her from him and demanding to know what lark had taken her into the woods in the first place. But he never even thought of doing so then. She had run to him. Likely it was the ale made him unable think beyond that, or the feel of her, or that he had wanted to hold her for a very long time.

"No. I didn't hear anything," he murmured. "But I doubt it was human, if that was your worry. Foxes scream sometimes, when they've killed, and a screech owl earned its name from its screaming cry."

"An owl?" she said. He heard humor in her tone, but not as much as he'd have expected, for there was a wavering note just at the end. He did not have long to wonder at it, for she lifted her head. Moonlight spilled onto her face. It seemed as if he had forgotten what she looked like, for her beauty made the breath catch in his chest.

She straightened away from him a little, but Tristan could not seem to function ordinarily. At least he did not let her go, but kept his hands, albeit loosely, around her waist.

Either Marissa did not notice, or she still wanted the reassurance of his touch, for she did not break free of Tristan. Or even lift her hands away from his chest. They lay against him warm and right, too, somehow.

But she was not thinking of his touch or hers, either, it seemed. She was regarding him very gravely. "I swear to you that I did not break my word."

He had to think for a moment to understand what on earth she meant, for she might have sworn that she had not committed murder, she had spoken so seriously. And he knew he was lost to reason, on account of the drink and the abandoned spirit of that particular night, for with the sounds and sights of the unrestrained festivities in Penryn still swirling in his head, he was thinking he had wronged her, reducing her to such solemnity on a night when everyone else was gay and lighthearted and a little wild.

"Nor did I have a tryst with anyone," she whispered, still so serious that she sounded grim.

And looked grim, her silvery-blue eyes wide but shadowed. Whatever had brought her to the woods, she was afraid that having found her, he would revoke the permission he'd given her to ride. Still she didn't plead or cry, only regarded him intently with those beautiful eyes.

"Well then, if you did not break your word about riding without Ben, or tryst with someone in the woods in the dark then . . . you cannot have done anything unforgivable. This is Lammas Night, remember. A little errancy tonight is reputed to guarantee a good harvest later, though I am not certain precisely how that works."

Tristan was smiling. He felt like smiling. She felt good in his arms, and she was beautiful enough with her face turned up to the moonlight to take his breath away. But he'd not have known he was smiling from the look on her face. Her eyes were too watchful; her soft mouth a grave line.

"Do you have any idea, Marissa," he murmured, gazing down at her, feeling the soft silk of her hair brushing the hands he held against the small of her back, "how beautiful you are?" He took her by surprise. Her eyes flared, but her expression did not lighten. She only looked uncertain as well as distraught now. "But," Tristan went on meditatively, "you are even more beautiful when you smile. The corners of your mouth lift and transform your face." He lifted a finger to her lips and traced the Cupid's bow shape to the corner. "This line," he said and gently smoothed his finger along the length of the dimplish crease, smiling a little as he did. Her skin was satiny soft; her mouth perfectly shaped, and he could feel a muscle jump where he touched her.

She didn't smile, but regarded him, half warily, half wonderingly. "What are you about?" she asked, but it was difficult to talk with a long finger stroking the edge of her mouth.

Tristan's touch tickled, and Marissa did smile then. It was a small smile, uncertain, not bright and blazing, but it was enough to turn up those expressive lines. Tristan grinned down at her approvingly. His smile, even in the moonlight, was strong and white and though she clearly did not understand his mood, Marissa could not but smile a little more fully up at him as he held her in the moon-washed woods.

Tristan knew perfectly well what he intended to do. But it was Lammas Night, and he had found her in the woods, a fair maiden, just like in the old tales. Smiling at the whimsical foolishness, he trailed his fingers across the creamy skin of her cheek, then brushed them through the silk of her hair. When he came to the back of her head, he cradled it in his hand, and holding her lightly, lowered his head to kiss her full on the mouth that had turned up so winsomely for him.

He knew that rationales having to do with pagan festivals and a general wildness in the air would not stand up to the light of day, but they stood then under the light of the moon. She fit too well against him, and her achingly beautiful mouth tasted too sweet, and when it miraculously softened beneath his, when her lips parted, Tristan's kiss deepened. And pulling her closer, his hand traced her spine to her waist and almost beyond.

Perhaps Marissa sensed that he had to catch his hand back from the curve of her hips. Or that he was nearly lost to the sweetness of her mouth. Or perhaps she heard the cry far off on the drive. Tristan did not. He knew nothing but the taste and feel of her mouth, and when she suddenly pulled away from him, he could not quite release her.

His hands on her arms, she stood very still, staring up at him, her lips parted, breathing as hard as he found he was. And then, broader reality set in. Tristan heard Matt, come back out to look for him, because he had lingered so long. "Tris! Are you there? Ho! Tristan!"

The reckoning that was to have come with the morning had come a little sooner, it seemed. "Well," he said into the silence growing between him and the girl he'd had no right at all to kiss, "it is comforting to know one has friends, I suppose, even if they do come along at inopportune times. Come, let's lay Matt's worries to rest."

"No!" Marissa shrank back out of his hold. "Please? I . . . oh, please let me go without seeing him! Please?"

Was this how she got men to do her bidding, Tristan wondered, feeling as if he had sobered abruptly. She pleaded so urgently with such wide eyes to be left alone. And what was he to do? Force her to face Matt, who would not condemn her, but would surely wonder, and shrewdly, what had happened in the woods between them?

"I'll go to meet him, while you follow out of sight. That way you needn't be frightened again, but Marissa?" Her chin was high, but he thought that her lips trembled. Something tightened in his chest. Marissa undone? It did not seem possible, and when he looked more closely, he saw that she was biting her lip. Surely that was what he had seen: Marissa worrying her lip, impatient to be rid of him before Matt stumbled upon them and asked, as Tristan had failed so miserably to do, why the devil she'd been in the woods in the first place. "I shall have to talk to you tomorrow."

She nodded. There wasn't time for more. Matt called out again, sounding much closer, and Tristan wheeled about abruptly, feeling as if he must wrench himself away from her or what? He raked a hand through his hair. What did he want to do aside from dragging her with him? Kiss her again? Or throttle her for tempting him beyond endurance?

Chapter 17

Perhaps Marissa dreamed of Tristan's kiss. Certainly she thought of it each time she roused in the night, and was thinking of it already when she awoke the next morning. By then the memory of it weighed as heavy as lead in her mind.

She had reasoned out why he had kissed her. He had been three sheets to the wind, and she had run into his arms. On Lammas Night, yet, when he had just come from the village where revelers had been drinking and dancing with abandon before they slipped away into the woods with a partner. And she was not unattractive. Too many other men, young and old, had paid her tribute for her not to know she had some attractions beyond her purse. Given all three circumstances: the mood of the night, her dashing breathless into his arms, and his having had an unusual amount of drink, it was really no surprise at all that Tristan had kissed her. Indeed, he'd have had to be superhuman not to kiss her.

The kiss meant only that he was not so superior. He was a man, perhaps somewhat better than most, but no saint.

It did not mean he loved her.

Or even liked her.

Perhaps he did not dislike her so much as he had. After a month with her, he had seemed to find one or two points to commend. But no more than one or two, and she thought he disliked more about her than he liked. Quite certainly, he did not love her or feel anything even remotely close to it.

"You are up already, lamb!"

As Marissa was standing by the window, looking down into Lady Lynton's rose garden below, she could scarcely deny that she was awake.

"I wonder why it is," she mused, turning to accept the cup of chocolate Wren brought her, "that people use 'lamb' as a term of endearment. I have always thought them singularly dumb creatures. But then perhaps the difficulty is that I am dumb."

"Nay," Wren protested, sounding mild, though she gave her charge a searching glance. "I'd not say ye're dumb, m'lady, for ye're never at a loss for words."

Marissa rewarded Wren's attempt to rally her with a smile that while brief was also full of affection. "Very good, Wren. You are in fine form this morning, but let us leave the tedious subject of myself now. Tell me, how is Master Will this morning?"

"Long gone," Wren said succinctly, and nodded at Marissa's look of surprise. "Aye, the lad rises early, and not liking to be alone, found his father's room after he stumbled into his lordship's." Marissa held her expression perfectly still. She would not ask after his lordship. She could not yet trust how she would sound speaking of him, and Wren was shrewd. "As you might expect, there was an upset, but in the end, after a spot of breakfast, the pair of 'em left for Twyckham Hall, the lad lookin' bright as a new penny and the father lookin' dull as an old one. But I've a note for you." She dug into her pocket as Marissa's heart began to beat uncomfortably. " 'Tis from her ladyship," Wren clarified, causing the thudding in Marissa's chest to subside, and Marissa to lecture herself about the vulgarity of melodramatics.

Wren selected a jaconet muslin dress of a pretty peach color from the wardrobe. Marissa thought it cloyingly cheerful, but she said nothing as she turned her attention to the note from Lady Lynton. It began with an apology. Lady Lynton was sorry they could not have their chocolate together that morning. Dr. Richards had sent a note to say he had an unexpected visit to make near Tremourne and wished to stop by afterward to look at her ankle, and so she was obliged to make herself ready for him. The unexpected visit interfered with another matter as well. Before she knew of Richards' visit, she had promised Tristan she would write several important letters for him that morning. Would it be too much trouble, she asked, for Marissa to write them?

Marissa wadded up the note and flung it across the room. Wren's mouth formed an O but the look in her young mistress's eye kept her silent. For her part, Marissa sat down in a chair, sipped her chocolate in silence, and glared at the wadded ball.

When Wren had laid out all her clothes, Marissa abruptly announced she was going riding. The old retainer displayed no frustration at her charge's sudden change in plan. Indeed, she nodded agreeably. "Why it is that sitting upon a large animal should lift your spirits, I've no notion. But generally it does," she added, taking down Marissa's favorite habit.

As Marissa was slipping on her leather boots, Wren asked what reply she wished to send to Lady Lynton. "Tell her . . ." Marissa stopped. Taking a breath, she stood and looked at Wren. She did not apologize for the savage tone in which she'd begun, but when she spoke again, she was more composed. "Tell her, she need have no worry. I will write the letters as she requests."

Wren nodded approvingly. "Good, then. Now, enjoy your ride, lamb, and remember what your brother says: you're not to rush your fences but to take 'em in your own style."

It was what Kit always said to her. Marissa thought if she cried, as it seemed she might, that she would slap Wren. A wordless moment passed while she fought the prickling in her eyes, and then before she swept out the door, she leaned down to drop a light kiss on the older woman's forehead. "Thank you, Wren. I am sorry I am so impossible so often."

Marissa availed herself of the servants' stairs, lest she

meet Tristan, who might be lingering in the front of the
house after waving the Haydons off. She was determined
not to see him before she had her ride. She wanted to be
cool and composed in the face of whatever might come. It
might be nothing at all, but she would not risk testing her
composure just then. If she had almost cried in front of
Wren over nothing . . . it was best that she use the servants'
stairs.

Riding, as always, did Marissa good. Alone, as she did
not mean to leave Tremourne, and anyway Ben looked too
bleary after his Lammas Night celebrations to sit a horse,
she was free to think or let the wind blow her muddled
thoughts away as she chose.

For a little, she did not think, only rode hard. When she
turned Circe, however she found some silent part of her
mind had sifted through the chaff and come to conclusions.
Tristan had kissed her, as had other men. His kiss meant no
more than theirs. True, she had kissed him back, but was it
not time she did? If she was to be thought fast, then should
she not reap some of the benefits of her reputation? Tristan
was handsome. There was no disputing that. She'd no
desire to be an ice queen in truth, either. And so, why
shouldn't she have enjoyed their kiss? She thought he had.
She was the one who had pulled away, not him.

The thought pleased her, lifting her spirits, and when she
returned to the Lodge, Marissa went to the breakfast room.
She had scarcely been able to swallow her chocolate before, but now she was hungry, and she helped herself to
eggs, ham, and toast points.

When Tristan entered the room, she had barely begun.
He flicked his gaze from her to her plate and back to her.
Grateful for the laden plate, Marissa managed to regard him
as if she did not recall they had kissed the night before,
though in truth she had never been more aware of anything
in her life than she was that he had kissed her until her
senses swam.

"Good morning," she said, her voice beautifully even.
He did not look too much the worse for wear, though his

eyes, perhaps, were a little more shadowed than usual. And his mouth was taut, but she did not think the set of his mouth had anything to do with his excesses the night before, at least not the brewed ones.

"I wish to speak to you as soon as you are finished."

He did not say good morning, or I am happy to see you or . . . Marissa glanced down at the robustly full plate before her, blessing it all the more passionately. "Certainly," she said and deliberately waved a hand over the plate. "But as you can see, I am quite hungry. I'll be along when I am finished."

Tristan glanced at the plate again and then said levelly, "I am glad you are in appetite. I shall be in my study."

The moment the door clicked closed behind him, Marissa pushed the plate away, all her interest in food vanished. He was going to blame her somehow. She could tell it by the flat, inscrutable way he'd regarded her. And that, "I'm glad you're in appetite!" He might as well have come out and flung the charge of brazenness at her. Or said any proper lady would have feelings so sensitive and delicate she couldn't eat after being kissed. Or running, uninvited, into a man's arms.

Of course, Tristan would put the blame on her. Scalded, every fiber of her being shrieking in protest, Marissa rose. She did not care if he did realize she'd not been able to finish her breakfast. She wanted to tell him she thought he deserved as much of the blame as she. And she wanted the unpleasant interview over. She'd never thrilled to suspense.

He was not at his desk when she entered the study, after knocking with a deliberately brisk air. He was leaning against the wall by a window, looking out, and she wondered if he was brooding over their imminent confrontation. Evidently, he had been, for when he turned, he looked very grave, so grave, indeed, Marissa actually felt a rush of alarm.

"Thank you for coming so promptly, Marissa. Sit down, please." He did not appear to be angry. Indeed, he wore the expression of an undertaker and used the tone of a stranger, a formal stranger. "Would you care for more chocolate, or perhaps some coffee?"

"No." She could neither relax back in her chair, nor expend her increasingly tensed energies on simple courtesies such as a thank you. Tristan was so grim, Marissa felt more nervous by the moment and resented the feeling. Their eyes met and locked. "What was it you wished to see me about?" she all but snapped.

"Last night, of course," he said, and she was somehow gratified to hear impatience in his voice, too. She was not the only one whose control had slipped. "Marissa, I must apologize to you."

A muscle ticked in his jaw, but Marissa did not fault Tristan for betraying that the apology did not come easily. At least he was apologizing and not blaming. She felt suddenly magnanimous. "It is quite all right, I assure you. The night was an unusual one, and I . . . I know I am at fault for having been in the woods alone in the first place."

"Perhaps you ought not to have been there," he agreed, causing Marissa to stiffen momentarily until he added, "but I ought to have been discovering why you were there and escorting you safely home. Instead I pressed my attentions upon you."

It seemed a point of honor to Marissa that she hold his gaze, but the price was too high. Heat flooded her face. Marissa looked down at the sleeve of her habit and straightened it, as if a wrinkle had been annoying her. Only when she knew she was not red as a vulgar beet did she look up again. "It was Lammas Night, my lord," she said, as formal then as he had been before. "It was a night for embraces, and few of them, I imagine, so innocent as ours. Nor, in honor, can I allow your remark that you pressed your attentions upon me to go unchallenged. It was I who ran into your arms, as you know."

There, she had said it, but she felt no satisfaction at telling the truth. Indeed, she couldn't seem to breathe normally.

"You ran into them, because you were afraid," Tristan

said. Too softly. Marissa found herself looking down at her other sleeve, only to stop straightening it abruptly when she realized what she did.

"Marissa." Tristan sat down in front of her on the ottoman that stood before her chair. His knees brushed against her, and his hands reached for her hands. Marissa jerked her arms across her waist and tucked her hands out of his reach. "Marissa," Tristan said again. He paused, waiting, until finally she looked at him, then he went on quietly, "I compromised you last night."

"You did not," she contradicted flatly.

"Marissa, there were servants awake last night when I reached the house. They will know you went into the woods, and Matt announced to Hobbes that I had gone into them to investigate some noise we heard. Servants talk. Every household in the parish will know by tomorrow at the latest that you and I were in the woods together on Lammas Night. I know I ought to apply to your father first, but he is not here and you are. Marissa, we must wed."

She might have swallowed a rock for the way she felt then. And worse, Marissa understood why she felt ill so suddenly. His proposal . . . but she was a Portemaine and would not think how Tristan looked as he announced that he must leg-shackle himself to her.

"I will not marry you, Lord Lynton," she said emphatically, formally, decisively. "Never. I do not wish to be tied to you for life, nor do you wish to be tied to me, and if you have not, I have seen enough of wretched marriages to know my mind on this."

"Marissa," Tristan began, reaching forward as if he were going to pull her hands away from her body and take them whether she wanted him to do so or not.

But Marissa had had quite enough and violently pushed her chair back, not an easy feat, given that she sat in a large wing chair, and it stood on a wool carpet. "No!" she exclaimed, enough desperation in her voice to make it rough. "My mind is made up. Nor is there the least need for these heroics of yours." Her tone the more venomous because she saw clearly that he did, indeed, consider offering for her a heroic thing, she continued, "If your servants are so well informed as you believe, then they know I went into the woods for a good cause, though not one I am at liberty to divulge, and if they do connect you with me, they will think you came to aid me on that other business. That is what will be making the rounds of the breakfast rooms of Penryn, if your servants do gossip about you, which I would be willing to wager they do not." She was staring down at Tristan, for once. He looked large and strong and painfully handsome. "And so I will not marry you, my lord! I will not."

"I see," he said, rising himself. He seemed to tower over her as she scanned his face for signs of the relief he must be feeling. When Marissa saw only that he looked very grave again, she ascribed that grim look to disappointment with himself. The honey man had been reckoned strong enough to have virtual custody of her, but he had proven weak. Once. And he bitterly regretted even that little. Damn him, damn him, damn him! "Well," he went on, his eyes never leaving hers, "I daresay, a debt-ridden viscount is a poor match for you anyway."

Particularly as he did not even like her. "Quite," Marissa said in her loftiest tones. "And now, if you will excuse me?" It was the merest formality. She left before another word passed between them.

Chapter 18

"**R**issa, may I join you? You look quite content."

Marissa curbed an impulse to laugh. It would be a bitter sound, and Tory did not need ill humor. There were dark circles beneath her eyes, and she looked pale and drawn.

"I am frustrated actually," Marissa said, moving aside on the bench to make room for Tory. "I am having difficulty capturing the gracefulness of that tall grasslike plant across the lake."

"It is bamboo," Tory said in an emotionless voice. "Tris is experimenting with growing it."

Marissa put her sketch pad and pencil aside. Tory had not come to discuss bamboo or her brother's experiments with it. "Truth to tell, Tory, I am relieved you've come. I was not certain you would want to speak to me today. Do you wish I had not interfered last night?"

Tory's head sank forward, but she shook it. "I thank God you came, Rissa," she confided in a whisper. "I . . . I don't know what came over me."

"My influence, perhaps?"

Tory was not so lost in her own misery that she did not hear self-condemnation in Marissa's voice, and her head came up sharply. "You will not blame yourself, Rissa! I mean it," she said almost fiercely. "What I did had naught to do with you, and everything to do with me. You warned me in your way about Mr. Fitzhugh. You said young men have little interest in love. I just did not want to believe you. I wanted to believe what he told me! Foolish, foolish dolt that I am!" She flung away from Marissa, and grabbing a stick, tossed it violently into the lake.

Marissa would have liked to do the same, thinking of both Tristan and Fitzhugh, but Tory had already sat back down on the bench. Her hands were clenched tightly in her lap, and Marissa reached over and took them in both of hers. They neither spoke for a while. Tory fought tears. Her head once again bowed, she clenched her jaw and clung tightly to Marissa.

"You are not at fault, Tory," Marissa said quietly at last. "You have been surrounded by love and loyalty all your life. You had no reason to mistrust Mr. Fitzhugh until he proved you should."

"You were not taken in by him," Tory said in a small voice.

Marissa did not dispute her. "Between my cozy parents, suspicion and betrayal have ever been the order of the day. If your fault is that you trust too readily, mine is, surely, that I cannot but doubt. Lud, but we are a pair, are we not?"

Tory gave an unsteady laugh which was at least a laugh. "Perhaps if we could combine our natures, we could make do. Oh, Rissa!" She took a breath against the tears that welled up in her eyes. "He was so handsome and charming! When he looked at me in a certain way, I thought . . . I thought surely he loved me." Marissa had no ready, glib words, only her sympathetic touch. After a while, Tory asked in a whisper, "Do you think he laughed about me with Mrs. Lowell?"

Marissa thought she'd have liked nothing so much at that moment as to strangle Mr. Jack Fitzhugh with her bare hands. But all she could do was to answer Tory and do that with authority. "No! I don't think he was so cruel a person as that, Tory, or so heartless. I think in his way he did care for you, but in the end, no matter the woman, Mr. Fitzhugh cared most of all for himself."

"Beggin' your pardon, Miss Tory? M'lady?" It was the youngest of Tremourne's footmen. "Her ladyship asks if

you would come to the gardens. Mrs. Compton and Miss
Compton have come to call."

"Oh, Lud!" Tory exclaimed dismally. "This is all the day
needed. The Comptons come to flaunt Celia's Season.
Devil it a bit!"

Marissa had never heard Tory swear even mildly, but she
felt no inclination to laugh. Had she spoken, she'd have
seconded the sentiment, though not Tory's reason for it.

Marissa knew Celia Compton. Not well, but she had met
the girl during the first days of the Season, before she had
committed the unpardonable act of chasing her father to
ground at Mrs. Daviess' house of pleasure. Marissa
clenched her jaw, but she was not thinking of either Mrs.
Daviess or her father or even the Marquess of Salisbury,
the reason she'd chased after Exeter. Celia Compton had
light blond hair, green eyes, a heart-shaped face, and
though she was small, had as well, a delectably curvaceous
figure. By anyone's reckoning, she was very, very pretty.
Was she beautiful? Perhaps not, but what did that signify,
when she possessed exceptionally gracious manners, a conformable temperament, and was not, to boot, unintelligent?

A sense of such searing loss gripped Marissa that she had
to clench her hands tightly and fight for control as she rose
and accompanied Tory. He would be there in the gardens.
He almost always took time for tea with his mother.

He was there. Marissa heard his voice. He was speaking
to the girl so well suited to him. Marissa took a very deep
breath. She must gather herself, must forget everything but
Mrs. Compton. The harridan would present a challenge.
Marissa was certain of it. Mr. Compton's father might have
been a tin miner, but the old Cornishman had made it possible for his son to marry an Arbuthnott of the Sussex Arbuthnotts, one of the oldest families in England. Mrs.
Compton, secure in her lineage, did not stand in awe of
Marissa as did Mrs. Kendall or the Tregaron ladies, with
their only healthy as opposed to lofty family trees.

Though she was the guest, Mrs. Compton was holding
court in the gazebo, looking as smug and yet as haughty as

a cat that has just enjoyed a rich bowl of cream and a canary to boot. Celia's Season had been a grand success, as she informed Tory and Marissa after they were seated. Perhaps to be certain she would have a properly appreciative audience, Mrs. Compton had brought along Mrs. Kendall and Elise as well, for she had stopped at the Grange to announce her return, before driving on to the Lodge.

"I mean to tell you about Celia's marvelous Season, girls," Mrs. Compton declared in her distinctively high, even piercing voice. "For my darling is so modest, I fear she'll not say a word for herself when you young ladies have your coze together later."

"Mama! Please!" Celia Compton looked fetching, perhaps even more fetching than Marissa had recalled. The delicate willow green of her stylish silk afternoon dress brought out the pretty green of her eyes, eyes that were at that moment regarding her mother with a charming mixture of affection and reproach. "Lord and Lady Lynton will be bored to tears, if they must hear you go on about London again, and that is not to mention poor Mrs. Kendall and Elise for whom it would be their third recital."

"Well, we are very glad to hear you had such a successful Season, Celia," Lady Lynton said. Though Lady Lynton's dress was not dripping with the yards of lace and satin augmenting the costumes of Mrs. and Miss Compton, Marissa noted neither lady challenged her hostess for elegance of manner. "I am sure I speak for everyone in the neighborhood when I say that we are as proud of you as if you were our very own child, though, in truth, we all expected you would get on very well in town."

Celia could not but be pleased, and flushing with every evidence of true modesty, thanked Lady Lynton as graciously as that lady had spoken to her. Not to be left out, Mrs. Kendall echoed her hostess's sentiments and even went so far as to announce a proof of success that Mrs. Compton had not yet confided. "Though Hermione and Celia have not yet told you, I do not think they will mind my divulging that Celia has had the honor of receiving a proposal of marriage from Lord Durston, heir to the Earl of Chandos."

Durston. Marissa might have laughed. The viscount was as feckless as he had been five years before when he had hounded her so persistently that she'd resorted to trying to shock in the stables at Penhurst that day. Celia was welcome to *him*. But for all Durston's wealth and high title, it was not the future earl Celia wanted. Watching the girl flick a swift, discreet look in Tristan's direction to gauge the extent of his reaction, Marissa did not feel like laughing at all.

What Tristan's reaction was, she could not know. She had deliberately seated herself on the same side of the gazebo with him so that he would not be in her direct line of vision. All she knew was that Celia spoke next in a breathless voice, as if Tristan had looked taken aback or even angry. "The viscount was exceedingly kind to me in town, showing me every courtesy, but though he had exquisite manners and is so very nice, I am young, and after I consulted with Mama, I decided that I should wait a little to know my own mind before I gave him an answer. Gentleman that he is, he said he would be happy to wait until there was snow in London in July."

Sipping her tea, Marissa grimly commended her own insight. Celia Compton was no fool. She had deftly kept Durston on a string, and as deftly informed Tristan he had best come up to scratch soon or lose her. And had managed to smile charmingly as she did it.

Elise Kendall spoke up then, more concerned with the fashions Celia had seen, the carriages, the balls, and all the other trappings of life among the Ten Thousand in town. Mrs. Compton allowed the conversation to go on only a little while, for she was too shrewd to allow her hostess and host to become bored with what was essentially girlish chatter.

Smiling broadly, Mrs. Compton turned an indulgent eye upon Tory, who might well not have a Season in town unless her brother married an heiress. "Well, Tory, my dear, I hear that not all the triumphs of the heart occurred in London this Season. From what I understand, a certain very personable young man has paid you attention this summer."

Marissa simply dropped her cup of tea. She couldn't think of anything else to do after she felt Tory go rigid beside her. "Oh, Lady Lynton!" Marissa exclaimed then, making an unusual fuss. "Forgive me! How clumsy of me, and Tory! I have soaked your skirts."

Lady Lynton was not deceived. Marissa received a brief, probing look from her, but displaying a trust in Marissa for which Marissa was fiercely grateful, the viscountess rose gracefully to the occasion, waving off the apologies and sending Tory off to change her dress, while Dorcas scurried forward to clean up the mess.

With Tory gone, there was no one between Marissa and Tristan. And one less body between Marissa and Mrs. Compton.

Mrs. Compton had greeted Marissa courteously enough at the first, but she had been content to allow Exeter's notorious daughter to languish half hidden beside Tory. Now that the duke's daughter had thrust herself onto center stage, however, the look Mrs. Compton gave her was narrowed.

"I trust, Lady Marissa, that you have behaved yourself here in Penryn," she said, as if she were on close terms with Marissa and had the right to say such a thing.

"I have enjoyed myself very well, Mrs. Compton," Marissa replied, as if that had been the question. She held the older woman's gaze effortlessly, for in all, they both knew that Mrs. Compton was merely an Arbuthnott of Sussex, while Marissa was Exeter's daughter. "Everyone has been most kind and gracious to me."

"Well, I am certain your mother must be relieved that you have not indulged your penchant for . . . exceptional doings here. After you left town so, ah, suddenly, Lord Salisbury turned his eye in Lady Anne Mortimer's direction, but I believe that being a confidant of Her Grace's, as he is, Salisbury would redirect his gaze if you returned to Exeter

House reformed. If you do not, I am bound to warn you, Lady Marissa, that I fear you may end on the shelf."

Marissa smiled coolly. "I never fail to be amazed at the power my affairs have to interest others, ma'am. I would not think a young girl fascinating to anyone of experience, but as you have taken it upon yourself to advise me in place of Her Grace, my mother," Marissa continued as calmly as if Mrs. Compton's eyebrows were not lifting to her brow, "I should advise you that I have always thought the shelf a most underrated place for a woman to languish, and as to Salisbury, specifically, if the marquess wishes a wife, then he would be well advised to keep his gaze fixed upon Lady Anne Mortimer."

Marissa punctuated the end of her speech by flicking her fingers at an imaginary piece of lint on the sleeve of her dress. She did not have to remark into the silence that she would do the same to Salisbury if he bothered her again.

But the ladies were not allowed much time to follow her dismissive gesture or even to contemplate whether Mrs. Compton's overbearing manner justified such an acerbic reply from a young lady. Tristan spoke, addressing Mrs. Compton pleasantly, but firmly.

"Lady Marissa has been a great help to Mother this summer, Mrs. Compton. Among other things, she relieved Mother of the burden of maintaining my correspondence, and we are all very grateful to her here at the Lodge."

"Indeed we are," Lady Lynton spoke up, giving Marissa a fond, indulgent smile. "Thanks to Lady Marissa I've had delightful conversation all summer and my gardens are thriving as never before."

Marissa was blushing, though she did not know quite why. And floundering a bit, she had no recourse but to admit the unusual embarrassment. "You put me to the blush, my lady, as you can see. The pleasure in our cozes was mine, and as to the other, I was glad to help."

She did not look at Tristan even then. And he seemed content to ignore her as well, for he looked to Miss Compton when he spoke and on an altogether different subject.

"Will you tell us of your trip from town, Miss Compton? I am expecting some shipments from London, and wish to know if the roads were in good condition."

Marissa did not really fault him. He had come to her defense. And of course, as a proper host, he would now change the subject to smooth over the prickly moment. Honey man, addressing a girl as honey-tempered as he. Celia would never skewer anyone with her tongue, even a tartar who had richly deserved the skewering.

No, a blush dusting her pretty cheeks, Celia tilted her head and kept the floor, describing in rather extensive detail her trip, which included a delay in Plymouth that had had the consequence of forcing the Comptons to drive through Penryn on Lammas Night.

At that point in her story, Celia shuddered delicately. "It was quite shocking, really, to see the people forget themselves so! Why, they were drinking and dancing around a great bonfire like pagans of old! Mama had me pull down the shades in the carriage."

Marissa wondered slyly if Tristan would admit to being one of the shocking people, particularly when Mrs. Compton shrilly proclaimed that the custom of Lammas Night was a heathen practice that ought to be forbidden. Marissa did not think he would.

"I am surprised I did not see your carriage," Tristan said to Mrs. Compton, reminding Marissa that she had called him brave. "I was in Penryn as well last evening, as I have been for many Lammas Nights. I agree that the revels are not for polite ladies, but for the people who toil diligently on our behalf, I think them a fair enough recompense." He was smiling, and to her wonder, Marissa saw Mrs. Compton, even, was not immune to the power of Tristan's smile. Or perhaps Mrs. Compton did not forget her dear Celia's interest in the man, who was, after all, a viscount.

Mrs. Compton smiled, albeit chidingly. "You are a gentleman, my lord, and I do understand that gentlemen have differing views on these matters from ladies. But I hope you were not too lost to the revels! That would not do."

"Only a little, Mrs. Compton. Only a little."

And he smiled again, Marissa observed from the corner of her eye, as he described kissing her as being only a little lost to the revels. But then what would he have said? That he had been lost in love of her? When he was smiling so heart-stoppingly at Mrs. Compton and her daughter? Marissa sipped at her tea and did not contribute further to the conversation.

Chapter 19

Twice, Marissa read the scrawled notes Tristan had made for a letter to a friend, the Earl of Derby, indicating interest in investing in a new canal that would run from Liverpool to Manchester. She could scarce keep her mind on the words, however, for she was obliged to listen for sounds from the hallway that would forewarn her of his return to the Lodge. If she heard them, she meant to shoot to her feet and be on her way out the doorway, leaving as he entered.

She would not be in the small study alone with him. She could just imagine how it would be to sit across from him with nothing passing between them but the awareness that the day before he had asked her to be his wife, wearing an expression suited to a burial service.

Not that she thought she needed to worry that he was any more eager to be closeted with her than she was with him. He had left Tremourne shortly after the Comptons yesterday, presumably to go to Matt Haydon's, for he had later sent a note home from Twyckham to advise his mother he would take his dinner there, and had not been in evidence since, having either stayed the night with Mr. Haydon, or kept to his study.

It was Wren who casually mentioned that his lordship had ridden out with his bailiff just after luncheon. Marissa could not remember why Wren had spoken of him. She had been thinking her own thoughts, but as those thoughts revolved around the recollection that she had promised the day before to write the letters Lady Lynton had indicated were important, she went down at once to Tristan's study.

Finally, forcing herself to concentrate, Marissa absorbed the content of Tristan's notes and went strangely cold. Where would he get the money to invest in a canal project? The sum asked of him was not small. Had he had more reason for his proposal to her than concern for her honor or his? Was the honey man as calculating as all the rest?

It was obvious that he admired Celia Compton. True, he had spoken a few words in Marissa's defense, but his smiles and conversation had been addressed to Celia and her mother, and the Kendall ladies from time to time, of course. Marissa stirred restlessly at Lady Lynton's desk. She'd not only felt hopeless and tense at once with Tristan sitting next to her yet virtually ignoring her, but she'd been bored to tears. She had thought she might scream, if there were even one more word said about the shops in London, Celia's principal topic of conversation after her social triumphs.

But Tristan had seemed to bear up very well. Would he have married Marissa for her money, all the while secretly yearning after pretty, well-mannered, conformable Miss Compton?

The girl was the only child of a very wealthy father. Marissa had quite forgotten that fact, until she read the notes for the second letter Tristan wished written for him, and learned how he intended to finance his investment with Lord Derby. It was a letter to the moneylender in town from whom he had borrowed, informing the man that he would send only five hundred pounds per quarter, the amount they had originally agreed upon. Obviously, he had set himself to repay his debt early, but having found a good investment, he had reconsidered his thinking. He had not thought to marry Marissa, or even Celia, when it came to it, for monetary reward.

Marissa groaned aloud precisely because she felt relief. She was allowing her thoughts about Tristan to run on so they were becoming a tangled mess. And that was utterly preposterous. She was not marrying him. It did not matter if he was a saint or a devil. He did not want her. Celia Compton or another would have the pleasure of him.

The door to the room swung open. Marissa spattered ink across the page she had almost finished. At least, though, she'd the consolation that Tristan did not witness her reaction. Mr. Thompkins accompanied him, and Tristan was speaking to his bailiff as they entered.

It was Mr. Thompkins who faced Marissa, and who glancing her way as she was tucking the smudged sheet of vellum out of sight, registered surprise. Tristan swung about abruptly. And froze, but for only a second, certainly not long enough for Mr. Thompkins to drag his surprised gaze from Marissa and notice.

But Marissa noticed. She could not have missed how her presence made Tristan go stiff. Her eyes had locked with his.

To her frustration, she felt her face warm.

Immediately, Marissa forced herself to do what she felt least like doing. She smiled graciously at both men. "Good afternoon, gentlemen. I was just writing some letters for Lady Lynton, but I don't wish to disturb you. I'll return . . ."

"Nonsense." Tristan's voice sounded harsh. Marissa felt her chin lift a notch in response, but then the man who had kissed her and subsequently offered for her though he'd not the least desire to marry her, ran his fingers through his hair. "Forgive my tone, but Thompkins and I are in a dilemma as to what to do about water in a low-lying field. You won't disturb us, and I should like to post those letters today, if you've the time to finish them."

She could scarcely say she did not have the time as she was obviously in midletter. And at least Thompkins was there. Marissa inclined her head, and the two men adjourned to the couch, where Tristan had left a large, rolled paper. Marissa, craning only a little, could see it was a diagram when Tristan unrolled it over a low table, and the two men fell to studying it as they discussed the best way to manage the field.

She liked Tristan's voice. It was a small thing and easily denied, but the realization crept over Marissa before she could deny it. She was following it, enjoying its low, attractive register, before she realized what she did.

He couldn't know she had been listening to him, of course, but nonetheless she darted a quick glance to him from under the cover of her lashes. He was not looking at her, of course. He and Thompkins were absorbed by their project, and so her gaze lingered.

Celia Compton was fortunate. Her husband-to-be was a leader, commanding Thompkins' respect not because he was the man's titled employer, but because his ideas were intelligent and well-considered. Nor was it only Tristan doing the talking. Assured as he was, he demanded Thompkins' thoughts and listened attentively to them with the result that his bailiff was as committed to the success of the drainage project as he.

But Marissa eavesdropped too long. Perhaps she could not have forced her attention from Tristan, but she berated herself for a stupid fool when Thompkins rose and after saying some last thing to his employer, murmured "m'lady," in farewell to her.

As the door closed behind the square-set bailiff, Marissa stared down at the half-empty page before her with growing tension. She could hear Tristan rolling up the diagram. At any moment he would be finished. What would he do? Stay? Go?

Where was he now? What was he doing? All was still in that section of the room. At least she thought all was quiet. It was difficult to be certain with the loud throb pulsing in her ears. Blast her heart for pounding so! She could not think clearly. And what was he doing?

She simply had to know and lifted her head.

Marissa then had the singularly odd, and not so pleasant experience of having her mouth go a little dry. He had been watching her all that time she wrote she knew not what on the letter before her. Leaning against the back of the couch, his legs crossed at the ankles, his arms crossed over his chest, he had been waiting for her to finish and look up at him.

When she did, he said in a calm, level voice, "What am I to make of you, Marissa?"

She could not control her expression. He took her by such surprise she could not keep her eyes from flaring and resented betraying more emotion than he ever did. "I don't know why you must make anything of me, my lord," she snapped. "Do you want to sign this letter now?"

Marissa held the letter out to him. When he took it, she planned to leave.

Tristan ignored the letter. "Perhaps I've no imperative to make anything of you, Marissa, but I feel the need, none-theless. Ascribe my desire to an expected taste for puzzles, if you like."

"I do not like." There were other things she wanted him to call her, and the contrast bit her. "Nor do I care to be called anything so common as a puzzle." Rising, Marissa thrust the letter out to Tristan, forcing him to take it.

It was comprised of only four sentences, and he read it in a glance. Marissa hadn't time to do more than straighten the other papers on the desk, a task she executed only be-cause she'd not have him think she fled the room, though that was precisely what she wanted to do.

When she glanced at him to calculate whether she could pass by him while he was still reading, Tristan looked up with a frown. "What is the matter?" Marissa demanded. "Have I made an error?"

"I'm not certain." Now she thought there was the faintest hint of a smile in his eyes, and she waited, mystified, her compulsion to leave put aside for the moment. "You have followed my notes exactly, except that you have left off the word 'please.' "

It was nothing. Marissa shrugged negligently. "You are a viscount writing to a cit. I see no reason that you must say 'please,' sir, take my money."

"He is a wealthy cit, though," Tristan pointed out.

Marissa shrugged her aristocratic shoulders once again. "Anyone may have wealth. But you will always have what this Mr. Greeley will always lack: title and name. I would wager that he would give his eyeteeth merely to be invited to Tremourne for a week."

Tristan's amusement became more obvious. He smiled a quirky, beguiling, lopsided smile. "Perhaps if I invite him for a month, he'd cancel my debt entirely."

"It might be worth a try, if you've the stomach for moneylenders." She knew she was smiling, too, albeit faintly, but couldn't seem to stop. Any more than she could seem to make herself look away from him.

A moment passed, then two, and all the while Marissa was telling herself she *must* go.

"If I invited him, and he forgave the debt, I should be indebted to you twice over."

She assumed Tristan meant that he was indebted to her in the first place for declining his offer of marriage and was taken by surprise at the pain that tightened her chest. She had always professed that she preferred plain speaking to gallantry. "You are not indebted to me for anything," Marissa said, unable to moderate the curtness of her voice.

"But I am," Tristan insisted quietly. "On Tory's behalf, that it is. Had you not all but thrown your cup of tea at her, Tory maintains she might have burst into tears right before Mrs. Compton's ferret eyes." Ferret eyes? He described his future mother-in-law's eyes so? And they were ferrety, but then, too, they were nothing like her daughter's. Celia's green eyes were more ingenuous than not, and in all trusting. "And if she had burst into tears," Tristan was continuing, "then it might have come out that she went alone to meet Fitzhugh on Lammas Night, and would perhaps have been persuaded to elope with him, but for you."

"That is all rather far-fetched," Marissa said stiffly.

"Almost as far-fetched as the possibility that it would be you who saved Tory from ruining her good name on Lammas Night. Would you ever have told me?"

Marissa looked truly surprised. "It was not my story to tell."

"And so, out of honor, you would have allowed me to believe what I would. Do you know what I believed?" She did not want to talk about that night, of all nights, but her head moved from side to side, answering him despite her, just as her feet remained still behind the desk. "I thought you were walking to Penryn to spy on the festivities when you became frightened in the woods and turned back."

And ran into his arms. The very arms that were now crossed over his chest. Marissa's heart raced, and she looked down at the desk, but saw nothing of the paper there, the pen, or the ink. She saw his strong arms, his lean body. And remembered how they had felt.

"Thank you, Marissa."

She had not needed that soft thank you. It made something ache inside her and in reaction, she fixed Tristan with a cool look. "And so what is your puzzle, my lord? The far-fetched fact that I would look after Tory? Or that I would not sing my own praises to you?"

"As I have never known you to sing your praises to anyone, Marissa, it is the former that puzzles me: the queen of the lark foiling my sister's attempt at the same."

Queen of the lark. It was too absurd, and she could feel the corners of her mouth, the very lines he'd traced with his finger that night, lifting. Oh! Why had she not left the study? There was no point in speaking with him, unless she liked to ache. And she did not.

"The answer is simple, actually," Marissa said, stepping briskly around the desk. "Putting oneself in the hands of a fortune hunter—or influence hunter, in this case—is never a lark and nothing I would ever do. Your other letter, the one about the canal project, is there on the desk, awaiting your signature. Until this evening, my lord."

She had to walk close to him. He could reach out and catch her. But, of course, he did no such thing. He likely wanted her to go. Wished she would.

"Wait a moment, Marissa." His voice tugged at something in her. For pity's sake, she even liked the way he said her name. "I've something for you."

She turned, mistrust in her eyes, but Tristan pushed away from the couch and proceeded to his desk. It was just as well he had not seen her expression. Marissa knew the mistrust was for herself. She wanted him to want to keep her with him.

He had not fabricated an excuse, however. The moment Tristan removed the sketch pad from his drawer, Marissa went hot. She had been looking for that particular sketch book since yesterday, but had never thought to ask him if he had come across it. Dear God, she could only pray that he had not looked at it.

But God could not work retroactively. There was a glint just there in the depths of Tristan's amber eyes that made everything inside Marissa churn. "I found it on the bench down by the lake. I hope you'll forgive me, but I could not keep myself from looking through it. Your work . . ."

"Of course, I forgive you," Marissa interrupted, reaching for the pad. But Tristan did not release it. Marissa looked up at him then, her jaw so tight it would ache later. "I thought you were returning my property."

"Not before I say that I am flattered."

The gleam in his eyes, not to mention the slant of his mouth, sent a scalding heat surging into her cheeks. And he saw it. She saw him flick his gaze over her fair, revealing skin, and she thought she might well hate him. "You may be flattered, if it suits you, my lord, but I have drawn almost everyone in the neighborhood, even Hobbes."

"Did he fare half so well as I, I wonder?"

He was smiling now, all his considerable charm fully in evidence. Marissa's eyes narrowed. She had never been curious as to how the mouse that is stalked by the charming family cat feels. "It was an exact likeness, just as yours was, my lord. You may decide for yourself whether you think you are more attractive than Hobbes. Oh, Lud!" she cried suddenly, as a clock chimed two o'clock in the distance. "I said I would be at Rose Cottage in a quarter of an hour." The excuse had the vast virtue of being quite true. Emboldened by the thought of escape, Marissa all but jerked the sketch pad from Tristan's hand. "Thank you for returning my work," she said over her shoulder. "With any luck, the Tregaron ladies' likenesses will be as exact as yours."

Chapter 20

And good riddance, the decided crack of the closing door seemed to say.

She was angry. Tristan stood staring at the door as if it might answer why she was angry. Because he'd seen her sketch of him? Because it did flatter him? Why should she care whether he knew she thought him not unattractive?

Could she care for him?

Surely not. She had never given the least sign that she did.

True, she'd flown into his arms, her heart pulsing like a bird's, but she had been afraid then and running from whatever she had imagined to be in the woods.

Still, she had run to him. Would she have run into Matt's arms? Gerald Kendall's? The arms of someone in London?

Would she have allowed the man to kiss her?

Someone had kissed her sometime, for she hadn't been shocked witless by his kiss. To the contrary, in fact. She'd returned it. Would she have returned any man's kiss?

No. Not Marissa. Of all the people he knew or had ever known, she might well be the least indiscriminate.

Tristan dropped into his chair, and shoving his long legs out, raked a hand through his hair. He must try to think coherently, never, ever an easy thing where Marissa was involved.

But if the one kiss, even one so sweet and fiery as that one, could be dismissed as the result of Lammas Night and fear, the sketch could not. She had made it for herself, and she had drawn him smiling charmingly. It was not the image a person who did not admire him, or at bottom did not care for him, would draw.

And she had been furious to learn that he had seen it. Why? Because she did not want him to know she cared for him?

But she had refused him. Firmly.

He raked his fingers though his hair again, considering his proposal to her.

He had been so angry with himself that morning, flailing himself for lacking even a modicum of self-control. She had been entrusted to his care. She ought to have been safe with him, of all people, but he had taken advantage of the night and the place and led her astray.

And he had thought she would not be well pleased by the memory of the kiss the next day, though, in truth, most of his thoughts had centered on how she would respond to the proposal of marriage he had felt it his duty to make. His expectations had made him grim. For he had been certain she would refuse him. Only the manner in which she would reject him had been a matter of debate. He had not known whether she would lift those delicately arched eyebrows disdainfully or lower them pityingly.

But she had adopted neither attitude. She had been quick to reject him, true, but she had not scoffed. Now he considered it, he thought she might have been more than a little frantic in her manner. Retreating, she had nearly knocked over a heavy chair. That was not like Marissa. And Tristan distinctly remembered seeing the pulse in her throat throb almost as if she were frightened. She could not have feared he would physically force her into marriage. Had she feared herself? Had she feared she wanted to say yes?

Tristan threw back his head and breathed deeply. The very idea made him want to jump from his chair, race to Rose Cottage, and demand, before the Tregaron sisters' delighted eyes, to know if she was susceptible to him, did care, did want him as he wanted her.

Yes, he could admit it now. He wanted her. Had wanted

her from the first, perhaps, though he had fought her allure. Before she had come to Tremourne that had not been so hard. There had been her decided dislike of him, and he'd had no desire to doom himself to a place among her rejected suitors. No, the thought had not appealed, and so out of self-defense, only half admitting his weakness toward her, he had fastened upon her faults. They were not inconsiderable. Tristan smiled but the smile soon faded as he recalled how adamantly he had wanted to send her away when he had seen her standing on the stairs that first day. In his heart he must have known he could not escape unscathed if she lived for any length of time under the same roof.

Tristan gave a dry laugh. Clearly, he had not escaped unscathed. But he had learned a great deal, too, and most of it to her credit.

She was wise. At least when it came to the affairs of others, he amended, a faint smile lifting his mouth. But it was true. Marissa alone had gone to the heart of his turmoil over his father. She had seen he was ashamed. No one else had, and no one else could have addressed the feeling he'd hidden even from himself quite so uncompromisingly. She was nothing if not self-assured. And determined, too, as Matt had said. She'd all but shaken her finger at him that day.

She was intelligent, too. He'd have known from the questions she'd asked about his estate had he never had any other conversation with her. And she had listened to every word he exchanged with Thompkins earlier. He had watched her try to listen without appearing obvious. Tristan smiled briefly, lopsidedly. He ought to have asked her if she'd an opinion on how to prevent flooding in that field. At the least, she'd have asked thoughtful questions.

She had guessed Tory's intent Lammas Night. Tristan's hands closed around a letter opener on his desk. He had gone straight to Tory's room after the Compton party had left, and from her room, where he had found her with her head buried in her pillow, he had gone to Jack Fitzhugh's, but the Irishman had flown. Wisely, Fitzhugh had departed for points unknown, but Tristan promised himself an accounting should he ever see the man again, though Tory had wanted him to do nothing. She had said there had been no harm done, but her eyes had been red-rimmed as she said it. Damn, but he blamed himself for not paying closer attention to her affairs! He had thought Marissa needed watching, and yet it was she who had done the watching over.

And would never have told a soul, if it had been up to her. She was loyal. No one would ever have known that Tory had crept out of the house on Lammas Night to meet a man had Tory not given herself away to him at the tea. Marissa had diverted the guests, but Tristan had never known Marissa to be clumsy, and so had flicked his gaze back to Tory and found her nearly parchment white, far paler than a simple spill could possibly warrant. Some of Tory's tears had been shed out of gratitude for Marissa's sensitivity and quick thinking.

Tristan thought how frequently he had visited Penhurst and Exeter House over the previous five years and how little he had allowed himself to understand about Marissa. She had been right to say he had been determined to see the worst in her. Certainly he had never considered that some of her most flagrant behavior might have been the only means she'd had to fight her mother's schemes for her, and her father's utter negligence in regard to those schemes.

Not that Tristan did not have some sympathy for the duchess. Marissa would not have been an easy child. She was too intelligent and too spirited. He had only to think of her at that cockfight to feel nearly as sick with fear as he had that night. Or after she'd brought the Kendalls' curricle to a halt. Had he looked deeply within himself, had he had the courage after the cockfight, say, he'd have realized what lay beneath his anger. She was the only person who could make him so furious, because, of course, she had the power to make him so afraid for her.

But, Lud, he had not even admitted to himself the real

reason he had shown her his books. Oh, it was true he had not wanted to think himself ashamed for his debt, yet there had been more to the sudden decision to bare all. He had understood his deeper intent only that morning as he rode about Tremourne seeing nothing but Marissa's face. In some secret recess of his mind, he had thought to use her response to his debt to fight the interest in her that was increasing to the point that he could scarcely deny it. He had been so aware of her in his study that he had thought not even to go there, only to find he could not stay away. When she had asked about the ledgers, he had, without admitting it even to himself, seen his opportunity. He had expected his indebtedness would put her off completely, that she might even draw back physically as if he were tainted. She had done the opposite, of course.

Ever, ever surprising, ever intriguing, Marissa. She would not make an easy wife. Celia Compton would. Celia would chatter sweetly and incessantly about shops and fashions and also marry Durston, if Tristan did not ask for her. She had made that plain. Tristan knew Durston better now than he had five years ago, when Marissa had plotted to fend off Chandos' heir. He now knew Durston to be, not to put too fine a point on it, slow-witted company. Celia would manage him neatly. Marissa would have put a period to the feckless boy in a week.

Tristan laughed aloud, imagining her response should Durston, gone somewhat to fat now, heave himself down on one knee to propose to her. Very likely she would mock the boy pitilessly for his efforts. She had not mocked Tristan, however. She'd said something about how he had never liked her, and by inference how intolerable marriage to a man who cared nothing for her would be.

Little wonder she would have that particular opinion. She would know better than most how important reciprocity was in a marriage. Even mutual dislike would be preferable to Marissa, Tristan imagined, than an imbalance in affection. She had seen how, for a woman of strong character, love, if it was scorned, could turn to hate and bitterness.

Oh yes, Marissa would protect herself from her mother's fate at all costs.

Which reasoning implied . . . was he mad? Tristan rose, restless now. Had he allowed the talk at the Sea Maid on Lammas Night to influence him? His woman? He was grinning before he caught himself and could not seem to stop even then. Devil it, but there was no other woman like her. She had made his blood roar from the first.

He thought of riding down to Rose Cottage. He could accompany her home. And propose differently? Gauge her mood first? Tristan laughed. She was a slip of a girl, and yet he was thinking of treading carefully. Ah, but he did not think he would tread too carefully. He began to grin again. He had seen that sketch.

Half absently, Tristan glanced out the window to gauge the time that had passed since she had left his study. What he saw made him frown. Thompkins had predicted that they would have a storm that day or the next, but he had forgotten his bailiff's words—likely at the instant he had seen Marissa at his mother's desk. Thompkins had been right, however. Heavy clouds were already darkening the sky, and the wind was rising. When Tristan heard thunder rumble in the distance, he turned on his heel and left the room.

His mother and Tory shared a real fear of storms. And he did not know if Marissa had safely returned from Rose Cottage. Glancing at a clock in the hallway, Tristan saw it was nearly five o'clock. He had spent far more time than he'd realized coming to his decision.

He found his mother stoking a fire in her room, and when he entered, she gave him a rueful smile. "I may be safely tucked away under the hill near the river now, but as you can see, I still have need of a good fire to ward off the fright of a storm." There was more thunder, closer. Lady Lynton clapped her hand to her heart. "How I detest all that rumbling and cracking! I am all right, however, Tristan. You needn't take my hand. Tory is coming to sit with me.

She has just gone to see if Marissa wishes to cower together with us."

Tristan laughed as he went to pull the curtains across the window. Marissa had returned then and was safe. "I find it hard to imagine Marissa cowering."

"No, it is not an image that comes to mind easily, but one never knows." Lady Lynton shivered a little. "This is her first true Cornish storm, and I know she'll not have experienced the like in tame Suffolk."

"No, I doubt Exeter would allow them there." Tristan smiled, and if the little joke about the duke's power and wealth did not produce a smile that reached his eyes, his mother did not notice.

"Will you bring me my shawl?" She gestured to a chair near the window of her sitting room. "There. But where is Tory? She went after Marissa ages ago."

"She'll be along shortly then," Tristan assured her, tucking the shawl around her, and she sighed.

"That does feel good. And I know I am an imbecile about storms. After thirty years in Cornwall, one would think I'd have made my peace with them. Of course, I am certain that Tory has not been struck by lightning, and Marissa is likely as thrilled by the raging of the elements as you are."

Tristan was in the midst of murmuring some assurance when Tory burst into the room. "Oh, Tristan! Thank heaven you are here. I have been looking everywhere for you. Marissa is out in the storm."

As if on cue, a bolt of lightning flashed across the sky, lighting the room despite the drawn curtains. Lady Lynton gave a cry, though whether on account of the bolt or the thought of Marissa outside, it was impossible to tell. Tristan took her hand, but his eyes were on his sister.

"Do you mean that Marissa has not returned from Rose Cottage, Tory?"

"Yes! Wren said she ought to have returned at least an hour ago, but Rissa often dawdles on the way, if she sees something she wishes to sketch."

"She'll have noticed the storm building if she was out-side and will be along shortly, I'm sure," Tristan said, though even as he gave the assurance, he knew he would go to look for her.

Tory gave him good reason. "It's likely she stopped in the woods, as she'd have been riding through them, and if she did, it is equally likely that she did not notice the clouds building over the Channel. Nor have I ever warned her how quickly a storm can break here. I didn't think of it, and so if she felt the wind rising, or even noticed the sky darkening, she'll likely have disregarded the signs, thinking it would be some time before the heavens opened on her. Oh, Tris-tan, I hate to think of her all alone! Hobbes said he felt in his bones this would be a bad storm."

"Hobbes' bones creak the same tune every time," Tristan said calmly. "But I will go out to the stables to see if she got that far."

"Oh, Tristan! Will you go after her if she is not there?" Lady Lynton regarded her son in distress. "I don't know which thought frightens me more: you riding out into the storm or Marissa huddled under a tree, bearing it alone."

Tristan bent down swiftly to kiss her cheek. "If she hud-dles under a tree, she'll be there a long while. Whether the storm will be bad is impossible to predict, but that it will last through the night, we know from experience. And yes, I do mean to go and look for her. You are right to say that she'll not have experienced the like of this before. I'll not waste my breath urging you not to worry." He smiled, his eyes gleaming as if he were still the boy to whom he re-ferred next. "But I would have you recall, if you will, that you were never angrier with me than the time I rode out into a storm for the excitement of it."

He was gone even as she was calling out to him to take care.

Marissa was not in the stables, and Tibbs was readying a horse for Ben Hawkes when Tristan strode through the doors.

The older groom's grim expression lightened. "I see you've your taste for storms still, m'lord."

Tristan laughed. "Yes, though I can say my enthusiasm for getting wet has abated somewhat, but actually, I've come looking for Lady Marissa."

"I was just goin' after her ladyship, m'lord," Ben said, respectfully touching the brim of his cap.

"You know where she is, then?"

"Aye, m'lord. She rode to Rose Cottage to draw the Misses Tregaron. As it's so close, she doesn't take me with her there. She doesn't go by the road, you see, but through the woods and across the fields, and so she stays on Tremourne for all but the last quarter mile or so, and that's a corner of Twyckham land. I hope I didn't do wrong, m'lord."

"No, Ben. No harm would come to her in the normal way of things between Rose Cottage and here." Tristan paused, frowning thoughtfully. "But if she rode through the woods and stopped along the way, then it is possible she did not see the storm building until it crashed around her. Does she know of the hunting box?"

"She does!" Ben exclaimed, looking suddenly brighter. "She had me show her the way there once, m'lord."

That Marissa had had an interest in his little retreat surprised Tristan, but as Ben could scarcely satisfy his curiosity, he merely nodded. "Good, I'll go there first, then."

"You'll go, m'lord?"

Tristan couldn't tell if the young groom felt relieved that he was not to be asked to ride out into the storm, or deprived that he would not have the honor of rescuing Marissa. Grimacing wryly to himself, Tristan wondered whether Marissa might not prefer to have the groom come to her.

Someone was in the hunting box. Tristan caught a whiff of smoke on the wind as he approached. If it was Marissa, and not some trespasser, it seemed she had managed to look after herself. Tristan found he was not astonished, and once again he wondered if he had not engaged in a long bout of very wishful thinking after she had left him that afternoon. Would she welcome his presence? Or would she prefer another? Someone from London, perhaps? A sudden particularly fierce gust of rain caused Stockings to sidle. The question, it seemed, was moot. He was to be her company, whether she liked it or not.

Chapter 21

Marissa blew softly on the kindling. Kit had taught her how to start a fire during a summer spent at a castle of her father's in Scotland, but it had been years ago, and she was struggling to remember his directions. Finally she produced an eddy of smoke and a flickering spark. She was lucky the kindling had been so dry. And that she had remembered the hunting box. Outside the wind lashed the cottage with rain, and shivering, Marissa nursed her fire more intently. Her sopping clothes worse than useless, she had already stripped them off and found a clean blanket on the bed that was one of the few pieces of furniture in the simple room. Though a thin, summer weight cotton, the blanket was better by far than nothing at all. Marissa pulled it tighter around her shoulders, holding it in place with one hand, and did not allow herself to think whom else the blanket might have warmed. She could not afford to tear the thing off.

Her flame flickered then caught on a second piece of the kindling. Marissa was bending down close to coax the fire again when the door of the box exploded open behind her, banging hard against the wall. Marissa surged to her feet, clinging to the blanket. Her small fire flamed then fizzled before the torrent of wind-lashed rain that blew in the door and drove a man into the cabin.

Marissa caught her breath, gaping at the sight of a man wrestling the door shut. She wore nothing beneath the blanket, but even as she backed a step toward the small pile of wood near the fire, the only potential weapons she could see, she realized who he was. Tristan had come for her.

With the door closed against the weather, he turned, and Marissa was already taking a step forward, her face alight with relief and gladness that she would not be alone in a cottage that shook with the force of a storm more powerful than any she'd ever experienced. She could almost feel the warmth and strength of his arms, wanted them, wanted them so fiercely she almost did not hear the small, cool voice in her head that reminded her what had happened before when she had run into his arms: how she had given herself away and what she'd gotten for it, that stiff, forced proposal of marriage.

Her feet seemed to root themselves into the floor. And she could feel that traitorous gladness seep from her, from her spirit, from her face. Her mouth, in particular, lost its upward curve. She could feel it settle in a straight, unenthusiastic line, and spoke quickly, hoping he'd not have seen her initial response. The storm had brought on an early darkness, after all, and her back was to the fire. "What are you doing here?"

Possibly Tristan had not seen, for he did not smile either. "I came for you," he said simply, and flicked his eyes over her, perhaps looking for injury. Marissa told herself that the blanket was too thick to see through, and that the one arm she held beneath the blanket clutching its ends closed at her shoulder kept the blanket away from her body so that he could not see even the outline of her body. The logic sounded good, but nonetheless she knew full well she was entirely naked beneath the thin cotton covering, and she felt a flush sweep through her body. "Are you all right?" he asked.

"Yes. Only wet. The storm came up so suddenly."

Marissa knew she had rushed her speech. But he was regarding her still, his amber eyes shadowed by his hat, and she was too aware of her body. When he straightened away from the door, she stiffened, only to end by calling herself an overwrought fool, when Tristan simply proceeded to divest himself of his hat and long coat of a dun color he'd worn to protect himself from the rain. It had been effective. His shirt and breeches were only a little damp in places. His boots, however, he took off and set by the door. His coat he hung nearer the fireplace, an unexceptional choice of spot, except that every item of her clothing was there, hung on the back of a chair. His coat brushed her drawers and shift, and he moved the chair.

Another flush swept her. But even as it did, lightning split the sky directly overhead, and such a crash of thunder ensued that the cottage shook. Marissa jumped, then biting her lip for her cowardice, darted a look at Tristan. He was watching her, but all he said was, "I'll get the fire going."

He knew the cottage, of course, and with sure, unhurried movements took more wood and kindling from the wood box beside the fireplace, found the flint, and a screw of paper Marissa had overlooked. Putting the paper in the center, he made a pyramid of the kindling and striking the flint, soon had a fire blazing.

As he added larger pieces of wood, Marissa sat down on a small oval rug that lay before the fireplace. The larger pieces of wood caught soon. Tristan blew on them one last encouraging time, and then glanced down at Marissa. "Would you like some tea?" he asked.

Seated on the rug, with her knees bent so they made a tent of her blanket, she fancied she resembled an uninspiring block and secure in that feeling, was able to give Tristan a ghost of a smile. "At this moment I would gladly dance on the dome of St. Paul's for anything hot. Yes, please."

His smile flashed out at her, but before she could do more than blink, Tristan rose and went to a cupboard. There was not much furniture in the room, only a bed, a table, one straight and one comfortable chair, but there were two cupboards on opposite sides of the room. In the one closest to the hearth, Tristan found a canister presumably with tea in it and a kettle. Marissa had seen the hob in the fireplace, and had a vague notion one might hang a pot from its hook for cooking, but she had neither seen such a thing done nor known of the pot, so that she'd had no reason to think how to put the hooked piece of iron to work.

Water for the tea was easy enough. There was a large crock by the cupboard filled with water presumably brought from a nearby well. Tristan filled the kettle, then slipped its long handle over the hook of the hob and swung the arm of the hob back over the fire. As they waited for the water to boil, Tristan scooped some black tea leaves into a strainer.

"I did not realize you were so domestic," Marissa murmured, stretching her free hand out to the fire.

Tristan shrugged without looking up from his task. "The box is small. There is not much room for a servant."

Particularly if he were trysting here with someone. The box would be positively cramped with three people. Marissa glanced at the bed from the corner of her eye. It would accommodate two people easily enough, if they slept in each other's arms.

The tea kettle began to hiss, and Tristan drew the hob to the side with a stick, then used a cloth to remove the kettle and pour the hot water through the small strainer.

"There may be a leaf or two in it," he said, handing her the cup.

Marissa knew it was ridiculous for her to resent that Tristan might have—had prepared tea for another woman. Therefore she forced herself to smile, and pleasantly, too. "I would not care if there were a log in it, I think."

Why his chuckle should take her by surprise Marissa couldn't say, except that she'd been filled with thoughts of the other woman—or women—he had brought to the cottage she had had to find on her own. But he did smile, and his eyes glinted with unsettlingly warm amber gold lights as he regarded her.

"I do believe, Marissa, that you are as game as Tibbs says."

"Does he say that?" she remarked. She had half buried her face in the teacup, pretending to savor the heat of it, while in fact she was hiding from Tristan's smile. It made her hurt that he could smile at her like that when he did not like her, not really.

"He does, and you are." Tristan rose from the fireplace and came to sit beside her on the rug, cradling the teacup in his hands. He smelled of the rain and the wood fire. Marissa buried her face in the teacup again, trying not to dwell on how close he was. Had she not been sitting with both her knees folded up to her chest under her blanket, her leg would have touched the long leg he had stretched out toward the fire.

With a sidelong glance, she saw that his hair was drying, turning a lighter golden brown, and uncombed, feathered down over his brow in front. She had an almost irresistible impulse to smooth it back with her fingers. She knew the texture of his hair, knew the thick feel of it beneath her fingertips. Her heart raced, and biting her lip fiercely, Marissa jerked her gaze from Tristan to the bright fire.

Simultaneously, and because she had been distracted, her hold on the blanket slipped. Struggling awkwardly, grabbing at the falling end, she spilled some of her tea. "Devil it!" She exclaimed and flung a dark glare at Tristan, who was, as she had known full well, observing her difficulties. "This would be a great deal easier, if you were not staring."

Her snappish tone was excellent, and her glare all she could have wanted. But Tristan was regarding her in a way that was not unrelated to the way he had looked at her on Lammas Night, when she had run into his arms and he had caressed her mouth before he kissed her. She thought that if he looked at her like that another moment, she would melt before him. "Well?" she demanded, eyes flaring.

"Well what? You have caught the ends again." He spoke in a way she'd have thought entirely innocent and reasonable had she not been fully, overwhelmingly aware of a golden light dancing just there at the back of his eyes. "As you are covered literally from neck to toe. I cannot see the harm in my looking at you. You know already that I think you are beautiful, and game, too, as I said," he added, seemingly as an afterthought.

"What? You are being absurd." Marissa's tone had not warmed, but still it had, she knew with grim certainty, revealed her confusion.

She knew it because Tristan's mouth lifted. "You are game," he repeated low and quiet, and omitting "beautiful," leaving it to dangle between them, all the more potent for not being said. "I said I agreed with Tibbs that you are a game 'un. For proof, I point to the blanket. What did you do when you were caught in a sudden, drenching storm? Dissolve into helpless whimpers? Not at all. You found shelter for yourself, and peeling off your wet garments, found a dry substitute for them."

Marissa flushed again. She could feel the telltale prickling on her cheeks and tried to will it away, but her mind fastened on the thought that Tristan knew she had had literally to peel her underclothes away from her skin. And knowing that he knew was rather like having had him watch. The flush deepened, heating her so she scarcely needed the fire.

Marissa forcefully set down her empty cup on the floor between them. "I don't see what else I could have done," she said, tossing a sidelong glare at Tristan. "I'd have been struck by lightning had I not taken shelter. You ought to have known I would have the sense to save myself. I don't see why you came!"

She sounded half frantic, she thought, but then she felt more than half frantic, so she supposed she was controlling herself as best she was able. At least she was not looking at him, imagining him watch her undress.

"If I had not come, Ben Hawkes would have."

Marissa did not consider why Tristan might mention Ben. She was too startled. "Good Lord! His sense of responsibility for me approaches the ludicrous. Have you beaten it into him? He knew I knew of the box."

"I have never beaten a servant in my life," Tristan said, and as mildly went on to say with absolute certainty, "though I would have in this case, if Ben had not bethought himself, albeit belatedly, of his responsibility for you. Perhaps he did not need to ride with you to Rose Cottage. Though it is not Tremourne, it is close enough to be as good as, but the moment he saw the clouds begin to roll in, he ought to have ridden down to warn you. He knows, as you do not, how quickly storms can blow up here, and how fierce they can be in late summer."

"I'd probably not have listened to him," Marissa said, sounding wry and resigned at once, but when Tristan did not argue further, she added with noticeable alarm, "you do not mean to reprimand him, do you, Tristan?"

He rose to slip the kettle back onto the hob, evidently wanting more tea. The firelight played on his hair, making the lighter streaks shine like the sun. "You could have been badly hurt in this storm," he said with his back to her.

To Marissa, he sounded deadly serious. "But I could be hurt any time!" she protested. "Even riding with you, I could be hurt, if Circe stepped into a hole, and I sailed over her head onto mine."

Balanced with seeming effortlessness on the balls of his feet, his arms on his thighs and the tea kettle dangling from one hand, Tristan shifted to look at her. And smiled, though the smile did nothing to moderate something intense in his eyes.

"Ah, but I would adroitly manage to catch you before you fell, and so you would land safe and sound in my arms."

It was too much, that smile, that almost tense, glimmering look, and that ridiculous remark, all along with the unbelievable intimacy created by being alone in the cottage with him while outside the elements sounded as if they had gone mad. Devil take him, but he sounded as if he wanted her in his arms. Marissa smacked her hand against the floor. "Stop this nonsense!" she exclaimed, her voice high. "You don't want me in your arms. You don't even like me! And there is no point to it. You are not obliged to marry me on account of one kiss!"

The shutters rattled, the wind howled through the eaves of the hunting box, and the rain battered the roof, but still Marissa's voice echoed loudly in the small room, where the only other sound was the crackling of the fire. In the silence that fell after her outburst, she'd have given anything to repeat her words more calmly, if no less intensely, and she waited rigid, her eyes snapping with frustration for Tristan's reply.

He did not make it, at least then. The kettle had begun to boil and demanded his attention more insistently than Marissa. When Tristan turned from her to the hearth, Marissa felt almost as if she had been released from a physical hold. Weary suddenly, and still rattled by the intensity of her outburst, she bowed her head and rested it upon her knees.

In the quiet, she became aware again of the storm, the howling wind and rain, and the wild roll of the thunder. Through a crack in the shutters, she could see the unnatural dark of the sky and the equally unnatural, ghostly flashes of lightning that split it. Inside the cottage, there were only the sounds of her heart, the fire, and Tristan making them more hot tea. He was repositioning the hob as if he had done it a dozen times before, as he might have done, and might have done with as many women. She hated him, she decided, rubbing her forehead on her knee, and those women, too, by damn if she did not.

"Marissa, why did you go to the Daviess woman's establishment?"

So, she thought, that was the way he meant to respond to her a little too impassioned demand that he not put himself out to court her. He asked a question so entirely unrelated to anything that she wasn't certain she had heard him aright. When she didn't answer, Tristan looked around at her, catching her gaze.

"Will you tell me?"

He looked perfectly serious. His amber gaze was certainly steady enough, but she didn't trust him. He ought not have said that about her falling into his arms. "Why should

I?" she demanded in a tone so begrudging she was embarrassed by it, but she refused to apologize.

Nor was she given the opportunity. Marissa had thought the storm at its peak, but she had not experienced a late summer storm in Cornwall before. As if the elements had decided to enter the fray on Tristan's side, the storm intensified. The wind gusted suddenly, shaking the door and sending a tree limb crashing to the ground near enough to them that Marissa flinched. Though not really cold, she huddled deeper into her blanket and tried to wrap it more tightly about her.

Tristan rose. She thought he was going to bolt the door against the wind somehow, but he came to her, sitting down behind her and placing his legs on either side of her hips.

"What . . . ?" Marissa cried, trying to scoot away from him, but her blanket caught on the rug and slipped through her fingers. Before she could catch it, one side fell away, completely exposing her side, her shoulder, her back, and her breast. "Bloody hell!"

Tristan calmly took the blanket in hand. Pulling the fallen half over her again, he pulled the other corner from her fingers, and as if he did it every day, tied the two corners together in a knot that would stay without being held. "You needn't be embarrassed," he said, his breath warm on her cheek as he worked. "I did not see much of you that I have not seen in one way or another before. Now, come here. The gale's reached a feverish pitch and this fireplace is not the most efficient in the world."

Tristan did not allow Marissa much choice. Encircling her waist with his arm, he lifted her snugly back against him, and bending his knees, wedged her in on both sides. She shivered, he was so warm. Then he tucked his feet under her blanket. Bare, his feet were chilly, and Marissa gave a little yip when they touched her toasty warm toes.

"You see?" he said, a distinct note of amusement in his voice. "I am chilled to the bone and must share at least the bottom of that blanket. Now," he said after a moment of determined settling on his part and ineffectual shifting on hers, "that we are comfortable, tell me why did you go to La Daviess'?"

Wedged under hers, Tristan's feet felt like bony lumps of ice. So like bony lumps of ice, actually, that Marissa hadn't the spine to make him remove them from her warm cocoon. But she could and did jerk forward away from the warmth and attraction of his chest, and anchored her chin upon her knees.

"I told you that I went to taste the lobster patties," she muttered, staring into the fire. A draft of air found the top of her blanket and crept beneath it down her spine. Unconsciously, she scooted back an inch closer to Tristan.

"That is what you said once," he agreed. The low register of his voice seemed to touch some chord in her, and Marissa closed her eyes against it. "But, you see, I never saw you eat even one lobster patty at Mrs. Kendall's the night of her supper dance, and so I have come to doubt that reason."

He had observed her more closely than she'd ever thought. In fact she did not care for lobster patties. "Why do you care why I went to Mrs. Daviess'?" she demanded in a gruff, truculent voice.

"Because I am testing the notion that you do not always behave so thoughtlessly as I have accused you of doing."

Marissa looked around at that. Tristan was so near. Too near, but she couldn't help cocking a mocking brow at him. "You? Wrong? About me?"

He smiled lopsidedly. "I've never claimed infallibility."

Her heart thumped painfully in her chest. Half afraid he might hear the beat of it, Marissa abruptly turned back to the fire.

She had not been wearing her hat when the storm hit. It was sitting, ruined, on the ground near the flowers she had stopped to draw, and with nothing to protect her head from the rain, all the pins that had held her hair in a neat bun at the nape of her neck had been washed away. After she'd removed her clothes, Marissa had wrung out her wet hair, then twisting it tightly, had flung it over her shoulder and forgotten it. Tristan lifted it now off her neck and spread the thick, wet mass across her back to air it dry.

Immediately, Marissa shook her hair, as if to undo whatever he had done. Her heart was beating too hard. When she felt the touch of his hand upon the nape of her neck, she rushed into speech as much to distract herself as to divert Tristan.

"I went to see to Mrs. Daviess' to find my father. I had sent notes around to his clubs and the house where he keeps his mistresses, but he had not replied." Hearing a suspicion of bitterness in her voice, she added more crisply, "And so I went to him."

Tristan did not remark that a young girl should not know about, much less speak of, mistresses and particularly her father's. For one thing, it was time for honesty between them, but for another, all the world knew of Exeter's mistresses and the effect they had on his wife. "Will you tell me why you wished so urgently to speak to Exeter?"

Tristan was arranging her hair again, spreading it across her back. Marissa stifled the protest that rose to her lips. Already her hair felt more comfortable and as talking dispelled at least some of the unnerving intimacy of their position, she answered him. "Her Grace had accepted a request for my hand, despite my protests. I needed Father's support to oppose her. And if you mean to ask why my mother should wish to see me in a marriage to which I was not reconciled, I do not know with certainty. She says she believes marriage will be the making of me, but given her own, I think I can be forgiven for doubting her. Perhaps she has accepted that she will never make me over in her image and so simply wants me off her hands."

"And your father agreed, then, to refuse Salisbury's offer?"

For a moment Marissa could not think how Tristan knew it was the Marquess of Salisbury her mother had been prepared to force her to marry. Then she recalled that Mrs. Compton had said as much, and a sudden chuckle escaped her. "As it turned out, I had no need of Father's support.

Though I had given no thought to the possibility, Salisbury was also in attendance at Mrs. Daviess' gala. You should have seen his face when he came around a corner and found himself face to face with me. I was masked, of course, but recognizable to him apparently, and he, poor man, had a giggling, nearly bare-bosomed, Cyprian on each arm. Lud, he gaped so I thought his eyes would pop out of his head. He dropped the women, too, for all the world as if they had become hot bricks. One lost the top of her dress completely, and at that he went so red, I thought he'd expire on the spot."

"And he withdrew his suit?"

Marissa chuckled again. "The very next day and by note. Not only had I proven myself to be as scandalously inclined as I imagine he'd been warned, but judging by the Cyprians he favored, he's a proclivity toward lushness in his females."

"Cyprians are rarely designed for elegance," Tristan responded dryly, and without remarking on his own proclivities in that regard. "Now, tell me about your Grecian gown outrage. Who was importuning you then?"

Not "Was someone," but "Who." Marissa wasn't certain she wanted Tristan to understand her so well. On the other hand, she could not think clearly why he should not. "Leicester," she said quietly. "And his sensibilities were suitably scandalized, though his eyes did not seem to be," she added, lifting her head to look around at Tristan.

It was a mistake. She had done it unthinkingly, but now as she sat all but in his lap, they were both recalling that night when he had seen her dressed so that she had displayed the shape of her figure for any and all to see.

Marissa knew she ought, at the least, to scoot away from Tristan. But she recognized the thought as if from a hazy, disinterested distance. Immediate reality was Tristan, honey man, with the golden gaze that had likely entangled her from the first, but assuredly did just then, and she heard herself say, her eyes never leaving his, "Unlike you. You disapproved, but you were not much moved."

Perhaps it was the light of the fire that leapt to life in his amber eyes. "No? Not much moved? I had to fight an impulse to carry you off then and there to some remote tower where no one should ever see you like that again. But for me."

She had all but taunted him into saying it, and yet Marissa lashed out with her fist, striking Tristan on his chest. "Stop it! Stop lying!"

Tristan caught her by the shoulders and gave her a shake.

"What is it that you fear so, Marissa, that you do not want to believe me? I am telling you the truth. Great God, there is no man alive who does not think you beautiful and spirited. I am a man, and I've discovered since you've been at Tremourne how much more there is to you. You've a keen mind, are loyal and compassionate and so desirable, I cannot seem to keep my hands off of you. Rissa, I am not a nameless, titled cipher upon whom the duchess wishes to foist you in return for a regal settlement."

"No?" Marissa cried, wild that he should torture her with flattery he could not mean. "Whatever makes you think you are not? I certainly find it significant that she agreed to exile me to a home where there is a titled, eligible male, who is, surely not so by the by, in sore need of my purse."

Chapter 22

Marissa was hauled up, turned, and set down again on her knees. And none too gently. She gave a cry of outrage, but Tristan's response was to tighten his grip on her arms. "What the devil do you mean? That I could be persuaded to saddle myself with a woman for whom I cared nothing merely to discharge a debt I am whittling down nicely by my own efforts? You may take the amount your father will settle upon you and give it to Ben and Dorcas, if it pleases you! Never, not for one moment will I have you think I would marry any woman, even one who looks like you, for her money. Damn it! You might as well call me a whore and be done with it!"

In a dark moment, doubting herself more than Tristan, Marissa had wondered if he wanted the munificent settlement the Duke of Exeter would make upon her. But even had she not settled the doubt within a few minutes, recognizing that there was more than one heiress in England, Marissa could not have clung to it then. Face-to-face with Tristan, she could not entertain fancies, even dark ones, only the reality that she had come to know in the course of the five years since he had first stepped into her life. "You may cease glowering at me quite so fiercely, Tristan, for as it happens, you may well be the only man I know who would not pay the price of putting up with me for the pleasure of controlling my purse. I spoke in haste and awkwardly as well. I did not mean to say that you thought that way, but that Her Grace does."

"I see."

She thought he did see. His expression gentled. But he still held her, his strong hands on her shoulders, his thighs hugging her knees. She could count the creases at the corners of his eyes. And watch them deepen even, as Tristan slowly, slowly lowered his head to hers.

He kissed her. And she let him. She had berated herself almost ceaselessly since she had let him kiss her in the woods on Lammas Night, but not for having been lost to his kiss. That had been inevitable. Marissa had berated herself because she had run into his arms in the first place, and thus revealed she was not so immune to Tristan as she had wished him to believe. But now? He had come to her refuge, had turned her around, had put his hands on her . . . and there was no possibility at all that she would refuse him, not when he was already kissing her, and she felt as if she were drowning deliciously, dizzyingly.

Marissa opened her lips for him. Tristan pulled her up close to him, and she put her arms around his neck.

Outside the storm raged wildly still, but inside the small hunting box the storm was hot and so sweetly exciting they scarcely heard the furious wind and rain. And when Tristan stood suddenly, Marissa allowed him to lift her off the floor and carry her toward the bed. Inside she trembled at the enormity of what she was prepared to allow, but if she could not marry him, she could at least have this memory of loving him. Just once.

But Tristan did not lay Marissa down upon the bed and then lie down beside her. He sat down some distance from the bed in the room's only comfortable chair, and settled her on his lap. He smiled crookedly. "What did you think I meant to do? Take you on my gamekeeper's old bed without benefit of vows? I am sorry to disappoint you." Marissa could not believe she had truly allowed her disappointment to show, yet Tristan laughed softly. "You look as crestfallen as a child who has gotten switches for Christmas."

"You are a vain coxcomb, sir. I do not!" Marissa straightened, as if in umbrage, but Tristan held her by the

waist, and even had she wanted to leap from the warmth of
his lap, she couldn't have.

He considered the remark that had given her offense, let-
ting his eyes drift down slowly over her. The blanket had
gotten pulled tighter around her. Tristan's gaze touched her
breasts, her belly, her thighs, and then he looked at her
again, the gold of his eyes somehow dark and fiery at once.
"May I correct myself, Marissa?" he asked, his voice a little
rough. "You do not look like a child at all. You look like
the woman I want to marry. Soon."

Marissa caught her breath. For the first time in her life,
she felt a woman. A woman, full of a mysterious power
that could turn Tristan's steady, amber eyes hot and intense
and inflaming all at once. Had he only asked her to lie with
him, she'd have known her answer. But marry? She did not
believe he truly wanted to marry her. She believed he
thought it his duty, and that he was a man who would make
a virtue of necessity. If he must marry her, he would make
her believe he wanted her. No, that was not right. He
wanted her, as any man would want a half naked, not unattractive woman, but left to himself, he would never have
considered her for the position of his wife. He did not love
her.

"Tristan, you don't have to play at this." Her eyes
touched him briefly, but no sooner did their gazes connect,
then Marissa looked down to her hands. "I want you. I suppose that is obvious. But . . . but I cannot marry you."

"You cannot? Why? Is there some dark secret I do not
know? Are you really a fairy princess awaiting a carriage
driven by mice to take you home?"

"Actually"—the corners of Marissa's mouth turned up,
though she continued to address her slender fingers—"I
never wanted the part of a fairy princess as a child. When
Kit and I played at make-believe, I was Queen Elizabeth, or
some days, Jeanne d'Arc."

Tristan simply threw back his head and laughed aloud.
Marissa studied the strong column of his throat and his disheveled hair almost greedily, though she managed to smile

faintly when he looked at her again. "I ought to have known you would be nothing so fey and insubstantial as a fairy princess, Rissa. You are too much a flesh-and-blood woman, an intelligent, capable woman. I want to marry you. Tell me why you are reluctant, and I warn you that I know it is not because you don't care for me. You were too glad to see me this afternoon."

"It was, and is, storming violently!"

"But you are not afraid of storms. I would wager my life on it, Rissa. Just as I would wager that your eyes would not have lit like that for anyone else."

She couldn't hold his gaze. Though she had feared she had given her response away, she had not known how completely. He had guessed her feelings, and it seemed the only recourse she had was to tell the truth. She looked again to her interlaced fingers.

"I cannot marry you, Tristan, because I have seen what happens when one partner in a marriage feels more strongly than the other. Oh, I know you would never openly take mistresses as Papa has done. You've more feeling that that. You would always treat me or any other woman in your care with respect, but that is not enough for me, you see." She gave a soft but unamused laugh. "I am more like my mother than I care to admit. Only half a loaf would never do for me. I would make your life miserable."

She flicked him a sidelong glance. Tristan was regarding her intently, but Marissa had said all she could and made to get up from his lap and be done with it all. Tristan held her, though, one hand on her thigh and another on the small of her back.

"Whom do you believe I would prefer to marry, Rissa? Celia Compton, perhaps?" Tristan threw out the name with assurance and did not wait for Marissa's confirmation. "With all due respect to her, and she is a pleasant person, Miss Compton would bore me to tears. Never once has she moved me to want to throttle her. Unlike you. I have wanted to throttle you too many times to count, and never more than upon our first meeting, when I saw you in another man's arms. Rissa." His voice urgent, Tristan clasped Marissa by the arms and turned her to face him. "I may sound like a fool, but I have come to believe that I was half snared the moment I saw your sable hair tumbling so abundantly down your back. And when you turned about and I saw you full on, surely I was fully caught. Still I would resist my attraction to you, were it based solely on your looks. I have been resisting it, in fact, without really knowing what I did, until I was forced to come to know you better; to know there is as much to admire about your character, about you, as there is to admire about your looks."

Tristan slid his hands down Marissa's arms and lifting her hands, began kissing her fingers one by one as he told her why he wanted her and no other. "I want to marry you not least of all because you can speak of something other than London's shops if you discuss our capital. I want you for my bride, because you're a woman of spirit and so will never bore me; you are a fair woman, who will recognize an ostracized man, if for no other reason than that you do not believe the consequences of his sins ought to be visited upon his innocent son; a woman who will champion an old soldiers' home; a woman who will not think it beneath her to help me rebuild what my father lost and will help me to heal the scars he left on my soul. I want to marry you, Lady Marissa Portemaine, because I have fallen in love with you. And because you've the most irresistible mouth I have ever seen."

That last was supposed to make her laugh, but Marissa ducked her head. Tristan would not let her hide, though. He tilted up her chin with his knuckle to find that her eyes were suspiciously bright.

"I thought I was extraordinarily eloquent, but you have not believed a word I have said, have you?"

He looked so grave, she touched his cheek. "You were so eloquent and made wonderful listening. But Tristan, please, have done!"

"Have done?" Marissa flinched back from the blaze in

his eyes. "I am not about to have done, thank you very much. Tell me why in the deuce you think I do want to marry you, if not for love. We have agreed, I believe, that I am not hanging out for your money." She nodded slowly when he waited for an answer. "For your sweet temper, then?" His tone had changed. He asked it so softly and with so little sarcasm, Marissa felt tears prick the back of her eyes. Her temper was, in all, one of the foremost reasons she thought he did not really want to spend his life with her. She shook her head. "Why then?"

"Honor," she said after a moment in a gruff little voice.

"I see," he said and raked his long fingers through his hair. "You believe I've such a strong sense of honor that I would feel obliged to hound you into marriage after one kiss, but would not be constrained by that same sense of honor from lying to you outright when I say I have fallen hopelessly in love with you."

Marissa shot from Tristan's lap, before he could stop her. "Devil it!" she cried, frustrated and so hopeful of a sudden she was afraid. He had put the issue in a new light, and she couldn't seem to think clearly, at least not at that moment. "I don't know! You have always deplored me and my actions, and this is all so sudden!"

His hands were on her shoulders before she heard him rise, much less come up behind her. "Look at it this way," he said, his voice, his touch all too persuasive. "Before Lammas Night, I believed you cared for me as much as you might care for tripe stew." When Marissa said nothing, Tristan laughed softly in her ear. "You see? It is true, isn't it? We both were at odds. Great God, Rissa, it's a wonder you never drew blood with some of the looks you gave me over the years. And what did you call me? Did I not hear you say I had honey ears or some such?" Marissa wouldn't answer that, but Tristan ignored her silence. "And yet, despite that derisive epithet I know that you don't detest me now. Perhaps you did once; perhaps you never really did; but you do not now. Do you?"

"But I am ungovernable and hellish and shrewish even, at times, while you are good and reasonable!"

"Ah." There was an arrested note in his voice, beneath a certain humor. Marissa might have taken offense at the latter, but Tristan was moving his thumbs over the nape of her neck in slow, hypnotic circles, and it was all she could do not to fall back into his arms.

"I am pleased you think so well of me," he said gently, his breath fanning her ear, "but despite the risk I take of lowering myself in your eyes, Rissa, I am obliged to point out that it was I who clung to a generally unfair and undoubtedly precipitate judgment of you simply because I was turned topsy-turvy by a girl so beautiful and assured that I could not credit she was only fifteen. And I can be a coward, too. Ah, you try to protest, but why do you think I showed you all of my ledgers? Because without even admitting it to myself, I knew my interest in you was growing, and I wanted to prove to myself that you would never return my regard. But what happened?" Tristan gave Marissa a nudge, making her turn slowly to face him. The warmth of the fire had dried much of her hair, and the shorter tendrils curled about her face, framing it, presenting him a picture of almost unreal beauty. "What did you do? You looked at me with your silver blue eyes and told me without any sort of thinly veiled contempt—or coquetry, for that matter—that you thought I was brave. God help me, but I was so unnerved you'd have found me speechless had you not left my study."

Marissa couldn't control a smile. Tristan had spoken too feelingly for her not to believe him, and, too, it was funny to learn how awry his plan had gone. "Truly?"

"Truly. As has often been the case with you, I felt like one of those glass bibelots with the false snow in them: turned wrong way about and shaken."

An entire gurgle of laughter escaped her. Tristan did not laugh outright, only smiled steadily and so softly, too, that her heart swelled in her chest.

"Trust me, Rissa? If I must, I'll admit to you that when

we met Gerald Kendall on the path the day of the picnic and I thought of him creeping upon you and reveling in the sight of your pretty bare feet, I felt the strongest desire to rend the boy limb from limb." There was just enough savagery beneath the self-amusement that Marissa found herself believing Tristan might truly have been jealous. When he went on, she was convinced. "I won't tolerate even playful flirting, Marissa. You had best understand that. I count betrayal among the few unforgivable sins."

That was something they had in common, she realized, fathers who had taught them about the pain that is wrought by betrayal. "As do I," she said.

Tristan understood, for he knew her family too well to misunderstand, and he lifted her hands to his lips. "Good," he said with every appearance of solemnity. "We've settled that. I shall be in your bed every night."

"Oh!" She tried to snatch her hand back to give him the slap, albeit teasing, that his teasing deserved, but Tristan held on to her.

"I want to be in your bed every night, Rissa," he said, his eyes alight now, though not with laughter. "I want you, and I want to have a half-dozen little girls, who look exactly like you." When Marissa's eyes widened in bemusement, Tristan's expression softened. "Did you not think that I would want children?"

"Oh . . . I hadn't thought that far ahead. It's only that Mother has said with some regularity that I will not make much of a mother myself."

Assured, confident Lady Marissa Portemaine looked so uncertain, Tristan thought it a good thing that he would not see his future mother-in-law soon. "With all due respect to the duchess, Rissa, you were the only person in all the world, apart from his father, of course, with whom Will wished to stay. Nor was it Tory or Mrs. Kendall or Barbara Lowell who thought to visit him. Or thought to teach him to juggle and, necessity of necessities, to play dice. Only you, Rissa."

"Have you brought Barbara Lowell here?"

It was such a leap in subject matter that for a moment Tristan stared. Then he grinned. "Never say you are jealous of her!" he crowed—ungallantly.

Marissa freed a hand and hit him sharply in his chest. Probably her fist suffered more than he, but Tristan got the point. He moderated his amusement so that all that was left was an unholy gleam in his eyes.

"Did you? Did you meet her here?"

"No. Never. Nor have I bedded her anywhere else. She does not interest me. I prefer slender, regal, spitfires."

Marissa began to smile. She was all of those, she knew, and she was beginning to believe in his regard for her.

"I have used this hunting box to conduct some lucrative experiments with seeds. I'll show you what I have in the cupboard there, but later. Just now I want to tell you that I love you, Rissa." Tristan brushed her cheek with his knuckle. "You've skin softer than eiderdown. Come and kiss me, and tell me you will marry me, and then we will go home and make Mama happy. She has been angling for this, if I am not mistaken."

"She has?" Marissa did believe that Lady Lynton would not be displeased to have her for a daughter-in-law, but to have actively wished for her?

Tristan nodded. He was caressing the satiny skin beneath her ear, while with his other hand he smoothed the long hair that had attracted him from the first, but he did not ignore her doubt. "Curiously, when I asked Dr. Richards about her health after his last visit, the good doctor said he had never seen Mama looking better or stronger as she had this summer long. Now we shall have to ask her to be certain, but I suspect she claimed that so-temporary weariness in order to throw us together in my study, but . . . Ah, Marissa, I don't much care about anything else at this moment but that you kiss me."

She did then, and for a very long time, until, finally, Tristan lifted his head to murmur softly, "Will you make me happy, Rissa? Will you marry me?"

He waited, his mouth inches from her, but his eyes intent. She had to say yes. Had to trust him. She could not deny him or her heart. Not again. "Yes. Oh, Tristan, I . . . am afraid. I love you!"

"I know, my own." His strong arms around her, he pulled against him and held her as if he would never let her go. "I know, and you are being very brave to trust me, but, Rissa?"

She tilted up her head to meet his eyes and saw in them what he would say. She smiled slowly. "You love me. Dear God, but you really do."

He grinned, looking handsome enough to take her breath. "Oh, yes. I really do."